PLACES NO ONE KNOWS

PLACES

NO ONE

KNOWS

BRENNA YOVANOFF

DELACORTE PRESS

Text copyright © 2016 by Brenna Yovanoff
Jacket photograph © 2016 by Julia Presslauer
Jacket typography © 2016 by Brian Levy

All rights reserved. Published in the United States by Delacorte Press,
an imprint of Random House Children's Books, a division of
Penguin Random House LLC, New York.

Delacorte Press is a registered trademark and the colophon is a trademark
of Penguin Random House LLC.

Visit us on the Web! randomhouseteens.com

Educators and librarians, for a variety of teaching tools, visit us at
RHTeachersLibrarians.com

Library of Congress Cataloging-in-Publication Data
Yovanoff, Brenna
    Places no one knows / Brenna Yovanoff. — First edition.
        pages cm
    Summary: "Waverly Camdenmar, an overachiever in every way, seems
perfect, yet perfection is exhausting. She has not slept in days and then one
night she falls asleep and walks into someone else's life. She dream visits a
boy she could never be with and is forced to decide what matters most to
her" — Provided by publisher.
    ISBN 978-0-553-52263-1 (hc) — ISBN 978-0-553-52264-8 (glb) —
ISBN 978-0-553-52265-5 (el) — ISBN 978-1-524-70034-8 (intl. tr. pbk.)
    [1. Sleep—Fiction. 2. Dreams—Fiction. 3. Self-perception—Fiction.
4. High schools—Fiction. 5. Schools—Fiction.] I. Title.
    PZ7.Y89592PI 2016
    [Fic]—dc23
                            2015015299

The text of this book is set in 12-point Sabon.
Interior design by Heather Kelly

Printed in the United States of America
10 9 8 7 6 5 4 3 2 1
First Edition

FOR SYL, WHO EXPLORES
THE UNIVERSE WITH ME

WAVERLY

There's something awful about the sun.

It rockets up from the horizon like a hot-air balloon. One minute, you're looking at the shy, glowing sliver of it. The next, it's glaring down at you like the wrath of God.

Sometimes, if you spend too many nights staring at the clock, it gets hard to tell what's real and when you're only anthropomorphizing.

Every day, I walk myself through the sequence of events, trace my way back through the hours. If one moment logically follows another, that means it's actually happening.

It is 1:23 in the afternoon. I'm at my desk in Mrs. Denning's Spanish class, behind Caitie Price and in front of CJ Borsen, because that's where I sit.

I'm in Spanish because I have officially exceeded the allowable quota of French offered at Henry Morgan and I'm running out of elective options. It was this or home decorating. Sometimes when you show too much initiative, they have trouble knowing where to put you.

We're demystifying sports and activities, waxing inarticulate about our hobbies. So far, we have five aspiring musicians, three football players, and a handful of ill-motivated boys who enjoy taking apart cars and putting them together again.

My book is open to the chapter on *Deportes y Pasatiempos* and I know it's not a dream because the letters don't slide off the page. I know the answers to the review questions, and when Mrs. Denning calls on me, I know that I will not tell the truth about my recreational activity.

At the front of the room, she's wringing her hands, trying to figure out how her life went so wrong. "Emily," she says, looking hopeless, "how about you? What are some of your hobbies?"

There is a fantasy and it is this: during class, Mrs. Denning only speaks to us in Spanish. It couldn't sustain itself. Like all best-laid plans, it collapsed early, crumbling under the weight of its own ambition.

"*Me gusta bailar,*" says Emily Orlowski, and then goes back to painting Olivia Tatum's fingernails with Wite-Out.

Dutifully, I picture them dancing—a savage riot of eyeliner and cleavage.

"Very good," says Mrs. Denning, in a voice that implies it is not good at all and is, in fact, kind of horrifying.

Using her desk as a barricade, she settles on the back row. "Marshall? Would you like to tell us about your favorite recreational activity?"

Marshall Holt looks up. Then, just as fast, he stares back down at his desk and says in an impeccably accented monotone, "*Me gusta jugar a los bolos con mis amigos.*"

Mrs. Denning leans forward, sincerely convinced that he is not mocking her. *"Bueno. Y a donde juegas a los bolos?"*

"En el parque."

I enjoy bowling with my friends in the park. Brilliant. Marshall Holt, you are a genius. Also, mature.

Around us, people are snickering into their textbooks. Mrs. Denning is still watching Marshall in this sad, hopeful way, like she might eventually see the punch line.

For a second, he almost looks contrite, but the damage is done. She wilts, fidgeting with the plastic cup that holds her pens, searching the room for someone who won't betray her.

"Waverly, can you tell us another recreational activity?"

I am the bright, shining face she fixes on so she doesn't feel like she's drowning. So full of promise, so full of hope. Waverly will tell you the square root of any perfect number and how to conjugate the verb *quemar*. Yes, Waverly knows all about immolation. What is the significance of Bastille Day and who can list three thematic elements of *The Metamorphosis*?

Waverly will never tell you that her primary hobby is getting stoned in the play tunnel at Basset Park on a weeknight.

Waverly is a good, good girl.

Waverly is so virtuous it makes you want to die.

I keep my hands folded on my desk. People are looking at me now, looking at my helpful expression, my neat hair, thinking how good, how sweet, how nice. How fucking perfect. Thinking, who does she think she is?

When I answer, my voice sounds thin and almost doubtful. *"Me gusta correr."*

Wrong, says the girl in my head. *Incorrect. Woefully inaccurate.* I run, but not because it pleases me. What gives me pleasure doesn't enter into it. I run because the nights are long, and because I can't not run.

When the lights go out and the moon goes down, I slip out the french doors and through the gate. Down Breaker Street and along the median. I turn onto Buehler and let out my stride. From Buehler, I head for that one unreachable point on the horizon. Sometimes I run for miles.

Behind her desk, Mrs. Denning smiles. "*Gracias,* Waverly."

I make up a little postulate and write it down. Theorem of Perfection. The effectiveness of your persona is inversely proportional to what people know about you. I provide an illustrated example: two diverging trajectories, racing away from each other on the graph.

There are two Waverlys. One is well groomed, academically unparalleled, reasonably attractive, and runs the cross-country course at Basset in under eighteen minutes. Sixteen point five on a good day.

The other is a secret.

Secret Waverly is the one who never sleeps.

Maribeth Whitman is my best friend in the whole world, forever and ever, if you believe in that kind of thing.

The Watson to my Crick, the Donner to my Blitzen. We've taken all the same AP classes, joined all the same clubs, know all the same corollaries and equations and scandals. We have been making bracelets out of rainbow-colored string since kindergarten.

When I fight my way down the language arts hall and into our locker bay, she throws herself at me, arms flung wide, and even though the bay is full of roughly half the junior class and I hate being touchy-feely where people can see it, I reach back and let myself lean into her.

Maribeth knows how to arrange all her features to maximum effect. Her face is so sweet that if you look at her for too long, your teeth decay in spongy black patches, like time-lapse photography. Her hair is the kind of blond that makes you picture halos made out of kittens.

"God," she says, tucking my bangs behind my ear. "Your smile's malfunctioning again. Have you even been sleeping at *all*?"

I adjust my mouth to look pleasant and spin my combination lock. "Some." Which is the literal truth. I've been averaging roughly three hours a night.

She fishes a pencil from her bag and starts flipping through her notebook for a clean page. "Better get that sorted out if you don't want to look like the walking dead for homecoming. So, you'll be at the thing tonight, right?"

"Unless someone from cross-country sets practice on fire. No, wait—that's Huns. Yeah, I'll be there."

Her forehead wrinkles as she adds my name to her list, pencil scraping diligently across the page, and it's remarkable how well I know her—how she'll always make her notes in pencil, not because she ever needs to erase anything, but because pencils can be sharpened to a very fine point, and when she says *thing,* she means the dance-planning meeting. Just like she knows that I don't always sleep and I think siege jokes are funny even when no one else does. That my natural habitat is so deep inside my own head I don't always remember what expression I should be wearing.

With a conspiratorial smile, she leans so that her cheek is almost touching mine. "I think I'm making headway on the dance committee—for real, this time. You're going to be *so* proud of me."

This is the fascinating territory where Maribeth and I overlap. My greatest utility is my understanding of patterns and hierarchies. Hers is her relentless commitment to winning.

She taps the notebook. "I got Loring's minions to agree to have the meeting at my house instead of hers, and possession is nine-tenths of the law. Now, tell me I'm good."

There are two Maribeths, but unlike second Waverly, second Maribeth reveals herself to certain individuals at certain opportune times. If you are privy to her covert, secret identity, this does not make you lucky or special. The second Maribeth is a flaming bitch.

Her hand is nestled in the crook of my elbow and she smells like permanent markers and vanilla frosting.

Loring has been in charge of every nonathletic extracurricular event for our class since freshman year, and for the exact same span of time, she has always been terrible at it. That and her conspicuous lack of guile make her ripe for supplanting.

"I don't know if you know this," Maribeth says, giving my arm an emphatic squeeze. "But we're about to own every social function from now until graduation."

There is a single, perfect syllable forming in my mouth, unbidden. *Why?* Why are we focusing on this? Why is this desirable? Why are you so obsessed with organizing things?

But I don't have to ask why, because I know.

The dance-planning committee is something you submit to. The payout is another extracurricular activity to go on your Ivy League applications.

Your GPA is not enough. Your intelligence and your commitment are not enough. Cross-country means drive and discipline, the violin means that you do in fact have a soul. The food-drive committee means a devotion to service and community. Formal dance committee means that you are not socially defective.

Maribeth is drawing up her agenda for the meeting, pontificating on how we need to start making posters.

I am not listening.

I'm thinking about Loring and her wide, earnest smile. Her way of focusing intently, trying devotedly, and then failing. About all the ill-fated Lorings before her and the ways that Maribeth dismantles them.

"Come on," she says, reaching for my arm. "I have to fix my face before Chem so Hunter will ask me to the movies this weekend."

Machiavelli became enamored with Cesare Borgia because Borgia's ruthlessness fascinated him.

Maribeth Whitman is the most ruthless girl I know.

In the west hall bathroom, a few underclassmen are clustered around the sinks, but when we shoulder between them, they shuffle dutifully out of the way. They understand the pecking order, and it's only October.

I watch as Maribeth applies lip gloss in a cheerful rose-bud, then digs in her bag for a brush.

She was the one who told me in elementary school that people thought I was weird. Too quiet, too serious. "You should smile more," she said one day when we were in fifth grade, waiting in line for tetherball during recess.

"Why?" I said. "It's not like anything's wrong. I just don't feel like it."

And Maribeth had looked at me like I was some kind of new species, her head tipped to one side.

"Well, you don't have to *feel* like it," she said. "Smiling's on the outside. When you smile, it's for someone else."

Which, as revelations went, was kind of mind-blowing. I decided, there on the playground, watching Caitie Price lose her tetherball round to Cynthia Lopez who was a head taller, that maybe this was the whole point of extroverts—they understood how the outside worked.

Maribeth leans close to the mirror and rakes her fingers through her hair. Her gaze is shrewd, her paddle brush poised, but there's nothing there that needs fixing.

She goes to work on herself anyway while I stand by the paper towel dispensers, studying the collection of highly confessional graffiti that covers the spill wall floor-to-ceiling. This is where people come to tell their secrets. No names, no identifiers, but a wide variety of pens.

Some of the secrets are not secrets (*Mr. Cordrey has nose hair*). Some are too sad to contemplate and so no one acknowledges or mentions them.

Most are just the hard, ugly things that people feel, but no one says. Things like:

I only like guys who are
completely uninterested.
If they start to like me back,
I crush on someone else.
What if I'm alone forever?

I wish I was skinny.
If I was, though,
I know I'd be a total slut.

I think I lost my virginity on Saturday,
but I can't remember for sure and
I don't want to ask him.

The warning bell rings and Maribeth turns, leaning back against the sink. "I look good, right? I want Hunter to be intractably smitten."

Her hair is a shining curtain of Nordic genes and ambition. On the wall by the soap dispenser, someone has written in a cascading scrawl:

Fucked-up

Insecure

Neurotic

Emotional

The first letter of each word is printed in oversized capitals that align vertically to spell out *FINE*.

At my elbow, Maribeth is squinting at her reflection again, like something about it displeases her, even though she looks fine. Everything is fine.

"You look great," I say. The *i* in *emotional* is missing its dot. I have a completionist's urge to get out my pen and fill it in, but that seems excessive. I press my finger to the place where the dot should be. "Hunter will be powerless to resist."

Maribeth smiles, then rolls her eyes at the wall. "God, I can't even believe people write their private business in here. Don't they know this is the age of information? I mean, it's so obvious that *some*body will know, it's like they're just doing it so people will feel sorry for them."

"There are twenty-five hundred people in this school," I say, turning toward the door. "I guess they think quantity is the same as anonymity."

She nods, but I can tell she's not really considering it. She doesn't care about sympathy, or confession, or anything else she can't see the immediate utility in.

"Well," she says. "If that's what does it for them. I just think it's sad. Which, speaking of, you have tragedy duty next, right? Better watch out for all that unseemly emotion."

I answer with bland Waverly derision, the line I'm supposed to say. "What can I tell you? The slacker contingent is always in desperate need of guidance."

But my heart's not in it.

My last period of the day is spent behind the reception desk in the counseling office. It's a post reserved for well-behaved girls who already have sufficient credits, but are not so aim-less as to want a whole off-hour to themselves.

For the next seventy-five minutes, I will wear my helpful-person mask. Pretend I've had the requisite amount of sleep. My face feels cool and rigid, like it's made of marble.

By midnight, I'll have the voltage of a Tesla coil, but right now my legs are stiff and heavy. Things are hurting where they never used to hurt. I close my eyes and press my hands against my face. The counseling office is empty, so quiet you can hear the wires humming in the ceiling. In the computer monitor, my reflection is pale, ghostly around the edges. As much as I hate to admit it, Maribeth's right—I look half transparent. I look terrible.

I log on with the admin account and scour the Internet for relaxation techniques.

There are a lot of techniques. Some involve name-brand prescription drugs purchased at low, low prices from Can-ada. Others take a more holistic approach—recordings of white noise, incense and prayer candles. Counting back-ward from a power number again and again and again.

I make a list of possible solutions, complete with bullet points, notations on ease and convenience. Then I tear up the list and put it in the trash can.

Here's to admitting you have a problem.

I clear the browser and open my bag. Some people would use office duty to get a head start on their homework, but mine is done and has habitually been done for weeks. Not sleeping gives you all the time in the world.

Instead I take out a crossword puzzle. It's at that

obnoxious halfway point where all the easy ones are filled in, and the rest just sit there blank and mocking.

Forty-five across. Name. Renaissance-era poisoner. Fourteen letters, begins with *L*.

I'm staring at the squares, counting them over and over, when the door to the reception area wheezes open and someone slides a lavender hall pass across the desk. Big hands with long fingers and bony knuckles. Boy-hands. He smells like a mixture of detergent and something complex and peppery. He doesn't say anything.

After the silence lasts so long it stops being annoying and starts being awkward, I look up. Marshall Holt is standing over me. He drops his gaze and mumbles something incoherent.

I lean back in my chair. "Excuse me?"

He's not imposing, but his chest and shoulders look bigger when he folds his arms.

"I'm supposed to see Trunch," he says, louder this time, but only marginally.

The Trunchbull is one of three guidance counselors tasked with the academic and emotional well-being of the entire Henry Morgan student body. Of the three, she's the biggest, the loudest, and the meanest, and she's probably been here for as long as the school has existed, which is approximately as long as people have been calling her Trunchbull.

I drag the logbook across the desk and pencil in Marshall's arrival time. His expression is unreadable.

"You can go in," I say when he doesn't move. Suddenly, my heart is beating too fast for no good reason. I keep my eyes fixed on his face until he turns away.

As soon as he's disappeared into the office, the reception area feels manageable again.

I push my chair in a circle, listening to the murmur of voices. Trunch can usually be counted on to sound semi-inconvenienced at best, but through the door, her tone is strange—not irritable or impatient. Instead, she sounds almost tender, and *that* is interesting.

There's a place just under the ceiling vent where everything that happens in the guidance office is clearly audible for one square foot. I roll backward in time to hear Trunch sigh and do something organizational with a stack of paper.

"Let's talk about your plans for college," she says in her smoker's rasp.

For a second, there's silence, and then Marshall does the strangest thing. He laughs. "Yeah, that's not going to happen."

I expect Trunch to argue, or at least try and talk him into taking some classes at the community college, but she lets it go. She waits a full ten seconds before she says, "Regardless, you need to do something about your grades."

"Like what?" he says, and as bored as he sounds, I think I can hear him smiling.

I'm dubiously impressed that someone could accrue this much academic misfortune only a month and a half into the semester.

"Well," Trunch says dryly. "You could start by employing a few simple tricks. You know, show up now and then? Maybe try some of that fabled classroom participation, turn something in once in a while."

Marshall's voice is lower, but just as clear. "Maybe I'm not that bright."

"I have two years' worth of standardized tests that say otherwise."

"I thought those tests were supposed to be biased or something."

That makes her laugh—a hoarse, cawing sound. "Generally, the issue of bias doesn't come up when you decimate every section. Your English scores are phenomenal."

"Yeah, well, I speak English."

She laughs again, but it's short this time, and bitter. "Have you been to a remedial comp class lately? I'm not talking about them, Marshall. I'm talking about you. What about math?"

"So, I can count. Big deal."

Their conversation devolves into a catalog of teachers and course numbers. Instructions for him to at least take home some applications, at least look into financial aid. I stare at the crossword, but no answers present themselves. I feel heavy, like I can't lift my hands.

When Marshall finally comes back out of the office, he doesn't look at me.

In the shallow pool of appealing boys at Henry Morgan, there are two kinds: the ones who are not to touch, and the ones you might possibly think about touching if you were bored at a party and there was nothing on TV and you wanted to see what the big deal was, but didn't really want it to go anywhere because they don't know who George A. Romero is and anything more than five sloppy minutes would probably end in homicide.

Marshall is the first kind.

He stands over me with his arms folded and his gaze

averted, waiting for me to check him out. This task may be completed in several ways.

Appreciate:
    His mouth
    His wry self-deprecation
    The way his T-shirt complements his shape
    The way he smells clean and disreputable at the same time

Decline:
    His laziness
    His wry self-deprecation
    The way he dozes off in class
    The way he's looking past me, over my head, like I'm almost too trivial to stand

When I stamp his pass and slide it across to him, he meets my gaze for the first time. His eyes are a dark, complicated brown. Suddenly, I'm convinced that he's going to say something and it's going to be scathing. But he just turns and walks out, letting the door sigh shut behind him.

I stack the hall passes so their edges are flush, perfectly parallel to the keyboard and the monitor. Pens in a tidy row, pretend that order equals tranquility—already looking ahead to cross-country practice, the next predetermined activity, the next unit of the day. Everything perfect, everything in its place.

Somewhere, there's a merit scholarship in all of this.

•

Between cross-country and the twice-weekly meeting of the Most Hallowed and Venerable Homecoming Committee, I go home and shower. Then I walk over to Maribeth's.

All of the best people have gathered in her living room, sharing gossip and takeout containers. Maribeth is at the center of their orbit, their beaming sun. Everyone clusters around her, basking in her radioactive glow, soaking up the light-years until star-death.

When I step down into the split-level rec room, she smiles and holds out a felt-tip marker. "Here, you can help with the stencils."

Maribeth does a lot of things involving markers. I sometimes suspect this is her own socially approved form of drug use. No need for misappropriated liquor or illicit substances. Petrochemical vapors go right to your brain.

She's flipping through a catalog of formal dresses, supervising the poster construction with good-natured detachment. Loring is perched on the corner of a velvet ottoman, smiling hopefully like Maribeth is not usurping her authority in greedy gulps.

I sit cross-legged beside them, ready to spend two or three hours in mute, agreeable productivity. My skull is echoing, like I left my conversational abilities someplace else. My whole body feels vacant.

"Like you mean it," Maribeth whispers under her breath, and I adjust my expression automatically. A smile is for everybody else.

"I hate short hair on girls," she says, folding down a corner of the page and then folding it up again.

The magazine is open to a picture of an androgynous model with no hips and a spiky Mohawk, bleached and razored. My first impression is that the way she's slumped artfully on the little brocade fainting couch makes her look disassembled. My next is that her hectic cheeks remind me of how Edgar Allan Poe was obsessed with girls with tuberculosis and I still need to find another secondary source for my AP lit project.

I finish stenciling a twinkly star, and the way I can tell that sleeplessness is getting to me is that for three or four seconds, I'm oblivious to the fact that Maribeth is watching the side of my face, waiting for me to say something.

When I finally look up, she acts like I've reproached her. "Oh, shut up, Waverly! I didn't mean on *you*. Your hair looks fine."

Once, Maribeth told Kendry Epstein that she hated when top-heavy girls wore clingy shirts—it accentuates the way their bra straps dig in. Kendry hasn't worn her Carl Carringer blouse since, even though she bought it with her own money and I know for a fact that it cost two paychecks.

The way Maribeth can cut through someone's entire

being with just a sentence or a glance is something close to magical. She knows, with unerring acuity, how to pick a thing apart like she's not even trying. I used to find this impressive, but lately there are times when I don't think she even knows that she's doing it.

My hair is smooth and sensible, low-maintenance. It looks the way it always looks. I draw a circle and try not to think about the larger implications.

A primary component of the dance-planning committee is simply the opportunity to socialize with the right kind of boys. The varsity kind, college-bound, muscle-bound.

Maribeth is showing pictures of formal dresses to her future boyfriend, Hunter Pennington, asking him what he thinks about bubble hems. I can kill the suspense right now: Hunter does not think of bubble hems at all.

I spend most of the evening trying to deflect the attentions of CJ Borsen, who is on the soccer team with Hunter, and is, in his own way, just as blandly datable—tall enough to wear heels with, polite enough to never point out that you've stopped listening. Attractive enough that if I showed up somewhere with him, everyone would glance over and nod approvingly.

Taking advantage of a lull in conversation, he leans across the coffee table. "Hey, I don't know if Maribeth already told you, but student council is talking about maybe starting the canned food drive early."

I hate student council.

When I actually take the time to think about the situation and the circumstances, to think about what is happening right-now-this-minute, it's not that confusing.

We planned this, Maribeth and I. We built it, orchestrated it—me, the sly strategist, and her, the smiling, gleaming princess—all purely by design.

Back in eighth grade, Taylor Cassidy was the most popular girl in school. She was head of yearbook, captain of the volleyball team, cool and effortless and golden.

We . . . were not.

When Taylor found out she was moving to Tennessee at the end of the year, Maribeth saw the opportunity I'd never even known we were waiting for.

We were sitting on the floor of her walk-in closet, playing Reversi. Back then, she still liked to do things like that.

She said, "When Taylor leaves, I want to be head of yearbook. I want to be her."

"Why?" I said.

"Because when you're the prettiest and the most popular, then you're in charge of everything. You can do whatever you want."

And maybe I was never very socially inclined—but that? That made sense.

Maribeth wanted to take the summer to properly transform. She had this vision of coming back changed and everyone falling down at her feet in awe. She'd been watching too many movies.

"No," I said, and I only meant it in a practical sense, but she frowned anyway.

I didn't care. I was already planning it in my head, arranging the Reversi disks to form a war map of the three most relevant cliques in school, knowing that this was what Henry V knew. Sometimes, it doesn't matter if you're outnumbered ten to one. With the right strategy, the right weather conditions, and the right men, you can still take over France.

"Do it now," I said. "Do it before Taylor leaves, and then it won't be provisional." I was in accelerated English for the first time, proud of busting out *provisional* in conversation. "If you do it now, no one can take it away from you."

We made her what she is, step by step and piece by piece. Half the tricks she knows? I invented them. Or at least, I stole them from Machiavelli and Sun Tzu and *Heathers*.

We did it, just like I knew we would, moving into the delicate ecosystem of student organizations like an invasive species, making the territory ours one biweekly meeting at a time—student council, Key Club, mock UN. Formal dance committee looms imminent on the horizon.

And now, Maribeth's world is also mine, and every time the hours move too slow, or the conversation makes me want to punch a baby bunny, I just remember that I brought it on myself.

When I get up to forage for something to drink, CJ follows me into the kitchen and I experience a gloomy premonition.

CJ's face is so symmetrical it seems vaguely unnatural. He's proportioned like an ad for something patriotic, with thick, reddish hair, last year's midrange Volvo, and a dimple in his chin.

The way he's looking at me now is too blatantly *significant,* and I already know exactly what's going to happen.

Once when we were fourteen, Maribeth got the very backward idea that I had a crush on this boy named Jarett Fitz. She told everyone.

On the first day of this charming debacle, I pulled her into the bathroom and tried to explain that she was wrong, and she laughed and said I must really like him if I was making such a big thing about it.

So I stopped making a big thing, but it was too late. Everyone was talking about it, and after another forty-eight hours, it just seemed easier to decide that I wanted to date Jarett.

Except—and here's the thing. I didn't. At that point, the only boy I had ever wanted to date even a little was this skinny blond kid in my accelerated math class who liked Mandelbrot fractals and walked the scary line between prodigy and genius. He won the science invitational, and the next year, he got sent to one of those private schools where everyone owns their own graphing calculators, and I never saw him again. This is not the touching point of the story.

The point is that the unfortunate Jarett asked me out, which in ninth grade essentially means that you meet someplace, hold hands, and kiss with way too much tongue. Then he tells all his friends you gave him head, even though you didn't get remotely close, and no one really believes it, but they repeat the story anyway, because it's just that delicious.

I told him no.

Then Maribeth got mad at me for making her look unreliable and undermining our social endeavors. She told me

I was being unreasonable, which is something I am definitively not, and that I wasn't being loyal to the plan.

I stood my ground for a week. Then I apologized, and she forgave me.

CJ is looming over me now, gazing down with hopeful good cheer. "You were good in Spanish today."

"Thanks," I say to the eight matching canisters of dry goods on Maribeth's counter. *Coffee* is full to the top, but the *Tea* and *Sugar* levels are down.

"Waverly." He's very close and smells like spicy Cheetos and something sweet that makes me want to sneeze. "I was wondering if you wanted to go to the dance with me."

His eyes are green like spring foliage or breath mints, and the point of having a date for the dance is having something to be smug about.

I watch him so long that he starts to squirm.

"Yes," I say, because it's easier than saying something else.

By the time I get home, my nighttime restlessness is starting to set in. I'm ready to peel off my sweater and shrug out of my day. Shrug out of my life. Night is when I mind the most that everything feels fake.

My mother is standing in the kitchen with her phone pinned between her shoulder and her ear, drawing tiny rows of dichotomous flowers around the logo on a Zoloft promotional notepad.

"Stephanie," she says with absolute authority. "You can't expect a person who's already established this kind of baseline to spontaneously change. The fact is, no matter how much you might want to see an improvement, it's going to be her own choice."

Stephanie is the other clinical psychologist at the mental health center. My mother doesn't have friends, she has colleagues.

"Waverly?" she says, giving me a little wave. "Oh, she's fine. She just walked in."

The word *fine* blossoms in my brain, appearing out of nowhere for the second time today, but that's hardly surprising. People use it so much it barely has meaning. They use it so much they might as well say nothing at all.

My mother seems untroubled by the emptiness of social conventions. She holds up her index finger, looking off over my head. "Stephanie—Stephanie, I have to go."

When she hangs up, the air in the room is suddenly insufficient. The effort of turning her full attention on me demands outrageous quantities of oxygen. I peel the top sheet off her notepad and drop it in the trash.

She sighs, taking a saucepan out of the cupboard. "Stephanie's daughter is having trouble at school again," she says to the can opener. "And Stephanie thought that if she could just get her feet under her, maybe if she transferred to State—which, let's be honest, *that* wasn't about to fix the problem. Anyway, it's disappointing."

I don't bother to respond. Stephanie's daughter is a moron.

"You're home late. Do you want something to eat? I'm about to heat up a can of chicken broth, maybe sauté some liver."

My mother believes that I am her in chrysalis form. That I will one day emerge, brilliant and dysfunctional, to psychoanalyze Ford commercials.

"We had takeout at Maribeth's. The dance-planning committee went long. Do we have any candles? I need to do an experiment."

I don't point out that she's possibly the only person on earth who is comforted by her comfort foods. It would be too much of a shock.

My mother nods and starts ticking her fingernails

against the lip of the sink like she might be counting. "I think we have one or two tapers left over from the holiday party last year. In that bottom drawer of the credenza."

I turn to walk out, but she stops me in the doorway and kisses me quick and light on the cheek.

"You know," she says, with her hand on my shoulder. "Sometimes I forget how much trouble kids are. I've just never had to worry about you. Even when you were little, you always thought before you spoke."

And that is precisely why I don't talk. Too much thinking.

Far from one or two candles, the credenza is dangerously infested. White tea lights that radiate anxiety, and tall Christmas tapers, steeped in the aroma of spiced cider and seasonal depression. And far at the back, a fat brown candle that smells reassuring and capable and faintly familiar. There's an undercurrent of cracked pepper, mixed with something sharper that might be licorice. If I concentrate, I can imagine other elements—notes of fabric softener and smoke, a tiny olfactory snapshot of being back in the front office—the signature scent of a certain kind of boy. The kind with a sullen, sculptural mouth. The kind whose jawline is worth admiring, but for display purposes only. The kind who might look enticing, seem intriguing, but never actually satisfies.

I take the candle anyway, because it seems the least likely to tip over or collapse or melt into nothing and burn down the house.

MARSHALL
Stupid

Waverly Camdenmar is so hot that when I see her in the halls, I want to put my hand against my chest and make sure I'm still breathing.

Not that I'd ever say that out loud. I'm not an idiot.

Waverly is just this place I go when everything starts to be too much. Sometimes people in offices keep a poster of a vacation spot over their desks. Waverly is like that, like an inspirational quote or one of those music box ballerinas. Something private. Quiet.

I lie in bed and think her name, even though thinking it gives me a guilty feeling.

It wasn't always like this. Before last year, she was just another girl—hot like other hot girls, but completely un-touchable. The feeling was whatever. I could deal with it.

Now it's bad. Every day I have to decide whether or not I can stand to go to Spanish. I tell myself over and over how I'm not going to look at her or think about her or notice her or *any*thing.

And every day, there's Waverly, third row from the front

and one seat over, with her pens lined up and her mouth open. Hand in the air, reaching for the answer.

It starts at my heart and spreads fast and hot up my neck, until my face goes red and my ears feel like they're about to catch fire.

I'm thinking about this, even though it's past midnight and I should be thinking about homework, but everyone else is still up, which means everyone else is still shouting, and I left my history book in my locker.

Out in the hall, my dad is telling my mom all about how pointless and needy she is, and she's not telling him he's wrong. If she did, I think it would break something. It would be the thing that dissolves whatever disgusting glue is holding them together. It would be exactly what they need.

I have to get out of the house. Not for a cigarette or a couple of hours, or to spend the night at my brother's, but for good. The Trunchbull had this whole fantasy about college applications, but my family's in chaos, my grades are a disaster, and college is just one more thing that doesn't happen for the Holt boys.

The scene with Trunch was hazy in that dizzy-high way, where all the main parts are hard to remember, but then random things will stand out with freaky Hollywood clarity. Let's be honest. I was really stoned.

And as long as we're being honest, that's pretty much an ongoing thing.

I know the motivational speeches and the public service announcements. The front office has all kinds of posters and pamphlets about making good decisions, and when counselors or teachers or whatever tell me I'm wasting my potential, I know it's the truth. I can watch it slip by, but that's an ocean away from having any idea what to do about it.

I know I could destroy English or history—especially English. I could do respectably in pretty much everything else. I just don't.

When I close my eyes, there's Waverly again, sitting behind the reception desk, looking at me like I'm defective and she's the one with the final answer, worth ten thousand points. Like she's just waiting for the goddamn tiara.

She was working this crossword like it was the most important thing, and only put it away when she condescended to check my hall pass. It was one of those hard ones that you get out of a book or the *New York Times*. There was a long word across, with a *Z* and a *C* and two *A*'s. Her eyes were bored and her bottom lip looked pink and kind of untouched.

Then I went into the office and Trunch told me all the things I already know, like how I'm not living up to my potential and I need to start applying myself. Like it's just that simple, and now that I officially know I can do the work, it's only a matter of getting the work *done,* when everyone knows that's the hardest part.

"Marshall," she said, right as I was getting up to leave, in that voice that sounds all sad and quiet, *I'm not blaming you.* "I was talking to some of your teachers. I hear that neither of your parents came to parent-teacher night last month."

I just nodded, trying hard not to look tragic.

"Is there a problem with involvement at home? It might help to talk to them."

But the reason they didn't show up is because I didn't tell them. They have their own shit and I'm old enough to do my own homework. There are plenty of problems, but none of them have to do with involvement.

"It's no big deal," I said, and I wasn't talking about parent-teacher night, but everything—the missing assignments and the participation points, the tardies, the absences. All the bullshit.

I came out of the office feeling like my surface had been chipped away. See-through, like if Waverly just raised her head, she could have looked inside me and she wouldn't have seen lungs or bones or blood, she would have just seen how messed up everything is.

I didn't have to worry, though. It wasn't like she cared.

She still had the crossword out, but hadn't filled in any new boxes. Number forty-five still sat there, with its *Z* and *C* and two *A*'s. I read the question upside down while she stamped the pass, and suddenly, I knew the answer. I knew it and she didn't, and that was the one thing I had that made me worth anything.

If I hadn't been completely chickenshit, I probably would have said something, but just then, she looked at me. Her eyes were sharp—*piercing*—and I had to look away so she didn't see the answer sitting right there for her to pick apart and stare at.

I picture it now, alone in my room. Imagining the way the back of her neck always looks smooth and I want to touch it.

I think of possibilities and they are fucking terrifying. I could have made her see me. I could have impressed her. There's just the little issue of how my voice stops working when I look at her.

I say it now, just to myself, just whisper it. The answer to the question, the feeling of having something she doesn't. Something that she wants.

I close my eyes, and when I open them again the room feels less empty. For a second, I think I can actually see her, standing in my doorway, soft and pale in the light from the street. Then I squint and she's gone and I'm stoned and lonely, and it's late—so late.

I roll over, feeling tired and stupid.

I want to punch myself, because I know girls like her— the kind who act like I'm some disease, like I might get them dirty if I stand too close. I want to tell her she's not that smart, that being perfect isn't the only game in town.

That I'll be something else, something good. I'll clean myself up if she wants. I'll be anything.

She is never looking in my direction.

WAVERLY

1.

Some people are born wakeful.

When I was little, the reason I couldn't sleep seemed simple. I was too full of thoughts. The problem would work itself out when my skull got bigger. I didn't know yet that the ideas just get bigger too.

Back then, when I'd brushed my teeth and said good night to my stuffed lamb, exhausted every jigsaw puzzle and game, read all my books and the drowsy weightlessness still wouldn't come, I'd go to the moon. That kind of inter-orbital travel is easy when you're little—the membrane between real and pretend is still semipermeable. Your imaginary friends seem just as solid as anyone else. When they pinch you, it hurts. When they disappear, you wonder what you did to make them leave.

Late at night, I'd stare at the ceiling and imagine myself on the moon. Up there, I would lie on my back, making angels in the drifts of pale lunar dust, peering down at my neighborhood with telescopic vision.

Because it was pretend, the tiny roof of my tiny house would dissolve and then I'd be looking at myself where she lay under the sheets, wishing to be a physicist and a manticore and Carl Sagan. And sometimes, if I stayed there long enough, her face would go slack and she'd close her eyes. She'd fall asleep.

That trick is broken now. The moon has disappeared, replaced by other allegories—mushroom clouds that bloom and expand in radioactive billows, and gleaming knives balanced on their points, rotating in perfect symmetry. I don't need an expert to tell me that's not normal.

Some people are just born wrong.

In my room, the urge to climb out of my skin is suddenly so big it feels criminal.

I turn out the lamp and light my candle, illuminating the only place where nothing about me is for other people. A draft sends the glow flickering over the bed, desk, chair. My bookcase, home to three hundred comic books, thirty-seven collectible horror movie figures arranged in alphabetical order, Norman Bates to Xenomorph, and a pair of two-gallon terrariums that house my tarantulas, Franny and Zooey.

Maribeth said once that it was fitting, how even my pets can't be in the same room with each other without risking fatality, but the arrangement seems equitable. They're just enjoying each other from a distance.

When I lie down, my bed feels miles away. Already, I want to be up again, on my feet and pacing the room a few hundred times. But I need to sleep, and if I can't have that, then I need to achieve some kind of doze or trance or hypnotic state.

Courtesy of the Internet, some things I've learned today: insomnia is a harmless phenomenon that affects everyone from time to time, and it's the sole province of the clinically insane. It's a symptom of a physiological, possibly life-threatening condition, and it's all in your head. Mainly, though, I've learned that the Internet is alarmist, uninformative, and full of contradictions and the only practical option is to pick some relaxation techniques and start trying them.

I have my candle from the credenza, even if it's just an outsized Thanksgiving votive. Now all I need is a number to count backward from until my brain bows down to the hypnotic power of repetition.

Eleven seems like a good choice. It's a Lucas number, an Einstein prime, and the preferred visualization number in my mother's guided meditation book. Downstairs, the TV is murmuring and then she switches it off and the house goes silent.

I lie back, arms at my sides, trying to clear my mind.

But trying not to think is much harder than it looks. At once, I'm ambushed by the faces of the people who inhabit my world every day—my mom and Maribeth and Jamie the cross-country coach. They hover in front of me in a noisy flock, voices overlapping, blending together until I can't even tell who's saying what. If it's Jamie who likes Cattaleya orchids for the corsages, or if Maribeth thinks I could qualify for State.

I understand in a muddled way that the reverse counting technique must be working. Ordinarily I'd still be wired to the core, staring at the ceiling with hot, itchy eyes and humming skin. And instead, here I am, all my thoughts slipping away, slipping away, my hands heavy and numb.

I'm beginning to suspect that thinking is overrated. There are all kinds of people at school and I'm reasonably sure they rarely think at all. How nice it must be to have low expectations. No one wants anything from you. If you succeed in not getting arrested, they're happy for you.

Except for the Trunchbull . . .

The Trunchbull—I hear her voice suddenly, as clear as if she were standing in the room. *I'm not talking about them. I'm talking about you.*

Marshall Holt is a burned-out loser who just happens to have nice features, good skin, and well-shaped eyebrows. And surprisingly good test scores. The smell of the candle is much stronger, suddenly—a dark, complicated array of dryer sheets, deodorant, smoke, and indifference. It's undercut by something sweet and pungent and all its own. Pot, maybe?

All at once, I'm back in the office, sitting behind the reception desk with my stack of hall passes, and Marshall Holt is waiting for the stamp.

He's looking past me, and his mouth is wide and soft in a way I've never noticed. Then he smiles, but it isn't friendly. "Little miss perfect isn't so perfect after all."

I stare up. The sound of his voice is realer and sharper than everything else, almost accusatory.

The scene changes, the way it does in dreams. Now the room is small and poorly lit. I can't make out the details, but there's a smell of tomato sauce, onions, dog, and laundry.

He's sprawled out on an unmade twin bed, still looking at me, but not aggressive now, not arrogant. His eyes are fixed on mine, so dark I think I'll drown there. Somewhere close by, people are talking in raised voices, but the sound is indistinct, nothing but a murmur.

He smiles again, and this time it almost looks regretful. "Forty-five across is Lucrezia Borgia."

I sit bolt up, clutching my blankets to my chest.

The clock says 1:29. My pulse is frantic.

Somewhere down the street, a dog is howling like its heart will break. On my nightstand, the candle flickers. I lean over and blow it out.

Lucrezia Borgia. How could I have missed that?

•

When I meet Maribeth in the commons for a cup of coffee before homeroom, she and Loring are already waiting at our favorite table.

There's a party supply catalog open between them and Maribeth is bent over it, running her finger along the pricing column for confetti. The way she's biting her lip tells me everything is still proceeding to plan, a coup is imminent. One more advancement in a series of delicate maneuvers.

I know what will happen next. Maribeth will check off an order for crepe paper streamers in the color of her choice, like it was a foregone conclusion, and Loring will slip farther and farther toward the edges, until she simply disappears. The separation will be neat—no mess, no blood—and Maribeth is always so charming, and so, so warm. All the way up until she's not.

She waves me over and I know Loring can already sense the vibrations as the balance of power shifts. She gives me a smile like a bank-job hostage. Her mouth moves just fine, but nothing's happening around the eyes.

Maribeth reaches for me, moving so that Loring is

effectively boxed out, and flutters her lashes meaningfully. "*So?* I heard you had a little talk with *CJ* last night."

I ignore the seat she offers and slide into the one across the table. "He wants me to go to the dance with him."

"Oh my God, he just went up and asked you?" She sounds affronted—nearly scandalized—but her smile is fueled by pure, high-test pride. "I *told* him to do it like a normal person, with hearts and flowers and something *cute*."

Ducking her head conspiratorially, she runs her finger over the little brass key hanging on a chain around her neck. Hunter didn't give it to her, but I know the key must represent some meaningful encounter—that one time at the beginning of September, they conversed or flirted or did a group project on locksmithing or maximum-security prisons. I know her well enough to know the key is aspirational. A symbol of their bright and productive future together.

"It's fine," I say. "I don't think I would have liked that."

"Oh, you would have—you *would*. It would have been adorable!"

The way she can be counted on to tell me what I want is irritating, but for once, it doesn't strike sparks off the phosphorus strip in my chest. I'm not operating on a lot of sleep, but *some*. After my weird little pseudo-dream, I got four or five really decent hours. I feel okay.

The sun is out now, and everything seems new and clean and soft. I smile, thinking how nice it is that Maribeth is smiling and I'm here in the commons with her. I have a cup of coffee and it tastes sweet and dark and bitter, exactly how I like it.

She reaches across the table and holds my face in her hands. "You look better this morning."

The way she says it is cozy, reassuring. Just tender enough to remind me that the rest of the time I look terrible.

But maybe I'm projecting, thinking my own thoughts instead of hers. She didn't mean it like that—can't have meant it like that—and there are so many things to enjoy. I'm glad that Maribeth always wears her hair loose down her back like a Disney princess, and she hasn't changed her perfume since eighth grade, and her face is lovely and familiar. I like my laugh when I'm with her, and the way we've been glancing sideways at each other for our whole lives.

I even like Loring, although her ideas, organization, and execution are always terrible and she needs too much validation from people like Maribeth. That, more than anything, is a critical indication that it won't be okay. As soon as you need something from Maribeth, it's all over.

The way she's watching Loring now is openly appraising. She does the vaguest, subtlest thing with her mouth—halfway between a smile and a frown. "Loring, that thought you had about the table decorations was really interesting. Did you read that in *Ladies' Home Journal*?"

Maribeth's face is angelic. She waits. Does she pause the tiniest bit before she applies the adjective *interesting*? Does she draw the word *really* out a beat too long? No one can say for sure. This is the magic of plausible deniability.

I know the trick because I invested time and energy into understanding it. Maribeth knows it because she was born with the ability to slice through a person's self-assurance without even thinking.

Afterward, what recourse? Just shrug and smile and say you don't care about glitter or crepe paper or being included. Whether your existence has value.

Loring is looking over at the floor-to-ceiling windows, staring out at the cars in the parking lot and trying to decide if she's just been flayed.

It will sink in soon enough.

Don't kid yourself. Everybody cares.

•

The cross-country team: home of tiny nylon shorts and school-sanctioned eating disorders.

Within the distance runner demographic, I'm something of an aberration. I don't run to keep my weight down. I run because there's nothing better than going for miles with everyone else strung out in little clusters behind me.

I win because I have a good understanding of strategy, the long game, pacing myself.

No, wait. I lied.

I win because I'd rather hold a needle in the gas flame and stick it in my eye than lose. In fact, in the event of an eye-skewering tournament, I'm relatively certain I'd take first. Make it a competition, and I can do just about anything.

Over by the sinks, Kendry Epstein is braiding Palmer LeRoy's hair. They're talking about calories.

"But protein," Palmer says. "Maybe not beef. But soy? How many calories does tofu have if it's baked?"

"I don't know, but it's supposed to be good for your

boobs—I heard it makes them huge. Waverly knows, right?" Kendry says it over her shoulder, giving me an ironic look.

I laugh because that's how the script goes, the little joke, the little giggle. A smile is for everybody else. I have no breasts to speak of.

I open my locker and get out my cross-trainers and my shorts, thinking about homecoming posters, sleep deprivation, hearts and flowers and Maribeth's stupid necklace. Thinking about crossword puzzles and Lucrezia Borgia, right up until I hear Kendry say, "Okay, Autumn—for real. You can't keep putting your psychotic flyers on the bulletin board. Just, can you please take it down?"

Autumn Pickerel is sitting alone on one of the low benches, staring at a battered notebook with paper flowers decoupaged all over the front. Her legs are stretched across the aisle, and the laces of her sneakers have been wrestled into sloppy bows, grimy from being stepped on.

Behind her, the bulletin board is huge, covered in photocopied pep rally announcements and ads for letter jackets and class rings, only now, there's something that looks like a hand-drawn bingo card tacked in the exact center of it.

Autumn is slow. Not in the sense of being stupid—I have no idea about her mental capacity—but her cross-country times are terrible.

Strictly speaking, the level at which she sucks doesn't matter. Distance running is one of the only sports with an open roster. A social free-for-all. Anyone who wants to can sign up.

I just have no idea why she wants to.

Girls like Autumn don't go out for sports. They sulk around the drama department or the art hall, fidgeting with their piercings and drawing tragic water lilies on their shoes. They write poems about how they're in love with sad, androgynous musicians who wear eyeliner. They don't just show up to Extracurricular Involvement one day and start loping along at the back. Or anyway, they never did before.

She's looking up now. Her hair has fallen in a reddish spill over one eye. The way the fluorescents glint off all the metal in her ears makes her look like she's holding an electrical charge.

"You can mark off the square for *Fascist to Be Fascist,*" she says. Her voice is soft and husky. "I mean, since you're the one who fulfilled it just now."

She says it very clearly—just tosses it out there, without missing a beat.

Working theory: Autumn is so socially bizarre that she's exhausted all obvious channels of expressing it. Clearly, she has joined cross-country because the only way left to prove her eccentricity is by doing something normal.

Kendry plants her hands on her hips. "God, what is *wrong* with you? Do you have any idea how weird you are?"

Autumn just stares back, and in that moment, I'm almost sure that something is going to happen and I have no idea what it will be. Autumn looks mysterious, but not the way other girls look mysterious when they're trying to flirt with boys or keep secrets. Nothing about her face tells me what's coming. She's not angry, not anxious or hurt or apologetic. I don't recognize her expression, and *that* is interesting.

"Come on," I say, taking Kendry's arm, turning her by the elbow.

For a second she resists, still staring down at Autumn like she wants to eat her. Then she sighs through her teeth and lets me do it.

In the hierarchy of our glossy, snarling pack, I'm the beta. This is the end result of having built Maribeth Whitman. The privilege of being carnivorous.

Kendry twists away from me. Most days, she has a face like a happy pie, but now she's looking thunderous. "The bulletin board is for office-approved flyers *only*."

"I'm sure people have enough reading comprehension to recognize that the school isn't sponsoring"—I examine Autumn's contribution, which represents a fairly damning selection of things I have actually heard various girls on cross-country say, and bite my lip to keep from smiling—"Bitchface Bingo. It's fine."

Kendry clearly believes it is *not* fine, and doesn't appreciate how the card is obstructing people's view of the sign-up sheet for synchronized swimming, but she huffs once, then catches hold of Palmer, dragging her out of the locker room, stepping ostentatiously over Autumn's outstretched feet.

After they've gone, Autumn stands and saunters back toward the sinks. She takes her time, swinging her hips from side to side and singing under her breath, "One of these things is not like the others. . . ."

At first I think she must be talking about herself, but the way she's looking at me is too purposefully cool. Too bland to be accidental.

As she passes the bulletin board, she stops in front of me, holding the notebook against her chest—not like she's protecting herself with it, but like she just needs a place to rest her arms because they really are that heavy. She's taller than me, with a good build and long legs. I wonder why her cross-country times are so bad.

"Cute how they all jump," she says, sounding almost sleepy. "Did they come with that built in, or did you teach them how to do tricks?"

I stare back at her and don't answer. The truth is, it's a little bit of both.

The warm-up is flat and slow, heading down the east side of the park and out along the road. In the haze of car exhaust, my heart beats harder. When I begin to sweat, it's the slick, ghostly kind, drying off my face and arms as soon as it appears.

There's an ugly word beating in my blood. The word is *tired, tired, tired.*

Even before I look up, I can tell I'm lagging. My feet throb with a tight pain that wasn't there a week ago, and for half a mile, it's enough to keep me at the back with the Autumns. The aimless and the slow. Girls who joined to please their parents or get in shape or just to be able to say they played a sport in high school.

But I have no right to be tired now. I slept last night,

really and truly, for the first time in days—deep, unconscious sleep. And sure, maybe it wasn't eight hours, but it was actual. Functional.

As I cross Spooner Street, my stride gets longer. Now I'm shaking off the torpor, powering through it, rising up and up—above the road, above the trees. I'm flying. Running is like music. It requires rhythm and focus. It requires dedication. It requires a dogged ability to shut out everything else. The herd is strung out below me, keeping time with the thump and slap of their cross-trainers. I hold the sound in my head and subtract cars, trucks, motorcycles, voices until it's nothing but a song.

By the time I reach the corner of Wentworth and Sixth, I've left them behind. I move like patterns of air and light. I float.

Sweat blooms in a thin film across my back and my stomach. My skin feels cool and smooth, like I'm turning into stone.

I hit Grant Street and the ache starts, gnawing at my heels, the backs of my ankles.

Let me tell you about blisters: they are irrelevant. They tear, they weep, they scar, but they do not keep you from getting to the finish line. Pain is a series of impulses. It leaps from your nerve endings to your brain, telling you to move your hand off the burner, to get that gash stitched up. It's an evolutionary function, a language of survival.

Pain as a concrete, factual thing does not exist.

•

If my mother is concerned with the deep dark heart of things, my father is the opposite. He's in commercial advertising. His job is to spearhead campaigns for products like ammonia-based hair color and high-protein weight gainer and denture adhesive. I am typically not in his target demographic.

He and I communicate using an elaborate system of sticky notes. When he's working on a new concept, he writes down his thoughts and sticks them to the counter. Some days, the kitchen looks like it got hit by an exploding piñata.

The product of the day is a box of granola bars. The note is a bright, wholesome shade of blue, shorthand for emotion. How do Sun Valley granola products make you *feel*?

I peel down the wrapper and bite into it. It tastes crumbly and reminds me of the oatmeal cookies they gave us for snack in kindergarten.

I scribble *nostalgic* on the sticky note and go upstairs to shower.

When I come back down for dinner, two new notes have appeared on the counter. Orange is thank you for your participation. Green means a face-to-face. The green one says, *Pizza in the TV room? Olives and banana peppers.* At the bottom, in red ink, courtesy of his trusty four-color pen, it says, *Destroy this message upon receipt.*

My mother must be out. We are ordinarily not allowed to eat wet or colored foods in the TV room.

I like eating with my dad because he doesn't have a preconceived notion of how things should be. The conversation isn't measured in correct dosage, no prescription recommending that the napkins match the place mats.

He's sitting on the floor with his back against the couch and a yellow legal pad propped on one knee. When I come into the room, he looks up. There's a pizza box on the coffee table.

"What do you think about mutual funds?" he says.

"I don't, really."

He nods and makes a dutiful note. "So you're saying the seventeen-to-twenty-five market is untapped."

"Dad."

He smiles, leaning forward to flip open the box. "Speaking of the jaded-youth demographic, isn't it Friday? Shouldn't you be out doing something *involved*?"

I shrug and reach for a slice. "Involvement gets old."

He waves his pen in a way that's calculated to conjure images of my mother. "I see. And do you feel that as a contemporary American teenager, freshness and novelty are vital to the development of your psyche?"

"Dad, stop. We've been working on color schemes for the dance for two weeks. Do you have any idea how long two weeks is when you're talking about napkins?"

"Ah, and do you have a date for this dance?" His hands are clasped on the coffee table now, legal pad forgotten.

"I'm going with CJ Borsen."

"And just what are this CJ's qualifications?"

"Aspirations of law school, and a five-star safety-rated fuel-efficient car."

"And would you say the match is socially advantageous?"

I nod and rearrange the olives on my pizza for more even distribution. I don't point out that all my contacts are socially advantageous.

His expression is open and receptive. I just don't know how much of that is the marketing consultant, and how much of it is my dad. He makes up persuasive copy for a living. It doesn't really matter that he's joking. Advantageous contacts are still just another fact of life.

After pizza and two episodes of spin-off *Law & Order,* I double-check the answers on my trig homework. Then I go up to my room and get out a new book of crosswords. I pass four or five hours filling out the puzzles in English, and then again in Spanish. Some of the words aren't in the translation dictionary. I have to look them up online. Some don't even have a Spanish equivalent. The vowels are unpredictable and all over the place.

When the book starts looking like the work of a serial killer, I shove it back in the desk and take out my candle and my matches.

The sleep I got last night was insufficient, but it was real, and the true test of any good experiment is whether or not it's repeatable. I lie on my back. The flame burns low and steady. I close my eyes and start to count.

MARSHALL
Tripped

It's not like I think the acid is a good idea. I don't.

But my brother Justin has this thing about parties and if I don't look like I'm out-of-my-mind happy, he'll always take it personally.

He offers me the tab, balancing it on a safety pin so he won't rub the dose off by touching it with his fingers. The blotter paper has a little Christmas angel printed on it in yellow ink. I wonder if it's supposed to be a joke, or if he's just confused. It's October.

Sometimes I get the feeling he's trying to piss off our dad, and this is just another way to do it—like Justin has me on his team and the sport is being more like him. Being exactly who my dad already thinks I am.

The theme for the party is Trailer Trash Showcase, which Justin came up with because he actually *likes* cheap beer, or because he started lifting over the summer and wants an excuse to wear a shirt with no sleeves, or maybe just as some kind of a misguided middle finger to everybody who ever made fun of us growing up for our clothes or our shoes or the street we lived on.

Now that I'm here, though, standing in his kitchen, the actual event doesn't really feel cool or edgy. Underneath, it seems more like giving up—you just say it first, before someone else can.

After too much time debating it, I reach for the acid.

"Atta boy," Justin says, smiling like I'm a dog who's done a trick, and then charging off to find a shot glass or a bottle opener or to bother someone else.

My friend Ollie gives me a look, but doesn't say anything. He's pretty good at seeing how things are going to turn out, but he'll usually keep his mouth shut.

Ollie's easy to be around, but sometimes hard to read. His mom left a couple years ago—just took off one day without warning. She said she needed to simplify her life, so she threw a bunch of stuff in the back of her Civic and moved to San Antonio, which is about the most screwed-up thing I've ever heard. In some ways, Ollie is probably as messed up as I am, but that's not why we're friends. Or at least, we've been friends longer than things have been shitty.

"Mars," he says. "Are you sure you're in the mood to go sailing tonight?"

Which is a hard question to answer.

The acid isn't a big deal. It's Friday night, so it's not like I have someplace else to be. Lately, though, my life is a little off the rails. I already feel like the walls are coming down around me. I want to feel different, sure. But I don't want to feel any more ruined than I already do.

Also, Justin's Trash party is not the greatest place to get chemically altered. A lot of people are walking around with huge ratted hair and their front teeth blacked out. I can picture several scenarios where the night doesn't go so well. They just aren't bad enough to make me change my mind.

"Don't," Ollie says, like he's going to give me a reason.

I put the square on my tongue anyway, because it's free, and because no matter what, it's a guaranteed alternative to feeling like I feel right now.

The party is loud, bigger than most of the ones at Justin's house, and everyone's swarming all over each other. The girls are sweating off their makeup and I know that before long, I'll have to go out in the backyard just so I can breathe.

"You didn't have to take it just because the Captain gave it to you."

In Ollie-speak, *the Captain* is shorthand for *Captain Cockjob,* but Justin doesn't know that. He thinks being the Captain is a good thing, which makes me half sorry. I'd feel all the way sorry if he wasn't such an unrelenting cockjob.

Tonight, though, he's at least acting like a brother, and he did just give me the blotter tab, for no reason except that he wanted to. "Come on, he's okay."

"Yeah, he's *fine,* as long as you're swinging from his nuts."

I laugh, even though that's so true it's not funny.

Ollie shrugs, then flinches as the Captain comes barreling back into the kitchen. "Whatever. Oh, hey, I was going to tell you. I saw Little Ollie in the art hall before Spanish today."

The Captain laughs and pounds Ollie on the back. "Wait, you're naming your junk now?"

But Little Ollie is a real person, this douchey freshman who looks remarkably like regular Ollie—not Ollie now, but Ollie when he was fourteen.

We ran into him in the quad one day at the beginning of the year and it was so weird and *Twilight Zone* that now regular Ollie occasionally keeps an eye on what Little Ollie gets up to.

Ollie shoves the Captain's hand away and doesn't answer. "Anyway, he was just lounging up against the lockers like a pimp, scamming on this little freshman girl. It was kind of crazy to watch."

"Is he smooth?" I say, not really caring, but already a hundred percent sure that I'd rather have this conversation than any of the ones the Captain has on offer.

Ollie shakes his head. "Not so much. When I passed them, he was looking like he wanted to jump down her shirt headfirst."

The Captain's still off on his own tangent like Ollie hasn't said a word. He hoists himself onto the counter, settling in between us. The way he's talking is loud and blustery, and I feel bad, because no matter how bad I feel, I can't help thinking that if we just ignore him, he might still go away.

I stand slumped against the kitchen sink, waiting for the acid to kick in and drinking a beer.

The Captain is telling the longest, stupidest story in the history of the world, all about how Hez, his roommate, wouldn't get out of the Captain's easy chair.

"—and he totally didn't believe that I'd do it, that I'd piss on him, but—"

Ollie sighs, leaning his elbows on the counter and staring down with his hair hanging in his face. "That's because you'd have to be a complete degenerate to piss on someone."

The acid is starting to come on in little tremors, like someone just threw a rock into water and now the waves are rippling out from the center.

When I look up again, Ollie's watching me.

"What?"

He shrugs and sort of smiles, but like a floppy cartoon character shrugging for something sad, and I know he's right—and I knew the score anyway—but it's too late now.

He says, "If it gets bad, think of something really boring. Like history, or something."

"I don't think history's boring," I say, and my voice sounds like nothing I've ever heard before, all sad and slow and musical.

Ollie shrugs again. "Deep-sea fishing, then. Or baseball."

But really he's saying, *We both know this is going to get bad.*

"You're right," I tell him, but I'm not sure I say it out loud. I might just be using my brain.

Then the two of us sit there being right, but not getting any satisfaction out of it. There's not really a prize for that kind of thing.

WAVERLY

2.

I've stopped counting down, but I don't remember when that happened. Voices echo from far away, getting closer. Everything feels cold.

When I open my eyes, I'm standing at the edge of a cement slab, surrounded by a horde of people. The yard is filthy. It has that ambience of total neglect that only frat houses and meth labs can sustain. The whole patio is awash in spilled beer.

The crowd presses in on me, boys in trucker caps and wifebeaters, the girls caked in makeup and squeezed into disastrously short daisy dukes.

There's nothing worse than the realization that everyone around you is adhering to some kind of unifying principle, and you're dressed in two-piece flannel pajamas. I clasp my hands under my chin and tuck my elbows close, gripped by the horrifying idea that I've been sleepwalking and have wandered into someone's yard.

No one seems to find my presence remarkable, though.

They don't even look in my direction, and as time wears on, I'm more and more convinced that they're not going to.

This is the functional opposite of dreams about delivering speeches to packed auditoriums while naked. It's like my subconscious is underscoring all the ways the world consists of tightly knit social biomes, and I am on the outside.

Everyone's drinking and laughing. I recognize a few of them from school, but mostly from the chatter and chaos of the passing periods. Everyone else is college age, but none of them really look like they're in college. Something a little too adult in their faces, a little too tired.

Close by, one of the boys is talking to a guy in his twenties, who's holding a bottle of beer and sporting facial hair that could use the delicate attention of a weed-whacker.

The boy is named Ollie Poe and he's in my Spanish class. He has lank, dark hair that comes down to his chin, and a nervous way of touching his collarbone before he talks. I had PE with him last year, and his crap badminton skills were rivaled only by his chronic inability to run the mile in under twelve minutes.

He's moving his hands too quickly, touching his forehead, his chin. "Look, is Mars gonna be cool or what? I mean, maybe you think this is *funny* or something, but he's down under that table picking at himself like a fucking tweaker."

The other guy nods and finishes his beer in a long swallow. He scrubs his mangy little beard with the back of his hand before answering. "He's okay. That blotter shit comes on big, but it peaks fast. Just don't bother him, he'll be fine."

Ollie twitches like a marionette, sticking a cigarette behind his ear, taking it back down again. "What if he gets cold? He's just in that beater. Shouldn't somebody check on him, maybe take him a blanket or something?"

The other guy shrugs, swinging his empty bottle in a meditative circle. "You go messing with him now, he's just going to flip his shit. Leave him alone, he'll work it out."

"He was rough tonight, though. Like, cut-up. Look, is something going on at your house, or what?"

The guy clenches his jaw like a nervous tic—one quick beat. Then he shakes his head, peering around the yard. "This *is* my house."

Ollie sticks the cigarette in the corner of his mouth. "Don't be a dumbass. You know what I mean."

The guy shrugs, scratching the back of his neck. I can't tell which parts of his sketchy ensemble are a costume and which aren't. "It's no big deal. My dad just got approved for long-term disability. Like, last week. Whatever. Untwist your panties. Mars is fine."

Ollie nods, looking unconvinced. He keeps glancing in the direction of the back fence, where lawn chairs sit piled between a picnic table and a rusting barbecue grill. The chairs look serviceable but the grill tilts halfheartedly on a missing wheel. It's a glance that says Ollie will watch out for his friend anyway, because he's just that kind of guy.

Across the patio, a pair of girls with way too much eye makeup are looking sleepy and drunk together, sharing a battered armchair and a can of PBR.

One of them looks over, and for a second, I'm nearly certain that she sees me. Her eyes go wide in recognition. Then a boy with a drawn-on neck tattoo and a pornstache—either real or fake—starts toward them and she jumps up, flinging herself past me and into his arms.

I turn away from them, and almost smack right into Ollie Poe.

He just stares through me like everyone else, eyes going back to the fence, back to where the table sits battered and forlorn, and a boy without a jacket is feeling rough tonight.

The yard is grassless, packed with dirt and wet, putrid leaves. They ooze sickly between my toes as I start across it. When the wind blows, it cuts through my pajamas like a surgical knife.

The picnic table is the stolen-from-the-park variety, gouged with pocketknife graffiti. When I lean down to look under it, Marshall Holt is sitting on the ground with his head bent and his knees drawn up.

This is not the indifferent Marshall in Spanish class, and not the cool crossword expert from my dream. He's got his arms around himself, holding the points of his shoulders. When he looks at me, his pupils seem to be swallowing his irises like spilled ink.

With a quick, electric pulse beating time behind my breastbone, I move closer. "Hey. What are you doing?"

His breath comes out in a strangled gasp, but he doesn't answer. His eyes are locked on mine.

I scoot up against the table, leaning farther into the dark. "Marshall, why are you under there?"

He flinches and turns his face hard against his shoulder.

"Hey," I whisper. My voice sounds careful and slow. I can almost feel myself sinking deeper into the dream. Letting it wash over me. I would never be so gentle or so forward in real life. "Hey, Marshall, look at me. Why won't you look at me?"

When he speaks, his voice is hoarse and cracking, barely audible. "You're not real."

I prop my elbows on the bench. "You should come out from there."

"No," he whispers, keeping his face turned away. Then, without warning, he swings around, eyes huge and dark in the shadow of the table. "It's bad—it's so bad. The ground is falling apart, it's peeling up all over the place. The moon's like a death's-head."

I sit in the dirt and look up. Above the trees, the moon is low, glowing orchid-white against the sky. Wispy clouds feather out, drifting in front of it, but in the dark, they appear to be reaching from behind it like spectral fingers. Or bones.

I keep expecting the scene to shift, the way things do in dreams, mutating from raucous house party to something else. Maybe, if I'm following Marshall's train of thought, a history lesson on Nazi insignia throughout World War II?

But the ground underneath me seems solid enough, and when I glance up again, the moon is just a moon. "It looks okay to me. Really."

He doesn't answer, working at the dirt with the toe of his sneaker.

"Marshall, relax. It's going to be fine."

"Please," he whispers. "Stop saying my name."

I nod, trying to look reassuring. "Okay, I won't say your name."

For a long time, neither of us says anything. He sits with

his arms around himself, breathing in long, whining gasps. Then he closes his eyes and wets his lips. "If you're real, then touch me."

I reach under the table, into the blue-black shadow, and after a second, he reaches back.

His fingers are warm, softer and more cautious than I expected, tangling with mine, and then he yanks his hand back, twisting away from me, covering his head with his arms. His breath sounds tight and panicked.

In my mom's clinician handbook, it advises that when people are operating under the influence of psychoactive drugs, you should ask them simple, manageable questions that will help you make their surrounding environment more comfortable. The bonus is that sometimes this lets you evaluate their mental state without sounding like you're interrogating them.

I stay right there in the dirt, leaning close, and don't say his name. The ground is wet and there's a soggy residue soaking through my pajamas. "Are you cold?"

He buries his face in the crook of his elbow. His shirt seems to glow up out of the dark like a lit bulb. All I can see is the curve of his back, the outline of his head. He's rocking now, swaying back and forth. His shoulders are shaking. His breathing sounds strangled.

"Do you feel sad?"

He keeps his face hidden against the crook of his arm. "Go away. *Please* go away."

I scrub my hands off on the tops of my thighs and stand up. "Okay, fine. Fine. If you want to wallow in the dirt, that's completely up to you."

I start back toward the cracked patio and the naked light. In the middle of the yard, I stop. Ollie Poe is coming toward me, elbowing his way through the crowd and carrying a gray army blanket. As he passes, his arm brushes my shoulder but he doesn't seem to notice. As soon as he touches me, though, a tight, creeping sensation blooms on my face and my bare legs, like something is very wrong.

Above me, the moon is smiling in its luminous, pock-marked skin. I shiver and wrap my arms around myself. Something about the moment is getting thinner, but I can't tell if it's me or everyone else. The feeling on my skin is chilly and squirming. Then it's nothing.

The light on my ceiling is unsteady. When I toss the blankets back, I do it so aggressively that the candle gutters out.

In the dark, I'm not entirely sure where I am.

The dream is still alarmingly vivid. Marshall Holt, with his bare arms, his bent back. The warmth of his touch as I reached under the picnic table for his hand.

It's difficult to hold on to these things, though, and the harder I try to inventory my surroundings, the more disoriented I feel, until I'm not sure of anything anymore, apart from a cold, scratching sensation whenever I move.

I flail toward the nightstand, fumbling for my lamp, then sit frozen in the circle of light, staring down at myself.

There are dead leaves plastered all over my feet like leeches.

•

The weekend gallops past in flashes. I keep coming back to the problem of my feet. I do the research for my mid-term paper, help Maribeth with the student council budget, win the mini-meet against the parochial school across town by almost forty seconds. I'm still thinking about my feet.

By Monday, the thought has stopped feeling like a thought and is more like a low-grade toothache, flat and tolerable, but always there.

I sit at my desk while cities fall, cells divide, the imaginary shadows of imaginary flagpoles make acute, useless angles when the imaginary sun shines down on them. I'm thinking about my feet.

The first order of business was to wash them. Then strip the sheets, pick twigs and scattered leaves out of my bed. I didn't put them in the trash. Instead, I carried them outside and walked up and down the block looking for a maple tree.

Maybe this is evidence that I've started sleepwalking.

Maybe relaxation does strange things to people. Maybe, unbeknownst to me, I've been attending redneck-themed keggers on autopilot.

Counterargument:

1) No one at the party seemed to see me except for Marshall Holt.
2) All the trees in my neighborhood are cotton-woods.

There's a formula for finding the volume of an irregular prism scrawled on the inside cover of my notebook, but I don't remember writing it there. The rest of the notebook is full of Spanish verb forms.

Marshall's attendance record is generally spotty, but today he makes it to class—a full three minutes after the bell. When the door opens, everyone turns to look at him. It's strange, how everyone is always turning to stare at latecomers, like just this once, there will be a mechanized dinosaur or a rhinoceros standing in the doorway, instead of some slacker who was smoking out by the baseball dia-mond and lost track of time.

His gaze rests on me for one scant second. By the time I meet his eyes, he's already looking away. Marshall Holt is just a boy I talked to once, for one excruciating second in the counseling office. There is no evidence that we con-versed the other night, even briefly, which leaves a very re-alistic dream. The kind in which you inadvertently get mud and leaves all over your sheets.

No, that doesn't work.

Superficially, it sounds neat and logical, but it doesn't prove out.

In the mirror over the locker room sinks, I check under my eyes. It's getting to be an obsession. Pat concealer in a dotted line, smear it with my fingertip. Usually, the full-coverage complexion perfecter in Porcelain Pure gets the job done, but today it looks chalky and unattractive.

"She's doing it again," Palmer says behind me, in a voice that could eat through metal.

When I turn around, Autumn is standing in the middle of the locker room with her shoulders slumped and her ankles crossed awkwardly. We have a meet today, but she's still wearing a faded black T-shirt instead of her uniform.

When the fluorescent tube in the ceiling flickers, she looks like someone out of a cheap horror movie—the girl who gets killed in the middle. Not the smartest or the prettiest or the most virtuous, but everyone thinks she's basically okay and they're sad when she's dead.

"Autumn," says Kendry, with her hands on her hips. "I thought we agreed for you to keep your random flyers off the board or I was going to have to report you for being too freakish to be allowed."

Autumn doesn't answer right away. A new flyer is tacked in the middle of the board. It says, in heavy block letters:

MISSING UNICORN
IF SEEN, PLEASE GO HOME.
YOU'RE TOTALLY FUCKED UP.

The drawing is good. It's of a Boston terrier with a horn taped to its forehead.

I think I catch Autumn looking at me from the corner of my eye, just for a second, but then she glances away, letting her bangs fall in front of her face.

After a lazy beat, she sighs and flicks her hair behind her ear with one coolly deliberate middle finger. "And I thought we agreed that you'd stop doing perverse things with tennis equipment."

"God," Palmer says, looking genuinely affronted. "You don't have to be a *bitch* about it. She was only joking."

Autumn just stares back with the same flat, sleepy expression she always has. Then she nods. "Oh. Oh, sorry, I get it now." Her voice is husky. "No, that *is* funny. I think you might have messed up the punch line, though. I think it's actually supposed to be *go fuck yourself*."

For a second, I'm almost hysterically sure that I'm about to laugh out loud. Palmer and Kendry are both looking incensed. I wonder if this is what international correspondents mean when they say tensions have escalated. The air practically crackles with angry static.

Then Jamie yells down the hall that we have five minutes until the bus and Palmer and Kendry snatch their Windbreakers and turn for the door. When they leave, the room gets so quiet it feels like it's starting to rust.

Autumn's still standing under the gently flickering light. When she speaks, she sounds almost drugged. "You know what I don't get? The fact that you do this shit voluntarily. I mean, forgive me, but what is the *point*?"

At the sink, I rest my hand on the faucet and take a beat before responding. "Excuse me?"

She covers the distance between us in four purposeful strides. "You. And them. Don't even tell me you think they're your same species."

"It doesn't matter."

"How very mercenary."

I lean away, trying not to look surprised, but I feel my eyebrows perk up anyway. "At least I know how to exist without antagonizing people."

"There but for the grace of God or whatever."

I splash some tap water through my bangs, pushing them off my forehead, using a strip of pre-wrap for a headband. "If you think it's all so meaningless, why are you even here? No one is making you."

She's different now, in the empty room. Her expression is cool and alert. "This whole sports and activities thing is just my mom's latest campaign for conformity, okay? Left to my own devices, I'm not a joiner."

The face I maintain is carefully neutral—my mother's psych face. "Shocking."

Autumn turns to the mirror, picking at her bottom lip. In the glass, her reflection looks stoic and mean. "I totally asked you a serious question just now, and you totally changed the subject. You, them, *why*?"

I shrug. Kendry and Palmer may not be astounding minds

of our generation, but they know how to navigate the terrain of empty compliments and small talk, and never seem to mind too much when I don't. "They have their uses."

Autumn twitches away from the mirror. "Jesus *Christ,* you are a sociopath!"

"I'm a pragmatist." The declaration seems too harsh for daytime-Waverly, and I add, kind of lamely, "There's a difference."

Autumn rolls her eyes. "Come *on.* Your friends suck so much it's criminal. What could you possibly get from hanging out with those guys besides the satisfaction of knowing you're better than them at everything?"

"It's not actually as satisfying as you'd think."

"*Wow.*"

I know how it sounded, but no matter how arrogant or mechanical I seem, the truth is worse. The alternative to formal dances and student council—to Maribeth and her minions—is to be deeply, unalterably alone. It's a hazard that has always been there, drifting in the background since elementary school. And so I study hierarchies and social norms, abide by the rules. I restrain myself, and even when I slip up sometimes and stop having facial expressions or start talking about spiral galaxies, most of the time, Palmer and Kendry don't actually notice.

For a second, I expect Autumn to scold me for my haughtiness the same way Maribeth would. Tell me, once again, the story of my own faulty wiring. But she just shrugs a broad, expansive shrug. "Hey, I get it. Your fatal flaw is that you have no people skills. Whatever, it happens to the best of us."

I stare back at her, shaking my head. "You make it a hobby to intentionally piss off *every*one, and you're blaming it on faulty *people skills*?"

"Oh, no—*my* fatal flaw is that I never lie. Totally different. If you want, though, I could probably give you a few pointers."

"Thanks, but I think I'd rather stick to just not talking."

She grins, but it's more like she's baring her teeth. "Waverly, please. It's not like I don't already know your dirty little secret."

I have a guilty recollection of wandering through drunk, oblivious crowds in my pajamas, waking up with rotting leaves stuck to my feet. Marshall, his warm hands reaching for mine from under the picnic table.

I cross my arms over my chest. "What secret?"

"That you're the smart one."

When I laugh, it sounds relieved. "*Every*one knows that. They print the honor roll on the back page of the *Courier* every quarter."

"I'm not talking about grades." She waves her hand at the empty locker room. "I'm talking about *this*. The dances, the clubs, the passwords and the handshakes. You know it's bullshit, and you play anyway."

I don't say anything.

"I bet you play chess," she says.

I shake my head. "I quit in junior high."

"Too dorky?"

"Yeah."

"You were good, though, right?"

"I don't do anything I'm not good at."

We stand looking at each other over the carved-up benches. She's wearing so much eyeliner that it's starting to flake off in waxy pieces, like crayon.

"You didn't quit," she says finally. "You just found yourself a bigger board with fancier pieces."

•

The run that night is long and dreamlike. I feel surreal, wired like a car battery, my engine clanking, my thoughts racing.

Autumn is unexpected. An unknown quantity.

I spend four blocks trying to anticipate all the ways her interest in me could end in disaster.

No matter what angle I consider, it's hard to see a motive. It's not that I'm guileless enough to believe she actually likes me. I just can't think of anything I have that she would want.

I need more information. I need to outline a presentation for my English class and ice my feet and find a dress for homecoming and maybe one of these days, if the oceans part and the stars align, actually start sleeping.

Since the night of the party and the leaves in my bed, I haven't been all that anxious to get back to my relaxation techniques. It means insomnia as usual, but at least I know I'm not going to wind up barefoot in someone's yard. I'm still not clear on the more esoteric aspects of what happened on Friday, but since I gave up on the counting and the candle, it hasn't happened again.

Running is enough to take the edge off, and if you just go far enough, a sense of unshakable calm will always set in. It leaves me rubbery-legged, but serene, and I slip in through the back door, weightless and euphoric.

By midnight, though, the rush of endorphins has already worn off. My feet ache. My vision is starting to sharpen like a telephoto lens, objects standing out with frightening clarity. There's nothing left to do but sit on the couch in the family room and watch *Fight Club,* and when all else fails, watch it again.

I am Jack's wasted youth.

MARSHALL
High, Low

The Captain's house is where I go when things stop making sense.

At home, the theme for the night is Pass the Blame: Who Gets It, and I'm in the mood for something that doesn't make me feel like I need to puke.

We're out on the sunporch, playing Hi-Lo around a white patio table. It's got four matching chairs and a canvas umbrella that barely fits under the sloped roof.

The Captain and Hez boosted it from the community pool in one of the new developments a couple months ago. It doesn't leave much space to use the washing machine, and it makes it hard to open the door, but they're so proud of themselves they won't get rid of it.

Hez is dealing, flipping the cards and taking the bets. He turns up the five of hearts and waits for me to call the next one.

On the other side of the table, Ollie and the Captain are going the distance for the millionth fucking time, mostly about Ollie's problem when it comes to closing the deal with girls.

"Low," I say, because the odds aren't great, but I just have a feeling and the feeling is low.

Hez flips the top card. It's a three.

"High," I say, and he flips the next card. Ten.

The Captain leans back in his stolen pool chair and squints at Ollie. "So tell me—if you're such a ladies' man and all—are you wearing that shirt as like a self-activating cock-block, then?"

Ollie's had the same clothes pretty much since his mom left. Jeans and old band T-shirts, and some collared button-downs with mangled cuffs. He makes a big thing of looking around the sunporch and the empty backyard, checking all the corners.

Then he turns to the Captain. "There are no girls here. At all."

Just like that, I'm miles away. Not thinking about girls, but one girl. The acid dream of Waverly in the yard. This pale hallucination that came glowing at me out of the dark, and suddenly everything seemed so real it was terrible.

Her face was the cleanest thing I'd ever seen, and everything else was so ugly and so dirty. The skin of the world was peeling back, showing all the bones. I had to focus on each breath, taking one and another, and then another. Otherwise, it felt like I might just stop.

And Jesus, by the time I saw her I was mostly gone. Fuck, I was an astronaut. I was already in orbit. After what seemed like centuries, she touched my hand.

"High," I say to Hez. The third card's a queen and my turn passes to Ollie without taking a penalty.

"In the mood?" Hez asks, tapping the pocket of his work shirt where he keeps his pipe.

I shrug and scrape the cards together. "I don't know. Maybe later."

Hez's real name is Isaac, but back when they were in middle school, the Captain started calling him Hezekiah for no reason and it stuck.

Across from us the Captain is still ragging on Ollie like it's a sport. "You're just picky, is all. Look at Marshall—he's a total bitch and he scores fine."

Ollie just gives him the kind of look that Ollie does better than anyone and slaps the top card out of Hez's hand without even bothering to call it.

The thing with the Captain is, you have to just shut up and let him do his thing. He was worse when we were younger, always beating on me over stupid shit or leaving me behind. Now he's just kind of a dick.

Hez picks Ollie's card off the floor and tells him to drink. Across the table, the Captain starts reciting some joke he heard from one of the guys who works with him at Grease Monkey. I suck down the rest of my beer, even though I should be waiting for the penalties.

Hanging out at Justin's on a school night is the kind of thing where the first time it happens, you don't really mind. It's like a novelty. But then, when you're not looking, it sneaks in and becomes your life, because nothing else is becoming your life.

Hez is packing his pipe now, looking at me with his eyebrows raised. He passes it over and I take it, even though I just spent fifteen minutes telling myself how I needed to get on track and I wasn't going to do that, not now, not tonight. Forget it. I'm too raw, too ready to dive into the heat and the smoke and the nothing.

It blooms in my chest and I feel guilty for—once again—choosing the easy way. I think about all the other people in the world who are stronger. Who face overwhelming odds and suck it up and raise themselves by their bootstraps to become effective leaders and the noble everyman saviors of third-world countries.

Then the warm feeling of floating, and at the same time, I'm too heavy to move. All the boredom and the awfulness is melting out of me and I sit there and let it go.

It's warmer than it was on Friday. The yard looks bigger without all the people.

Ollie's arguing with the Captain over whether two girls in one night counts as a three-way if they don't touch each other. The Captain says yes, if they're both on the bed at the same time.

Ollie says he could not give less of a flying fuck.

When the Captain finally gets bored with harassing Ollie, he leans across the table and punches me. "So, Mom still doing the sit-down dinner thing?"

I nod, looking someplace else. Not like he knows anything about it. He doesn't come over. And our sister Annie's always at work or school or someplace more important, so the heartfelt tradition that was supposed to bring the family together hasn't really got a lot to do with family.

Mostly, it's just me and them.

The thing is, when you grow up someplace shitty and angry and your parents fight all the time, you get used to the idea that it's going to end eventually, so when they finally sat down with us and laid it out, it wasn't a shock.

Our dad had been seeing this lady who worked in the back office at the chip-packing plant. The way he talked about it was flat, not like he was ecstatic or so in love, and my mom's eyes were red, but she'd already finished crying. They were getting divorced, and that was fine.

In movies, people are always acting ruined. It wasn't like that. I sat on the couch with Annie and started looking forward to my new, uncrazy life, like things were actually going to be better.

Except, there was the other thing. Our dad had been having problems—problems with his eyes, problems balancing. It wasn't devastating or anything. But it kept getting worse.

And then the tests came back and it was bad. There were lesions on his brain and his spinal cord, and suddenly, my parents were staying together. They were going to tough it out. Our mom was going to forgive him, and he was going to stop screwing the office lady he wasn't in love with and that was just the situation. They were going to keep doing exactly what they'd always done, only now they both felt guilty enough to pretend they didn't hate each other and we were all just supposed to pretend along with them.

Ollie takes the deck from Hez and puts it in front of me. "Your deal. Hey, you want to come over tomorrow? I was thinking—"

"That whole dinner insanity is such bullshit anyway," the Captain says, leaning back in his chair like it's no big deal. "One of these days, you need to just tell Dad to go fuck himself. Shit, tell them both."

The air in the sunporch seems electric suddenly, but the feeling in my chest is like nothing at all. I scoot my chair back and push the table out of the way so I can get out.

The Captain's still sitting on the other side of the washing machine with his beer in front of him. "Jesus—I'm just saying, you don't have to keep going along with it if it's so bad. What is your *problem*?"

But my problem is that right now, all I want is to be someplace he's not, and I could blame it on a lot of things, how he's always taking shots at people, and we never have anything to say to each other that really matters—or even just that I'm still messed up about Friday night, how I spent something miserable like five hours sitting under his picnic table and hallucinating every sick, fucked-up thing you can think of and he just keeps laughing about it, like me living out my grimmest nightmares in real-time was somehow hilarious. I need to get out.

The Captain's staring at me, but he doesn't say anything else. After a long, uncomfortable silence, I throw the cards down and go inside.

I could keep going, down the back hall and through the living room, out the front door. I'd walk around the neighborhood or maybe head home, or text Heather McIntire, see what she's doing.

Or maybe not. The thought of kissing her kind of makes me feel disgusted with myself.

Behind me, I can hear the Captain telling Ollie that pussy little bitches never get chicks. The house is empty and dark. I sit alone in my brother's living room and do nothing.

WAVERLY

My feet hurt.

They throb with a deep, constant ache that hits as soon as I swing myself out of bed. I get in the shower, and after standing there for fifteen minutes, the pain is better. My head feels numb, like it's stuffed with cotton.

All morning, my phone keeps buzzing in the side pocket of my bag.

Five texts. Count them: five. All of which are from CJ, who I've known for two years but do not *know,* not really. Not in any relevant sense. All of the texts are spectacularly content-free.

"What are you so homicidal for?" Maribeth says, prancing up to my locker after third period and leaning her chin on my shoulder.

I force myself to stop scowling and hold out the phone, offering: *skipped western civ do you hate tha romans as much as I do?* "CJ texted me this morning. A lot."

"So? That's ideal! I mean, doesn't it make you feel special?"

I think of the various ways to interpret that. The answer

is no. No, it does not. What's special about five text messages? He knows my number. He knows how to work his phone. Everything else is incidental.

"Don't you like knowing that he's thinking about you?" Maribeth says, and it's in this moment that I realize I'll never be able to answer her in any way that she would understand.

When I look at my phone and see a message from CJ that says *What up girl,* followed by three question marks and an exclamation point, I can tell we're not compatible. It's not that I'm a huge punctuation snob, or even very fascist about grammar. It's just that we are clearly not relating to each other in even the most fundamental way.

By the time last period rolls around, the day feels dreamy and bottomless. I think my heart is slowing down.

The counseling office is empty—its natural Tuesday state—and for the first fifteen minutes, I'm content to wipe down the copier with Lysol and rearrange the add/drop forms. Compulsive cleaning can only tide you over for so long, though. I put up the *Back in Five* sign, write myself a hall pass, and go for a walk.

I want to talk to someone and really mean what I'm saying. I want to put into words any of the frantic, tumbling things in my head and know that someone else in the world understands.

Instead, I wander in ever-shrinking circles until I wind up in the west hall bathroom, standing in front of the spill wall, looking at the secrets. There are so many of them—

so much realer than any of the things people say to each other's faces. A thousand truths about drugs and sex and friendship. Beauty, envy, bodies. Love. Even if I managed to read every single one, in an hour, they'll have already proliferated.

I don't know how to act like a normal person and it's making my life miserable.

My best friend doesn't like me.

My boyfriend isn't even nice.
Why is being alone so much scarier than being unhappy?

Down in the corner, next to the heating register, someone has written:

I'm not trying to starve myself,
I just want to be thin.
I never thought it would turn into a problem.

I study the handwriting, trying to figure out if it's someone I know—someone from cross-country, maybe?

But maybe it doesn't matter.

Maybe all that matters is that it's something true.

With a tight feeling in my chest, I unzip my bag. This is so stupid. It's absolutely not my business. My pencil case is stocked, though, filled with weapons of frank communication.

I take out a green felt pen I never use and uncap it like I'm watching from outside myself. Underneath the secret, I write, in neat block letters:

> *Go ask Sharon in the front office about*
> *the Healthy Choices program.*
> *You can see the counselor three times*
> *before they tell your parents.*

I leave the bathroom wondering if giving unqualified medical advice constitutes some kind of malpractice.

But the sentiment is right.

I decide that at most, it must amount to practicing common decency without a license.

•

Home—where the spring that's coiled inside me unwinds a little, where the gears stop grinding. Where no one is waiting or watching, or expecting me to be anything but bright and sharp and self-contained.

In the kitchen, there's a stack of takeout menus on the counter and everything smells warm, like ginger and lemongrass. My parents are standing in perfect symmetry with the island between them. They're eating Thai food out of paper containers and talking about determinist psychology.

No one else's parents like each other as much as mine do. They are charged like nucleons, paired like magnets. They communicate using a cool, coded language of theories and statistics, but their eyes are always locked in flirtatious combat.

"So tell me," she says, "about that Cambridge study on automatic eating." Her hair is shot with gray, and under the kitchen light, it looks silver. "I can't remember if it suggested industry-manufactured addiction, or just offered conclusive proof that people can be manipulated into consuming whatever you tell them to."

He smiles, gesturing with his chopsticks. "Does this mean you're going to try and convince me that volition is a flawed concept because of *peer* pressure?"

She takes another bite of pad see ew before launching into a mini seminar on social conditioning.

I climb onto one of the tall stools at the counter, watching as my parents conduct their courtship rituals. I eat green curry out of the plastic tub, thinking that I have never seen two people so in love, and so completely untouchable.

It's not that they fake the fake parts better than I do, because they don't. My mother is easily the strangest person I know. It's more like they know a language I've never encountered. A dialect you can only speak with someone who actually understands you.

Suddenly, I want to know what they'd think about the spill wall. Maybe one of them would understand the psychosocial appeal of confession. Maybe they could make the wall make sense. As soon as I imagine the conversation, though, it's an unmitigated disaster. Me, trying to explain that I wrote something there today—their hyper-rational, law-abiding daughter has defaced school property. Them, just as baffled by the entire concept as Maribeth is.

Answering someone's cry for attention is not in my character. I've never been one to involve myself in someone else's problems. But what I wrote today seems more like fulfilling a moral obligation. I think maybe if a person is asking—*begging*—for attention, it's because they need it.

When I leave the kitchen, I can almost feel my mother's eyes flick to the doorway after me. She knows I'm not there anymore—it's not that the information hasn't registered. It just doesn't mean anything.

In my room, I dust a pair of crickets with mineral powder and feed Franny and Zooey, watching them stalk delicately around their terrariums.

After the carnage, I sit with my knees drawn up and my physics notes scattered around me. I consider lighting the candle again—whether I should, whether it's safe. Whether I imagined what happened on Friday. If it's even possible to just *imagine* something as inarguable as a pile of dirt in your bed.

Maribeth would say that anything is possible if you set your mind to it. Except she's talking about acing the SAT, not late-night interlocational travel. I try to picture what she'd say if she knew I dreamed a dream so real I woke up with mud on my feet.

Maribeth has always been a believer in the power of persistence in the face of ambiguity. Don't understand a social situation or a sample set in pre-calc? No problem. Learn by doing. Want to be one of the most powerful girls in school, but don't know how to get there? Enlist a friend's help, devise a system and a plan, never look back. Pedal to the metal, full speed ahead, you'll figure it out. One thing follows another.

But I know something else, and it is this:

The world is under no obligation to be sane or orderly.

There was a regional meet in Baker once, freshman year, and the whole cross-country team stayed up way past curfew, crammed into a block of group-rate hotel rooms, eating Skittles and talking about who'd done it and who hadn't, the *it* in this context being sex. (It always is.)

I'd been rattling all day and was just getting worse. No one was remotely close to sleep, and I was beginning to feel jagged, like if I didn't get away, I was going to fly into shards like a dropped cup.

I took a dollar bill and a keycard. I went out to get a Coke and then kept going. My ears were ringing, my hands were tingling, and I walked faster. Out in the porte-cochere, the bellhops were wrestling with people's luggage, hurrying to get it off the curb because it looked like rain. Over the street, the clouds were dark and towering.

My pajamas were a rayon shorty set with tiny ducks all over them. I should have been shivering, but the sidewalk was warm. The wind gusted as I stepped off the curb. The street felt gritty under my bare feet and I started to run.

I'd gone six blocks when the lightning started, cutting the sky into a blinding network of cracks like a broken windshield, and I understood I was doing something reckless—dangerous, even. But it's so hard to tell when something's actually dangerous, or if it just feels that way.

I came around the turn at the end of a wide, residential street, and the sky seemed to open in one colossal thunderclap, so close the pavement shuddered. For a second, the world lit up white, and in an instant, the street was full of moths. They came plunging down out of the trees and surging up from the wheel wells of parked cars, like the night had exploded around me in tiny silver pieces. Then the wind tore down through the street, scattering leaves and branches. Scattering the moths. Thunder clapped like hands, and they were gone.

Afterward, I never knew if they were there at all, or something I'd told myself to make the night seem magical, or just my eyes. I raced myself back to the Hyatt. No one had noticed I was gone. I wiped the grit off my feet and climbed into the bed I was sharing with Kendry, not sure if the memory was real or imaginary. If I'd even gone out into the storm at all.

I push my homework out of the way and get out the candle. This is the world, and nothing in the world is ever truly inexplicable. But my heart beats harder just thinking about moths and dead leaves. I'm breathing too fast now for no good reason. When I work up the courage to strike a match, I hold it so long it gutters out, leaving me with a blackened strip of cardboard and a burned finger, trying to think whether or not it hurts.

I light another one and it flickers gently, reflecting off the votive jar.

Okay, so. Let's be logical. Consider the possibilities. Maybe sleep is miraculous—a strange doorway to something unknown. Maybe the other night, I accidentally dreamed myself into someone else's backyard.

Or maybe sleep is just a normal biological function, and I'm letting myself be intimidated by a candle.

I take a breath and touch the flame to the wick.

Under the covers, I count down like I'm preparing for liftoff. With my arms tucked close at my sides, I fall through darkness and cold murky air.

MARSHALL

Gloss

The thing about the Captain's house is, someone pretty much always winds up puking. This time, it's Ollie.

He makes it to the kitchen sink and then leans there, spitting into the garbage disposal. When I ask if he wants me to take him home, he shrugs and says he just needs to lie down for a while, which is Ollie-speak for yes, he wants to go home, but he's worried about puking in my car. I get him a glass of water and leave him lying on his face on the floor of Hez's bathroom.

Without him there to run interference, I'm fair game for the kind of life choices he'd usually keep me away from. When I scroll through my phone, though, Heather's name is missing from my contacts. Instead, there's a new entry all the way at the bottom: You Don't Want to Do This.

I laugh a little, but it's not a good laugh. It's short and dry, and even when he's not around to say it, Ollie knows the deal. How long has it been since I texted her? Long enough that her name could have been missing for months. Long enough I've nearly forgotten how shitty it feels knowing I don't feel that way about her. But her mouth is warm, her breasts are amazing, and she will always call me back.

I'm in the living room messing with the stereo when she finds me.

She's the girl I'm supposed to be with—the one who will always wait for me to call first, and maybe even notice that I've spent every night for the last week getting stoned at my brother's house, but won't make things weird by asking about it. She's the girl who will always have a joke or an excuse, and then back off if things get too close to actual.

She's clearly drunk and doesn't mind that I'm not in the mood to talk. It's easy to just lean into it. Make out with her. Enjoy it.

I can't remember if the Captain's story about Hez and the recliner actually involved him pissing on anything. Chances are pretty good that it did. The chair is more comfortable than the couch, though, and when I put my face down close to the upholstery, it smells okay.

We're tangled up with each other, sinking into the cushions, and then Heather starts running her hands up and down my shoulders. When she touches my chest, it makes me feel keyed up in a dirty way. I put my hand on her back, right above her butt, and she presses against me, leaning in for the kiss.

Her body is soft, and I wish that whatever I'm feeling for her would be more than just a crazy urge to put my hand up her shirt. The way I feel when she wedges her thigh between my knees kind of makes me hate myself.

"I'm not wearing a bra," she whispers, like I wasn't

already obscenely aware of it. She's getting lip gloss all over my ear.

I touch the side of her breast, the curve of her waist. There's nothing but a layer of shirt between us. I'm falling into it, getting lost in the feeling of her mouth on mine, when someone starts to laugh. It's a flat, scornful sound.

When I open my eyes, Waverly Camdenmar is standing in the corner with her hip cocked out to one side, arms folded, eyebrows raised. She's wearing blue pajamas, with a collar and a pocket and buttons shaped like birds. She has the weirdest look on her face—this mix of fascination and disgust, like she's watching something repugnant on TV. Like I'm the punch line.

WAVERLY

3.

Heather McIntire is in all the general-track classes at school and is exactly the kind of girl who wraps herself around boys like Marshall—too much eyeliner, not enough shirt. He's holding her in his lap, touching the outside of her hip, her thigh. I lean against the wall and wait for him to notice me.

As I watch, he moves higher, fumbling for her breast. I'm conscious of my mouth suddenly, how dry and empty it is. How untouched. CJ Borsen materializes in my head and stays for exactly one unenticing second. I can't even imagine kissing him the way Marshall's kissing Heather— all lips and hands and too much tongue. The scenario is impossible, not to mention vaguely repulsive.

Heather clearly has no such reservations about Marshall. He's got his head tipped back, eyes half-closed. She attaches herself to his neck, writhing against him like a squid.

He sighs, slipping his hand down the back of her jeans. And I can't help it—I laugh. I don't know what else to do. I laugh because the scene is so profoundly *uncomfortable*.

His eyes fly open and pin me where I stand. He goes rigid, sucking in his breath.

Heather must think he's demonstrating ecstasy, because she kisses him harder, apparently under the impression she's improving on her technique. He's staring over her shoulder, eyes fixed on my face. When I smile, he yanks his hand out of her pants.

"Hi," I say.

He flattens himself against the chair, shaking his head, and mouths the word *what?*

Heather turns in my direction, but her gaze doesn't quite connect. "Are you talking to someone?"

Marshall doesn't answer, only shakes his head and untangles himself from her arms. She slides out of the chair and onto the carpet, looking indignant, but he just stands up and steps around her.

"*Hey,*" she says, sounding shrill and confused. "Hey, what's wrong?"

The music is a thrumming racket of bass and suburban angst, and he walks out of the room and toward the back of the house.

"What the *hell?*" she calls after him, but she doesn't sound angry, just hurt.

After a minute, I push myself away from the wall and follow him. The house is dim and smells like popcorn. The carpet is itchy. Every surface feels very, very real.

I find Marshall in the little back-porch laundry room, wedging his way past an umbrellaed patio table to lean against the washing machine. I stand in the doorway while he lights a cigarette. He doesn't smoke it, though, just holds it. He's looking through the porch screen, into the backyard.

"You should put that out," I say, and his whole body jerks like I've electrocuted him.

I slip past the table to stand next to him. "Didn't you hear? They found tentative evidence suggesting smoking kills you."

He's huddled against the washer, leaning away from me. His mouth is so tight that his jaw looks wired shut. "What is *wrong* with you?" he says in a hard whisper.

I smile, but it feels breakable. "Nothing's wrong with me."

He laughs in a tired, breathless way that lacks conviction, but makes me feel small anyway.

I draw myself up—shoulders back, chin raised. "Nothing's wrong, except that you're breathing your sad chemical dependency in my face, and secondhand smoke is the silent killer."

"Seriously." His expression is rigid and he still won't look at me. "Why are you *here*?"

Under the reek of the cigarette, he smells like beer and pot and a girl's sugary perfume. I gesture behind me to the living room, where Heather is probably still sitting on the floor. "Hey, I'm not the one making a cornucopia of poor decisions. Why are *you* here?"

He glances at me, then mashes the cigarette out in a chipped saucer. "Why am I at my brother's house? He's my *brother*. Am I not supposed to visit my brother?"

I look at him so long he looks away. Finally, he scrubs his hands over his face and sighs. "Fuck, it's complicated. I mean, come on, don't you have problems?"

I don't answer. It's not the kind of question that you answer. Everyone has problems.

"Just . . . things are kind of shitty right now, okay? Sorry if I don't feel like talking about it with someone whose entire life revolves around good grades and being popular."

He looks angry, and under that, tired. I think of how he starts to doze in class, like there's no way to keep his eyes open when the transitive verbs come marching out.

"You could, you know. Talk to me." When I say it, my voice sounds very soft, like it's not coming from me, but from the girl who wrote well-meaning advice on the wall today. The one who has a place in her disposition for tenderness, even if it's small. "If you wanted."

He laughs dryly, turning to stare out into the yard. "Look, all I want right now is to go back inside and get a beer and act fine and okay and normal."

Act, he says. Act, not *be.* He's standing with his back to me, like he wishes he were still kissing Heather.

"It is completely appalling to get drunk and make out with strangers."

"It's *normal.*"

I raise my eyebrows. "Well, you know what they say— everyone loves a self-medicator."

"Shut up." He says it flatly and I can't figure out if he sounds bored or mad or just hopelessly, profoundly hurt. "That's not what I meant. And she's not a stranger. She's just . . . she's Heather."

His voice is scaring me a little. It makes him different from Marshall in class—the boy who gives bored, insolent answers or sleeps through unit review. The boy who shoved a hall pass at me and gave me a look like I was negligible. Nothing.

He's fidgeting with the dead cigarette, squeezing it, picking at it. The paper bleeds tobacco from a collection of little wounds.

I reach over and take it away from him, dropping it in the saucer. "Stop it."

Instead of arguing or taking it back, he squints at me. "What the shit happened to your hand?"

I turn my palms up. The porch light is dim, but it's enough to illuminate a dusting of soot, a small, shiny burn on my index finger. In the saucer, the cigarette has a black smudge on it the size and shape of my thumb.

"Nothing. A science experiment." I look away and wipe my hand clean on my pajamas. "I was lighting matches."

Out in the yard, someone is setting off a handful of bottle rockets. They tear across the sky, leaving a trail of sparks, followed by the small, hollow pop as they explode.

He doesn't ask what I'm talking about, just digs in the pocket of his jeans and pulls out a red plastic lighter. "Try this next time."

I move closer, a little, almost touching his arm. Here in the laundry room, it's just the two of us, me and my strange, nocturnal phenomenon. Everyone else is far away.

"I don't sleep," I say.

Marshall shakes his head, still holding up the lighter. "What?"

"You asked if I had problems. I never sleep. That's my problem."

He doesn't answer. He watches me so long I start to feel awkward, like he's actually seeing me.

"I could do better," he says finally. His voice is low, like we're trading confessions. "At school," he adds. "It's just that my whole life is completely buried under all this other stuff. But I *could*."

"But you don't," I say, when what I want is to whisper it like he's on his deathbed. Like the tragedy it is.

Marshall sighs and rakes his hair back from his forehead. "I don't want to talk about this."

"Because you know I'm right."

"Fine, yeah, you're right. Can we just skip this part?"

"Which?"

"The part where you tell me I'm lazy or a slacker or—or not worth anything. I already know how pathetic my life is."

Neither of us says anything else. I'm the one who looks away first.

Out in the yard, another round of bottle rockets goes off. The shower of sparks is industrial and beautiful, like someone's welding crossbeams in the sky. I wonder where a person gets bottle rockets, how much they cost. Maybe I'll invest in some. I like things that increase velocity and then explode.

"I look at you," Marshall says, and his voice is very gentle suddenly. "I look at you and I think, why is that girl so sad? Why are you sad?"

I turn to face him, crossing my arms over my chest. "I'm not sad."

Slumped against the washing machine, he looks broken.

His face is wistful, half lit by the dull yellow glow of the porch light. And he smiles. "I call bullshit," he says. "I'm calling bullshit all over that one."

I stand with my shoulders back. "Forgive me if I don't think unbiased evaluation of someone else's emotional state is really your area of expertise."

He shrugs. "Whatever. Not like it matters, but you're not *fooling* anyone."

"I'm fooling everyone," I say, and know it's the truth.

Everyone except him.

I can feel my blood thinning, becoming air or water. My hands are weak, losing my hold on the world, losing track of Waverly, and I dread the moment when I wake up in my own bed.

"I'm sorry," he says abruptly, staring out into the yard.

"For what?"

"For this—for not being . . ." He stops and takes a breath like he's about to say something else, but in a second, when the words stop eluding him. His mouth is open and I can see the frustration as he struggles for it. I want to jump in, start suggesting conclusions to his sentences, but I wait.

Instead, he holds out the lighter, offering it to me, but when I reach to take it, my hand is tingling and numb. The way he's looking at me is so cautious, so impossibly kind. Suddenly, I can't feel the cracked linoleum or the cold or anything at all.

"Better," he whispers as I start to disappear. "For not being better."

I wake up breathless, with a squeezing feeling in the center of my chest like my heart hurts.

•

I'm beginning to suspect that I can only converse meaningfully with strangers. My true, unfiltered personality is
unsuitable for everyday use, and the whole morning is just
one long object lesson.

In the commons before AP Lit, I told Maribeth that Kelly
green for the balloon arch at the dance was fine, when everyone knows that Kelly green is hideous, and in the last twenty-
four hours, I've been more honest with Autumn Pickerel
than I've ever been with any of the people I call my friends.
At night, in my dreams, I have the capacity to say and do and
be exactly what I want, but never in the daylight. Not in real
life. I spend most of second period considering all the ways
my ability to communicate is fundamentally broken.

Anyway, objecting to Kelly green would require me to
produce a compelling alternative, and I just don't care that
much.

When my daily stream of texts from CJ starts rolling in
before trig, I take out my phone and set him to *ignore*. His
persistence should be flattering, but it makes something
sink in my chest.

Slumped at my desk, I pretend it's Marshall texting me instead, and smile for the first time all day. His imaginary correspondence would be witty and surprising. He wouldn't talk about nothing. He would limit himself to one question mark per sentence. I can't decide if it's impressive or pathetic that even my wildest fantasies involve appropriate punctuation.

I tear a sheet of loose-leaf from my binder and compose a note I know I won't pass to him. It says things that seem largely self-explanatory and leaves out a lot of other things, which are too hard to put into words.

> *Hi,*
>
> *I thought about what you said last night. It's nice of you to ask, but I don't think that I am sad. I think I might just be tired. Also, I'm sorry I said your poor decisions were a cornucopia. That was probably uncalled for.*
>
>

Sincerely,

Then I tear it into sixteen tiny squares and put it in the pocket of my messenger bag. During the passing period, I throw away the pieces, despite the fact that no one's name is on it.

Maribeth meets me after Spanish and we walk down to the locker bay, talking about how we still need to go dress shopping and how hard the work will be when we have calculus next semester. Dependable, reassuring. That's the thing about Maribeth. She believes in a predetermined future.

Marshall wasn't in class, which was clearly a personal choice because when we reach the junior bay he's slouched at his locker, looking sullen and bored with his waster sidekick, Ollie Poe. His eyes are dark, and I look at him a long time before I look away.

Maribeth leans against me, draping an arm around my neck. "I'm thinking we should do something really intense and glamorous, like crystals or jewel tones, don't you think?"

From the corner of my eye, I see Marshall step away from the wall. And now he's coming over, crossing the bay. I turn my back on him and keep my expression neutral.

Maribeth soldiers on, explaining in loving detail how important it is to coordinate our corsages, but I can't focus.

Marshall's presence has the weight of an off-course planet. He's so close I can smell his crumpled T-shirt and his hair, that mix of detergent, pepper and licorice and deodorant and pot, but I don't look at him, and he doesn't say anything.

Maribeth is staring past me now, shifting her weight from foot to foot.

I focus on my open locker—my math book, sitting crooked on the shelf. The publisher's emblem is stamped on the spine in gold foil and he stays right there behind me.

Finally, when I can't realistically ignore him any longer, I turn, hands on my hips. "I'm sorry—can I help you?"

He's six inches from me, looking down with an expression like I've just hit him in the stomach.

He's holding a plastic cigarette lighter.

For one towering moment, I'm certain my heart will stop. My face feels numb. The locker bay is too bright. The lighter is cheap and cherry red. It's the same one he offered me on the porch last night.

We stand toe to toe, facing each other across countless fathoms.

Then he presses the lighter into my hand and walks away.

"Wow," says Maribeth. "What was *that*?"

I turn back to my open locker, trying to sound unaffected. "His name's Marshall Holt. He's in my Spanish class."

"But why was he like . . . completely *stalking* you?"

I make an ambiguous noise and line up my books by descending height. This gives the illusion of order.

Maribeth is wriggling with excitement. She pops her eyes wide, leaning in, grabbing for my wrist. "What is that? What did he give you? Did he give you a *present*?"

"Nothing. Just something he thought I needed. It's not important." When what I mean is, *nothing* is important. The most basic logic of the world is broken. Nothing will ever be important again.

"Waverly, seriously—what's in your hand?"

For a second, I'm sure we're going to wrestle over it. She'll pry my fingers open, get the story out of me one way or another.

But then she tosses her hair back and slips her arm

through mine, pulling me toward the bathrooms. "God, why are we even *talking* about this, though? I need to tell you what Hunter told me CJ said about you at practice!"

I want to sit down on the floor until I'm sure I'm not going to hyperventilate. I want to bolt for the science room and spend the next fifty years examining the lighter with a microscope to make sure it's real. Even after I manage to parse all her various pronouns, everything about that sentence is meaningless.

In the bathroom, Maribeth stands at the sinks, leaning close to the mirror with her compact open.

"What you've been needing is exactly this," she says to her reflection. "CJ will literally revolutionize your life. Now you can finally go on dates, like someone who is *not* destined to end life alone under a blanket of cats. And he's just nerdy enough about math and logical fallacies and stuff that you won't want to murder him. It's *perfect*. He is basically the most Waverly-appropriate thing I can think of."

I nod. The gap between myself and the facade of myself must be growing exponentially.

The lighter feels smooth and solid in my hand. Already, my pulse is beginning to normalize. I touch the surface of the spill wall, thinking how someone wrote these things, their confessions, their wishes, their hearts.

This is being brave or stupid to an alarming degree.

If someone put a marker in my hand, I could write, *I never sleep.*

For the covert New Ager in us all, I could write, *I transcend space and time.*

I could write, *Last night, Marshall Holt told me I was sad, and now I can't stop wondering if it's true.*

"Come on," Maribeth says. "I'll walk you down to the tragedy office. I need to make copies of the food drive information for Stu-Co."

When she says *Stu-Co,* it makes me want to get out a sheet of paper and tear it into little tiny pieces. I let my hand drop and follow her out of the bathroom.

By the time I finish my night run, there's a hot pressure behind my eyes. I'm moving too slow all the time now, too tired to run out the loose pieces rattling inside me. It's hard to get free with my legs so heavy.

Things have changed. The boundaries of the waking world have shifted, and even now, part of me wants to insist it can't be real. People don't just close their eyes in their bedrooms and open them someplace else. They don't start conversations in their dreams and finish them in the daylight. Everything about last night is impossible.

But the lighter is real. It came from somewhere. It used to be in Marshall's pocket, and now it's sitting upstairs on my desk. Everything's getting tangled in my head. I can't stop thinking about the way it felt to stand next to him on the porch, and the way he said *better.* The whole day feels like a dream.

I know this stage of sleeplessness—the unreality, the confusion. Insomnia is ruthless, but familiar. I have routines. Now is the point at which I eat a box of Popsicles and curate a personalized horror movie marathon. My blood is so wired my skin feels itchy. I've seen all the good ones a million times.

I fling myself down in front of the TV and flip through channels, looking for something bloody. It's not that I'm sadistic. It's just that things never really bother me. Nothing bothers me. And when it's hard to find things shocking, sometimes it's good to know that something in the world can still make your heart beat faster.

I click past *Seinfeld* reruns and ads for unusually durable blenders, and finally settle on cage fighting. It's a rebroadcast—after midnight, cable programming all starts to repeat itself.

The title match is Nikolai Federov, the Serbian Psychopath, against defending champion Andrew Saint John, and even though I've seen it twice and already know how it ends, I pull up my feet and cover my throat with my hand. This is the elemental truth of the world. It might be crude and senseless, but at least it's real.

Halfway through the second round, the door opens, making me jump. It's my mother. Her silhouette sends a jolt of adrenaline down my back like I've just been caught doing something shameful.

"What are you watching?" she says, tilting her head at the TV, where Saint John is grinding Federov's face into the mat.

I answer fast, and even sort of sound like I'm telling the truth. "I'm writing a paper on male dominance behaviors. For school."

The real tragedy is that this seems normal to her. "Well, I'm glad you're working on something challenging. It seems like so many kids would just pick the simplest topic and not really get anything out of it. And anthropologically speaking, human aggression is incredibly interesting."

I want to tell her that human aggression is not the easy one-two punch she thinks it is. Not every form of violence is a frontal assault. Aggression can be sitting in the cafeteria with Maribeth Whitman every day at lunch. The hardened criminals I know all deal in secrets and subtext. Maribeth's power is evident in the way that Loring hasn't come to a single committee meeting this week.

My mom is considering the television. "Are you almost done?" she says. Saint John has Federov trapped against the cage now, bleeding and squirming. "You should go to bed."

"I will," I say. "In a minute."

I know I don't have to lie to her. If anyone understands the deleterious effects of an active mind, she does. But still, there's a certain quiet defeat in telling the truth.

I could ask for a cure and she'd give it to me. She'd gladly point me in the direction of psychoanalysis and pills. It would feel like surrender, but it might mean sleeping through the night.

On-screen, Saint John is smothering Federov with the weight of his body.

My mom watches with her hands on her hips. This is her, Taking an Interest. "Will he give up, now that he's being held down like that?"

I shake my head as Saint John transitions into full destruction mode, lifting Federov half off the mat, then slamming him back down, dragging him along through a trail of his own blood.

My mom stands in the middle of the room, eyebrows delicately knit. "And they won't stop the fight?"

"Not while he can intelligently defend himself."

"Intelligent?" she says, and I hear the wryness in her voice—I get it—but she's not seeing everything and there are more elemental factors at work.

The fact is, blood is slippery. Blood can be a strategy all by itself. If there's enough of it, sometimes it can turn a fight.

Suddenly, Federov slips the hold and jerks his arm out. His fist plows the side of Saint John's head, once, twice. On the third impact, Saint John comes loose, rocking against the side of the cage and Federov is there, Federov is on his back with his arm around Saint John's neck and his other hand clutching his bicep.

The commentators are screaming over each other now. Saint John's face turns an ugly shade of purple, and suddenly the ref is sweeping in to save the day.

"Well," says my mother. "That will certainly make him think twice about knocking people's shoulders in the hall."

I don't answer. She means it as a joke, but the comparison is perfectly apt. High school popularity is a blood sport.

MARSHALL
Choke

I stop thinking about school somewhere in the middle of the second drink. By the sixth, I've stopped thinking about home.

Forget family dinners and report cards. Forget the way my dad takes about nineteen pills a day and it's still not enough to fix the way his hands shake or the way he slumps around the house like he's doing ninety-nine to life. Like everything is ending. Forget the way my mom ignores every shitty thing he says like she fucking owes it to him. Like she deserves it.

And yeah, the Captain can be a total asshole and his kitchen always smells like someone forgot to take out the trash, but at least with him, it's predictable. No fighting, no crying. No English homework, no one asking why I can't be more like my sister.

No setup for failure.

Except that's the biggest lie of all, because if I'm drinking bourbon in the Captain's kitchen, I'm clearly not at home applying myself.

Ollie's slouched next to me at the counter, picking at the

label on his beer. "You're looking good," he says, and he smiles, but it's a slow, ironic smile and in Ollie-speak, *good* means the same thing as *wrecked*.

But so what? That's the goal, isn't it? I'm getting there. Maybe after a few more I can even stop thinking about Waverly.

She took the lighter. I stood right in front of her in the locker bay, offered her my plastic Bic, and she took it. And sure, when someone hands you something, sometimes you might just take it without thinking. The way she looked at me was so shattered, though, like I was more than some random guy.

Maybe. Or maybe it didn't mean anything.

There are all kinds of bizarre things that could still actually happen. One of the smartest, most untouchable girls in school could show up at my brother's house in the middle of the night in her pajamas, and tell me to quit smoking.

She *wouldn't,* but she *could.*

The girl I write love poems to in my head could stand on the porch with me, so close I could smell her hair, and tell me she never sleeps. That's a thing that *could* happen.

But just because something's possible doesn't make it real. Girls like her don't actually walk into people's living rooms. They don't actually take a cigarette out of your hand and announce that you're a disaster area. But mostly, no matter how conversational they're feeling, they never just disappear right in front of you.

Maybe this is what hard-core burnouts mean when they talk about acid flashbacks.

All I want is to get to that point where you're drunk

enough that you can't feel your hands, because once you can't feel your hands, a lot of other stuff gets hard to feel too.

At the counter, Ollie's watching me. "Hey," he says, in a voice like he's trying really hard to sound like he doesn't care.

Normally, Ollie never has to work at sounding like he doesn't care. It's kind of his natural state. He hooks his hair behind his ears and looks away. "So, I was thinking maybe I should have a talk with that freshman. The one hanging all over Little Ollie all the time. She needs to know what she's getting into with him. He's one hundred percent about her global endowments, and she has to know that. I mean, I can just tell that she's going to be stupid about it—she *likes* him. It's going to end badly, is all I'm saying."

I'm about to pour myself another shot, or maybe say that sometimes people just need things to end badly so they can toughen up and get a clue, but right then, the Captain comes slouching over to us, all deodorant body spray and douchebaggery. He's smoking a cigar.

"Dude, you're scamming on a freshman? Are you out of your *mind*? Danger, Will Robinson, danger!"

"It's not like that," Ollie says, looking embarrassed.

The Captain snorts, taking another puff off the cigar and blowing smoke in Ollie's face. "Yeah, not like your dick's looking for a place to land. Not like that."

Some other night, I'd set him straight maybe, tell him to back off, but my thoughts are too slow and messy to string together and I don't say anything.

Ollie scowls and flips him off, throwing his empty bottle into the trash so hard the whole thing rocks.

I have this feeling I should ease up. Sober up. Get straight and go home.

When I tell him I think I'm done, the Captain laughs and whacks me between the shoulders. "I'm sorry, did you just say your name is *Pussy*? Because I just heard you say that your name is Pussy."

The cigar smell is everywhere, getting in my clothes.

"Man up," he says, reaching for a bottle and shoving it across the counter at me. Man up.

I keep getting blindsided by a bad, helpless feeling, like I don't want to be doing this. Which is complete bullshit, because if I really didn't want to, then I wouldn't be climbing aboard the blackout express.

Right?

Heather finds me in the kitchen, even though I don't remember texting her, and immediately, we're all over each other. And for a while I like it, because the kissing feels good in a way that paints over things that feel bad, and she tastes pink, like strawberry lip gloss, which tastes like candy and reminds me of being younger.

I'm going to feel like hell tomorrow. That's not a promise or a plan, but it's nice to have something you can count on. You know those people who say "Fuck my life," like they're these huge victims and the world is so completely cruel, like it's taking advantage of them? Well, I'm not that guy. I did this. Me.

I'm so fucking real that it hurts.

"I like your hoodie," Heather says, crawling into my lap. We're in the living room somehow, almost like magic. She's got her knees wedged down in the corners of the armchair so she's straddling me. "I love that song, how the part about the fish tank goes."

Her voice is high and soft, like a little girl, and I know she doesn't care about Pink Floyd, and she doesn't know that my dad gave me the hoodie for my birthday last year because *he* cares about Pink Floyd and thinks *Wish You Were Here* is a really good album and I'm such a loser that I should just love it automatically. And Heather doesn't know that, but she thinks she knows the words. She thinks she needs to love it because I do.

I know I should be careful about making out two nights in a row. She might start thinking we're like a real thing. Then she leans down and kisses me, and there's nothing but the kissing.

After, I stumble my way down into the basement where Hez has his bedroom and everything smells like socks. I lock myself in the bathroom and sit on the floor.

It's so hot in here I think I might melt and also, I'm starting to feel sick in that churning, sweaty way that gets worse every time I move my head.

The rush of saliva comes next, promising puke, and that's okay. I'll hold my breath and close my eyes. Get everything out, all the beer and the bourbon, the sloppy candy flavor of Heather's kisses, and then I'll feel better. I'll feel empty.

The tub is not the cleanest thing I've ever seen. It's got a crusty ring around the inside of it, but when I climb in, the ceramic is cool and I don't want anything except to lie down someplace that doesn't feel like a hundred and ten degrees.

I lean my head against the side. It's so cold it makes my teeth chatter. My skin feels tight and sticky and I can't think of anything except that I can't feel my hands and I'm starting to get the spins, and it's the best and worst feeling I've ever had.

I settle myself in the tub and lie back. My mouth tastes like failure. Like strawberries and bourbon.

WAVERLY

4.

When all my numbers dissolve into noise, I open my eyes.

I'm in a tiny bathroom with bad seventies wallpaper and no windows. Marshall Holt is slumped awkwardly in the tub with his head bent sideways. The floor is freezing.

"Marshall." When he doesn't move, I kick the side of the tub. "Marshall!"

He blinks up at me, scrubbing a hand over his face.

I crouch next to him, then flinch when I get a whiff of hard alcohol. "You're *really* drunk."

He nods, turning so that his head knocks against the wall. His eyes are red and he smells close to flammable.

Even this wrecked, though—this disreputable—he doesn't fit with the peeling linoleum and the wallpaper. His face is waxy, all fragile mouth and cheekbones. I've never thought this about a boy before, but he's too pure-looking. The floor feels ominously sticky. Everything smells like mildew, and the grim commitment to filth that can only really be cultivated by post-adolescent boys.

"What are you doing to yourself?" I hop awkwardly on

one leg, trying to wipe my foot clean on the back of my calf. "This is gross. It's stupid."

"Yeah?" he says, gazing up at me. "Well, it's still a fuck-load better than how things look the rest of the time."

There's an edge in his voice, and I glance away. The way he's staring at me is too honest. Everything is much too real.

"Are you a ghost?" he says suddenly, the words blurry and thick in his mouth.

"No."

"What are you, then?"

"A girl."

He drags a hand across his face, frowning like I've just presented him with a particularly difficult equation. "So at school when I see this complete fucking princess, Waverly Camdenmar, that's the same person? Like, tomorrow you'll be you, and you'll remember this?"

I nod. I'm not entirely convinced that *he'll* remember, but it seems indelicate to say so. I'm inappropriately pleased that he knows my last name.

He's struggling to his feet now, hauling himself up. He sits on the edge of the tub, dropping his head forward, closing his eyes. "Oh, God."

"Are you all right?"

He nods, keeping his head down. "Just really nauseous."

"Nauseated."

He squints up at me. "What?"

"Nauseous means something else. You're nauseated."

"Okay, well, *you're* completely pedantic."

He's clammy and pale, breathing through his nose, and

I'm secretly impressed by his use of the word *pedantic*. He sits with his hands braced on the edge of the tub, taking long, measured breaths. Then, without opening his eyes, he reaches over and flips the toilet seat up.

I wait for him to lunge for the bowl, but he doesn't. He stays perfectly motionless, eyes closed and head down.

Finally, he clears his throat and says in a halting whisper, "Can you do me a favor?"

From above, his shoulders are broader than I'd realized, muscular in a way that makes me feel awkward. I fold my arms over my chest like I could protect myself. "What kind of favor?"

"Turn the water on really cold and hold your hand under."

I stare down at him, trying to see a way for this to be some kind of joke or trick. His request is too simple, though. Too sincere.

After a second, I turn on the faucet and let the water run between my fingers. "Okay, I put my hand under."

"Is it cold?"

"Yeah. Now what?"

"Just—could you hold it against the back of my neck? Just for a little."

When I press my palm against his neck, he breathes out and starts to shiver. His vertebrae feel solid and knobby under my hand, just the right shape for my fingers.

I perch next to him on the edge of the tub. "Is that better?"

He nods, slumping sideways a little, resting his shoulder against mine. "Yeah. Yeah, it's nice."

His arm is warm through his shirt and I can feel him breathing.

We sit side by side without talking. Me with my hand on Marshall's neck, him with his head drifting sideways, closer, closer. Finally coming to rest against my shoulder.

He sighs. It's a soft, dreamy sound and I lean into him and let my cheek touch his hair, just lightly. For the first time all day, I kind of feel like I'm in the right place.

"Why are you so determined to destroy yourself?" I say, and my voice is very small.

"I don't know," he whispers back. "Why are you?"

"I'm not. I'm just . . . driven."

The inadequacy of this takes a second to sink in, after which it becomes unbelievably funny and I start to giggle in a way that sounds kind of hysterical.

And then Marshall's laughing too in little hitching gasps. "Yeah, right. You pile all this busywork and random bullshit on yourself, just so you won't have to actually deal with anything. Hey, I get it—you get to look perfect, whatever. But my way's easier."

I know I should correct his misconception that I'm not good at dealing with things, but I'm so much more incensed by the fact that he has just reduced the sum total of my life to *busywork*. "At least I don't degrade myself for fun."

Abruptly, he stops laughing. "Like you could even begin to know why I do *anything*."

His voice is harsh and I lean close, trying to see into his face. "Okay, why, then? What is so wrong with your life?"

He swallows hard, looking at the floor.

"What's wrong with your life?" I say in a whisper.

The question is a bad one, and I whisper because if the question is bad, then the answer is guaranteed to be bad too, and half of me doesn't want to know, but the other half, the brutal half *needs* to know, needs to hear the dirty parts.

Marshall doesn't answer. Instead, he twists away, hunching his shoulders, shaking me off. His face is a sick, grayish color. He looks awful.

Inexplicably, he's smiling. "You need to leave now."

"Excuse me?"

"I need you to give me some fucking *privacy*."

"Why? What are you going to do?"

He gives me a long look and holds up two fingers, the way saints bless people in religious iconography. Then he sticks them in his mouth like someone miming suicide and leans over the toilet.

"Oh my *God*. That is completely vile."

He takes his fingers out of his mouth. "*Leave,* then. It's not like this gets better with an audience."

I don't move. His gaze is confrontational, his challenge to me, and I don't want to watch, but I'm not about to be beaten by something so pathetic. It takes more than some drunk idiot puking to make me look away.

He repositions himself over the toilet and shoves his fingers hard down his throat, then retches and takes his hand away. Nothing happens.

With an exasperated sigh, he tries again. This time he gags, hanging his head down in the bowl so I can't see. The whole procedure is businesslike and surprisingly quiet, like he's done this before.

He flushes the toilet and leans his elbows on the seat,

holding his hand over the bowl and keeping his eyes closed. I wonder if I'm supposed to touch him, rest my hand on his back or pet his hair, but his shoulders are rigid and I stay where I am. I realize that I'm hugging my arms and make myself stop.

"So," he says without opening his eyes. "You just watched that." He sounds exhausted suddenly, like we're not engaged in combat anymore.

"Yeah."

He leans his forehead against the front of the tank. "What's wrong with you, Waverly?"

I stand over him, looking at his bent back, his damp hair. From this angle, I can see how his ears stick out too much, how the bones in his neck show. Drunk looks stupid and pointless on him, like it's bringing out his absolute worst features.

"That's a strange question, coming from someone who binge-drinks on a school night and then follows it up with a pretty good impression of a Pro-Am bulimic."

"I mean it," he whispers. "I wreck myself and I fuck myself up, and you just stand around and watch like it's nothing."

"Maybe debasement interests me."

"Functional. Really. Can you hand me a towel?"

I toss a faded bath towel at him and he catches it without raising his head. He swipes at his mouth and then his hand. The whole time he's wiping his fingers clean, he keeps his face turned away.

"How are you?" I say finally.

He sits back on the linoleum and looks up at me. Then

he laughs, sweaty and pale, eyes drifting shut. "Really, Miss Honor Roll—*really*? How am I? I'm fucking stupid, okay. Can you maybe stop enjoying it for two seconds and see if there's some mouthwash?"

He sounds so exhausted and so bitter that I don't quite know how to navigate the question. *Enjoying?* "Excuse me?"

"Mouthwash. Scope, Listerine. Look in the cupboard."

I open the medicine cabinet and hand him a giant bottle of something fluorescent that promises to lay waste to the menace of gingivitis.

He takes a gulp, then swishes it and spits a mouthful of green froth into the toilet. When he stands up, he does it slowly.

"Move," he says, shoving past me for the sink.

"You're revolting," I say. But I don't really mean it.

When he wrenches the tap, the faucet comes on full blast and sprays up against the side of the sink, splashing all over both of us. When I gasp and jump back, he turns the knob the other way, so the water slows to a trickle.

"You were okay before," I say, but I sound like I'm asking a question.

With his back to me, he soaps up and scrubs his hands. "In what universe was I ever okay?"

"You *were,* though. We were sitting there. We were fine. But then you had to go and turn it into some weird masochistic *thing.*"

He cups his hand under the faucet, then brings it to his mouth before he answers. "It's just about bad and worse," he says to the cracked ceramic basin and the floor. Water is running down his face and neck, dripping from his chin. "I can do it now and go to bed before I really start to feel it, or I can do it at home, tomorrow, with my mom banging on the door asking if I want a 7UP and feeling like my head's about to come apart."

"Or you could just not get drunk. That's always an option."

He shuts off the faucet and turns to face me. "Yeah, well, sometimes it's not. Sometimes you do things that feel bad later just so you don't feel worse right now."

The look he gives me is like he's sorry, like he's telling me some desolate and little-known fact and he wants to apologize for it. I want to tell him that I never put off unpleasantness. I always do the thing that feels bad right now. It's what makes me good at running. It's what makes me good at everything.

Out in the hall, someone's shouting and whooping, coming closer. A guy, yelling Marshall's name. He stops outside and then starts pounding on the door.

Marshall's still watching me, arms folded across his chest. Something about his posture makes me want to hug him suddenly, just wrap my arms around him and hold on. He studies me with that same helpless expression and I don't say anything.

More knocking, followed by a series of thumps. Someone's kicking the bottom of the door.

Marshall sighs, steadying himself against the wall. "Sorry, I've got to take this."

When he opens the door, his brother is lounging in the hallway. "Mars, you look like ass. Did I just hear you rallying?"

Marshall swipes his damp hair out of his eyes. His smile is wide and easy. "Yeah, I'm good."

"Not good enough! You've got five minutes to catch up."

"Nah, I think I'm done."

His brother pushes into the bathroom, holding up a bottle of cheap, oily-looking tequila. "Come on, man—don't puss out on me."

Marshall shakes his head and turns to look at me, but I'm already disappearing.

•

In class the next day, Marshall is ragged. His eyes are bruised-looking and he's wearing the clothes he had on last night.

I get out my compact and hold it so the mirror reflects the room behind me, trying to determine if this is what a hangover looks like. After roll call, he puts his head down and doesn't move until the bell.

If I had any doubts left as to the truth or untruth of my dreams, this effectively dismantles them. There is one way I could know what Marshall would be wearing. *Know,* with unerring accuracy, that his shirt would be blue, his jeans would be torn, and his complexion would be colorless. And that is if I stood over him in the bathroom of his brother's house last night and observed these things for myself. If I was *there.*

The lesson is on seasonal vocabulary, which it seems like we covered a year ago. I'm now five full chapters ahead. I was memorizing Thanksgiving verb forms back in the second week of September.

I'm not sure what's happening to me. In theory, I should be crumbling into chaos and madness right now, doubting everything I've ever known or believed. In practice, it doesn't feel much different from opening my binder to find my homework ready and waiting, even though I don't actually remember doing it. My body seems insubstantial. Made of smoke and vapor. Like responsible, studious Waverly is barely even a thing anymore.

I spend my shift in the counseling office staring at the clock, touching the dark showy grain of the reception desk, reminding myself that I am *here*. This is real.

When the second hand ticks and ticks and no one comes, I let myself out on a forged bathroom pass and read through the crop of new secrets that have appeared on the wall since yesterday.

It's mostly the usual fare—boys, bodies, self-loathing. The embarrassments and the crushes and the stupid crushing boredom.

And something else. Under my insider information about the access to confidential counseling, there's a new cluster of graffiti. In three different pens, in three different hands, someone has written:

Thank you.

• • •

After cross-country, Autumn waits for me in the locker room, standing at the sinks while I brush my hair and take off my running shoes.

"Hey," she says suddenly. "What are you doing right now?"

I glance up from the tangle of my laces, trying to parse the question. "Doing?"

"Well, do you want to come over or *what*?"

I zip my shoes into the side pocket of my track bag like everything about that sentence is normal, but my face keeps wanting to do strange things. A smile is working its way toward my mouth for no good reason. I don't understand what's happening. It's like she's just *deciding* to be my friend. "I can't. There's a meeting to discuss the dance budget."

"That sounds horrible," she says brightly. "I should definitely come with you."

"Are you even listening? It's a *budget* meeting."

"What, is it all secrets or something? Am I not allowed? You do realize you're just making it sound funner, right?"

I give her a sardonic look and shake my head. "If comparing discrepancies between spreadsheets is what does it for you, you have a weirdly specific definition of fun. Anyway, it's not the kind of thing where you can just show up because you feel like it. You're not on student council."

Autumn turns away, raking her fingers through her hair like she's thinking about that. Then she looks up. "If you don't even *like* your flawless little life, why bother?"

"I do like it. Kind of."

She stares at me, her mouth tugging to one side. "God, you are *so* fucked up. I *love* it!"

When I smile, it feels harder and grimmer than usual, like her attitude is catching. "The normalcy odds are kind of stacked against me. I'm the only child of an ad man and a shrink."

Autumn laughs, throwing her head back, hugging her sides. She's pretty when she laughs.

Her hair is messy, but a pleasing shade of burnt red that makes me think of foxes or fawns. Her willingness to just devote her attention to whatever comes along is fascinating. It's refreshing—like with Autumn, there's no such thing as in character, out of character. It's all just a question of *what next?* and *why the hell not?*

I put my hands against my forehead and consider what Maribeth might find acceptable. What she would call down vengeful thunder for, and what she would allow. What she wouldn't be able to actively prevent.

"You could," I say finally. "You could come. Not to student council—it's too late in the semester. But if you wanted, there's a volunteer meeting at Maribeth's next week. You could come help with decorations." Then, because I feel a certain obligation to be truthful, I add, "You won't like it, though."

Autumn gives me a patient smile. "Do you actually think I'm incapable of making my own fun?"

Her cheeks are flushed, like this is all just some delightful game we're playing, and a small, sensible part of me immediately regrets inviting her. The very idea of Autumn in the same room with Maribeth is alarming. But also just the tiniest bit thrilling.

"Look, there's something you need to understand. Maribeth is kind of . . . territorial. She takes this really seriously. You don't have to actually care about homecoming, but you have to at least pretend."

"I don't even know how to act like I care about letting Andrew Wiesman's frog eat the dissection worms in biology last year, and apparently *that's* going on my permanent record. Tell me more about this magical technique for faking your own feelings?"

I press my palms against my eyelids and sit down on the bench, considering how I'd approach this scenario if I were in Autumn's position. There are all kinds of ways to trick people into thinking you belong. "You'd need to seem deferential, but invested. Helpful. We still don't have a theme for the dance, so you could suggest one."

"What, like Enchantment Under the Sea or Love Among the Stars?"

"No. It would need to be a real one—not a joke, not from a movie. Also, it should have enough room for Maribeth to change the wording around and pretend it was her idea."

Autumn raises her eyebrows like I've just proposed something graphically offensive.

Her reaction shouldn't bother me, but still, I feel reproached. Overcome by a need to explain myself. It's vital, suddenly, to make her see that yes, I might sound cynical, but my understanding of the social order is unparalleled. It's supremely functional. It's really not as ugly as it sounds.

"Okay, I know this seems convoluted, but it's actually pretty simple. You'd suggest something like A Brief Moment in Time, which Maribeth will love, but she won't be able to use it because it wasn't her idea, so she'll change a phrase or a word, and then you'll wind up with Romantic Times or Time Stands Still."

The underlying mechanism is self-explanatory, but experience has taught me that other people don't always think about interpersonal dynamics the same way I do. "Or whatever. That part doesn't matter. What *matters* is that you're making yourself into a commodity. Most of being socially successful is really just being valuable."

Autumn is still looking at me like she finds me vaguely traumatic, chewing on her lip, but all she says is, "So. If I was going to be palling around with the Future Corporate Overlords of America, I'd probably need someone to show me how to do this whole . . . wholesome look."

"Are you saying that by *not* giving the impression I applied my eyeliner with a shotgun, that's a 'look'?"

"Of course it's a look. Everything's a look. Come on, it'll be fun—we'll hit City Drug and you can help me pick out a costume!"

I'm supposed to be going over the party rental budget with Maribeth and Palmer in forty-five minutes, but most of the big-ticket stuff is already paid for, and calculators exist. They'll figure it out. And anyway, it might be nice to go someplace with someone who doesn't expect me to manufacture transports of joy over color-coordinated barrettes.

We walk across Detmer Avenue to the drugstore and I make a brief itinerary in my head, laying out a shopping plan for Autumn as we go.

She needs new accessories and a different eyeliner. The one she has makes her look like a pissed-off raccoon.

In order to occupy Maribeth's immediate space, you can't look like you're faking it. Maribeth doesn't fake things, and so—my own carefully crafted persona aside—she has a towering disdain for anyone who does. It is absolutely crucial that Autumn appear to blend seamlessly into the environment. Like she has always been there.

Generally speaking, I prefer a sense of order. I like to have an agenda, but Autumn wanders the aisles completely unchecked. She's a dabbler. She has to try every lipstick, every variety of powder and gloss, even the ones that are glaringly wrong. She spends fifteen minutes comparing eye shadows, layering the testers on in rainbow strata all the way up to her eyebrows.

When she uses the little sponge to add a row of meticulous circles along her brow bone in Goldie Glitter, I finally intervene. "What are you *doing*?"

"I'm a peacock," she says, opening her eyes very wide and fluttering her lashes.

The look on her face is priceless, and I laugh even though I don't mean to.

It's sort of charming how entertained she is by lip stain and colored eyeliners. The makeup selection elicits far more interest than she has *ever* shown toward social customs or cross-country.

While Autumn deliberates between powder eye shadow in Platinum Glow and cream eye shadow in Pearl Perfection— shades that look identical to the naked eye—I kill time an aisle over, uncapping different brands of men's antiperspirant.

It makes me feel a little like an abject loser, but I take a few minutes, comparing scents until I find one that reminds me of Marshall. It's one element to his dark, complicated smell, and for a moment, I just stand there breathing it.

When Autumn peeks around the end of the aisle I almost drop the stick.

"What are you doing?" she says. She's wiped off all the powder and the glitter and her face is pinkly bare. She looks kind. Like someone who could keep a secret.

"Nothing." I jam the cap back on and feign interest in the wide variety of whitening toothpastes.

MARSHALL
Sick

The cough is nothing new, just a natural side effect of smoking. I've been working on it for months.

Only somehow, overnight, it's turned into a bad hacking mess.

Now I'm home, sprawled on the couch with the TV on. The light is nice, as long as the volume's down. The house is dark in unexpected places. Lightbulbs keep burning out and no one changes them. It's weird how fast the little things start to pile up. Dead leaves and dead batteries and slow, creaking hinges. The house is falling asleep like a cursed kingdom in a story. We're all just waiting for someone else to fix it.

Since my dad got disability, some things are still normal. My mom still goes to work at the power and water building downtown, comes home again, turns on the shopping channel or starts knocking around in the kitchen. My dad used to pack computer chips at AgiTech, and after work or on the weekends, he'd play guitar or build shelves out in the garage, but now he's on weekly injections and most of the time his hands shake too much to do anything fiddly. He sleeps a lot. Or else, pretends to.

In the kitchen, I can hear my mom cutting stuff up, making some stir-fry with free-range chicken and vegetables from one of the health food stores we can't afford, with no preservatives or dyes because she read on the Internet that chemicals are the reason people get sick.

I want a glass of water. I want a blanket. If Annie were here, she'd find me one. She'd probably sit around and watch bad cop shows with me and talk about college football until I fell asleep.

I want to be still and small, and not have to man up or act like everything's okay, but the thing about living in a house where someone's sick is, it's like they have a monopoly on it. If one person is always needing things, then no one else is really allowed to.

There's a family portrait over the TV, the five of us posed against a marble-gray background. It's from three years ago. Justin and my dad are at the back, matching baseball jerseys and matching sneers, while in front of them my mom pretends to be out of her mind with happiness and I work hard at being invisible. I stare at myself and wonder when my face got so hard, wonder when I stopped talking. Stopped smiling. Out of all of us, Annie is the only one just posing cheerfully like a normal person. In the picture, I look worried. Embarrassed by the fact that I exist.

The quieter and stiller I lie, the easier it is to be someplace else. I don't remember a lot about last night, but the part with Waverly is very clear, like it's the only real thing that's ever happened. I shouldn't be thinking about her. Mostly, I shouldn't be thinking how maybe, just maybe she'll come back.

I bury my face in the couch and picture her next to me, there on the edge of the tub. Her clean-smelling hair, her shoulder against mine. Ignore the other part—how she disappeared from Hez's bathroom in less than a second. It makes me feel too crazy. My head hurts like a car crash. If I close my eyes, I can still feel the weight of her hand on my neck and how fucking *hopeful* I felt suddenly, like maybe everything was pretty bad, but it was going to get better.

It's weird, the way she keeps asking if I'm okay when it's obvious I'm not. That night on the Captain's porch, she sounded sad as hell, and I could feel a tight, waspy buzzing coming off her. Something in her voice hurt like a bruise, but the way she looked was so untouchable. I think I get it now.

Asking someone if they're okay has got to be some dirty kind of genius. If you can prove someone else is a disaster, you never have to let them see what's wrong with you.

Our dog, Chowder, hangs around because she seems to think that if I sit in front of the TV long enough, the petting will start and food will appear, but I'm not in the mood to eat anything.

I take a couple NyQuil Cold and Flu and wait for them to work, to kill the pounding in my head. With my arm across my face to block the light, it's easy to be nowhere. Nothing. I think about Waverly and don't even care that I shouldn't. It doesn't matter. It doesn't matter. It doesn't. It can't. Because Jesus Christ, it's not like it's real.

I fall asleep and dream that someone's drilling into my skull with a power saw. When I wake up, it's time for another dose of NyQuil. I'm still waiting for the first one to kick in.

WAVERLY

5.

When I was eight, the woman who volunteered as the recess aide told me I wasn't allowed to show people the dead squirrel by the trash cans anymore because it was scaring the other kids and if I kept talking about decomposition, I wasn't going to have any friends and didn't I want people to like me?

I didn't know how to answer. I hadn't been trying to make people like me, but I hadn't been trying to scare them either.

As soon as I got home, I went into the study and told my mother what the recess woman said. Then I lay on the floor and waited for her to fix it.

"You don't have to stop thinking about autolysis and putrefaction," she said finally. I stared at her bare feet, hooked on the rail of her chair, as I lay under her desk, chewing on a pencil. "But you might consider talking about it less."

The way she said it was businesslike. She had analyzed the problem; this was the solution.

I pressed the pencil against my teeth, then bit down

hard. "What am I supposed to talk about?" I said, but it sounded tiny and indistinct.

My mom was quiet for a while. "Well, their interests, for example. I'm sure you can think of something." She took a deep breath and then I heard her close her laptop. "You're going to meet a lot of people, Waverly, and most of them just aren't going to be interested in the decomposition process."

The way she sounded when she said it made a gleaming web of circuits in my head. It confirmed everything I'd ever suspected, but hadn't been savvy enough to put into words.

My mom scooted her chair back and peered under the desk. I had stopped rubbing my feet on the carpet. I had stopped breathing.

"Sweetie," she said. Her voice was softer now. "There's nothing wrong with you. You're just ahead of the curve. You know that, right?"

It was a phrase I'd been hearing since kindergarten, and I nodded, but now I knew the truth.

I lay on my back, staring at the grain in the wood and sucking on the inside of my arm, even though it was something I'd mostly grown out of.

If we were having this conversation, that meant something was either wrong with me, or it was wrong with everybody else, and I had a basic enough understanding of probability to know that the odds did not rest with an entire planet.

. . .

In the glow of the candle, with my heart beating swift and shallow, I close my eyes and start to count.

The possibility that I'm becoming increasingly unsound—or else that the world is—should scare me, but it doesn't. All evening, I could barely wait for night. For every obligation to be over so I could light the candle and see if I'd wind up someplace else. My brain might be failing, the world might be unraveling, but no, it doesn't scare me. Because no matter how impossible, Marshall is the one place where I can be completely real and everything's still okay.

I can tell the truth, say all the worst, most honest things. I can scare everyone and never have to worry about the consequences.

When I open my eyes, I'm standing in the doorway of a small, low-ceilinged living room. Marshall is in front of the TV, stretched out across a very plaid couch, and there's a yellow dog staring at me with its head cocked to one side. That, along with a whole array of other landmarks, tells me I'm not at his brother's house.

The light from the television is flickering bright and dark. He's got one arm tucked awkwardly back behind his head and is staring at the screen like he's not really seeing it.

I stand in the door, just waiting, just watching. He looks tired. Abnormally young.

A girl comes skimming past me, wearing a red convenience store smock. Her hair is yanked back into a ponytail. In the light from the TV, she looks blurry and kind. She's carrying a stack of books, but the way she's holding them, I can't see the subjects. "Mars, go to bed."

He shakes his head, glancing at me, then away again. "*Storage Wars* is on. I think I'll just hang out here for a while." Then he winces and turns his face into the pillow, coughing hard.

She drops the books in a careless spill against his shins, then yanks the smock over her head, revealing a plain gray T-shirt. "God, yuck. If you've got another respiratory infection, tell Mom to get you some antibiotics."

She brushes past me again and disappears down the hall, returning a minute later with a blanket. When she offers it to him, Marshall takes it and drapes it clumsily over himself.

The gesture is weirdly tender and I have the sensation of a hook tugging at something in my chest. Then she scoops up the books again, juggling wallet and phone and car keys, nudging the yellow dog out of her way with her hip.

When she's gone, Marshall turns his head. "Hey, you. How are things in ghostland?"

I want to make some snarky comment, some remark about how insomnia is better than typhoid, but in the end all I say is "Hi."

He jerks his head toward the couch and I perch myself on the edge, careful not to lean against him or touch his worn-soft blanket. He scoots back against the cushions to make room, but doesn't rearrange his legs or sit up.

I hunch forward, pinning my hands between my knees. "Looks like you decided to stay in tonight. Are you really that hungover?"

He shakes his head. "Sick. Some chest thing. It's really gross."

There's a part of me that wants to tell him I don't think he's gross, but the words won't come. Instead, there's just my usual script—Waverly Classic. "Maybe this is a sign from God that you shouldn't be kissing girls indiscriminately."

When he smiles, the shape of his mouth looks like he's in pain. It's hard to know what I'm supposed to do. I'm not good with tender ministrations.

"Is there anything you need?" I say, and I don't sound tender, but I sound helpful. I just want him to see that when he hurts, I'm not enjoying it.

He looks up at me. His cheeks are flushed in hectic blotches. "Put your cold little hand on my neck?"

I feel self-conscious suddenly, and shy. "Do you want me to hold it under the faucet first?"

"No, I just want to feel it." His voice is low and matter-of-fact. Honest. "I like how . . . how *real* it is. I was kind of hoping you'd show up, you know?"

And the thing is, I do.

When I touch him, he squeezes his eyes shut and reaches out, fumbling across the couch for me. His skin is dry, furiously hot. His hand is blazing against my thigh and he leaves it there, rubbing his thumb over the place just above my knee. He looks ragged in the lamplight, hollow-cheeked and sunken-eyed from staying out every night. His touch is gentle and deliberate, like he means it.

"You need to stop being so rough on yourself," I say.

That makes him smile. He squeezes my leg and keeps his eyes closed. "Says the girl who doesn't sleep."

It takes me a second to realize he's talking about what

I said on the porch the other night. "Yeah, well, I never get sick."

He gives me a soft little pat, but doesn't say anything. His smile is knowing, sad in a way that makes me feel stupid and obvious. His hand on my thigh makes my cheeks prickly and too warm.

"Why do you do that all the time?" I say. "Getting drunk, getting high—I mean, I don't see the point."

He turns his face into the pillow and laughs. "There's no *point*. It's just a way to be."

"Be what, exactly?" My tone is flippant, implying a list of negatives. *Not* be important or productive. *Not* be a success.

He's got his face half buried in the couch, talking into the upholstery, but he says the next part clearly enough. "Here without having to be here."

He doesn't sound embarrassed, just weirdly factual.

I look down at his hand. It's softer, more delicate than I'd remembered, with clean cuticles and long, tapering fingers. Under it, the shape of my thigh is stringy. Utilitarian. The living room is bristling with furniture—end tables and recliners and terrible lamps—like it's supposed to be full of more people than just the two of us.

Marshall takes a breath like he's about to say something else, but halfway through, he's gripped by a ferocious coughing fit. He pushes himself up from the couch, sitting doubled over with his forehead against his knees. The way his face goes violent-pink, blood blooming under his skin, is slightly alarming.

"Are you okay? Do you need a drink of water?"

He shakes his head, still red in the face, trying to catch his breath. After a minute, he lies back.

I rest my hand on his neck again, rubbing my thumb over the smooth, burning skin, touching the hollow behind his ear. "You really shouldn't be smoking in your condition. Also, if you have a respiratory infection, antibiotics probably won't help. Most respiratory infections are viral."

He sighs, smiling a resigned little smile. "Waverly, you make me want to die, but it's in the best way. You have no idea."

"Mars?" A woman's voice drifts in from the kitchen. "Who you talking to in there?"

"No one," he calls back. "It's just the TV."

She creeps into the room looking pretty and timid, much too young to be the mother of three mostly grown kids. She approaches Marshall like she's weaponizing plutonium, bending over the plaid couch to feel his forehead. He doesn't make it easy. He was unresisting for his sister, accepting the blanket and the good-natured fussing, but his mother's hand on his face makes him flinch.

"I'm okay." He raises himself on his elbow, twisting away.

"Mars, baby, you're burning up. Let me get you some aspirin."

Her face is worried in a way my own mother wouldn't even comprehend. At my house, the concerns of the material world are purely secondary. I've been raised on the philosophy that once you can read the instructions on the Bisquick box and reach the stove, you're on your own. A chest cold is not life-threatening.

Marshall's mom is leaning over him, brushing his hair back like he's younger than he is. He lets his cheek sink into the pillow, but he's gazing past her, right at me.

I'm going now. I can feel my skin getting thinner. I hate the transparent feeling of already fading.

He gives me an imploring look and mouths the words *Don't leave.*

"I have to," I say, but when I move my lips, no sound comes out.

•

Marshall isn't at school. This should not be the focal point of my day. There's a bibliography due for the long project in English and a brace of practice sets for trig, and I don't have time to be thinking about someone else's questionable attendance.

His desk is uncomfortably vacant when I hold up my compact.

By the time office duty rolls around, I'm nearly climbing out of my skin.

I don't know whether to twirl or pace or start pulling out my hair. Instead, I write myself a pass for the west hall bathroom.

I have no secrets to confess, nothing clamoring to be heard. Even in kindergarten, I was never one for sharing. After six frantic laps between the wall and the door, I get out my pen anyway.

To the girl who thinks you can get pregnant from giving head, I write:

Please read an anatomy textbook.

Or an issue of Cosmo.

To all the girls who complain that their supposed BFFs are copying their style/mannerisms/catch-phrases/accessories, and then proclaim in self-satisfied tones:

I wish she'd just stop

I paraphrase a certain popular film and write:

You are not your Prada purse.

I write this only once, and then divide it—a collection of arrows spiderwebbing out, sprawling to touch the relevant grievances, all various permutations of the same problem.

To:

I think Austin Greer is my soul mate,
and he doesn't know I exist

I shake my head and write:

Just because you feel it doesn't make it real.

Near my first contribution, someone has written:

> *Bitch, I love my ED. It's the best*
> *decision of my life and I'm not*
> *going to change for anyone.*
> *Mind your fucking business.*

I consider this and write my longest, most truthful response to date.

> *I'm seventeen years old.*
> *I have no practical experience and*
> *no clinical training. For anyone who's confused*
> *or scared and looking for help, it's there,*
> *but you have to ask for it.*

•

Night is a long, unbroken sprawl, followed by another. And another.

It's been four days since Marshall lay on the couch looking up at me with hot, bleary eyes. Four days since I sat next to him and touched his neck and he rested his hand on my thigh. Four days since I've seen him. Since I got even the barest suggestion of a good night's sleep.

I've tried all the conventional wisdom—hot milk and boring books. A double dose of Benadryl, which left me numb, thirsty, and still very much awake.

The candle burns on my nightstand, but no matter how dutifully I count, nothing happens. After two hours and no luck, I admit that persistence isn't accomplishing anything, and blow it out.

Monday was supposed to be the day that sent everything clanking back to normal. No one can stay sick for more than seventy-two hours, right? That's impossible. It's inefficient.

But he still isn't at school. The assignment in Spanish is

a study guide, but it's just to pass the time. We don't have to turn it in because then she might have to grade them. Sometimes when I blink, the room goes shimmery around the edges. I draw spirals in all the spaces where the *-er* verbs should go.

The memory of Marshall's hand on my bare leg has its own kind of secret life. It creeps in, getting mixed up with lagging cross-country times and homework until suddenly, there it is, covering up everything else.

•

Tuesday. Tuesday is better.

And I know my debatable sense of well-being should be because when Mr. Aimsley hands back our Virginia Woolf papers, there's an A at the top of mine, or because Maribeth is waiting for me with coffee before trig and tells me the pattern I found for crepe paper flowers is a good one, but the reason it's better is because when the bell for sixth period rings, Marshall walks into Spanish, looking tired but upright.

I watch him in my compact and wait for him to look at me. He doesn't. When I accidentally make eye contact with CJ Borsen, he winks and rubs my ankle with the toe of his sneaker. I pretend to dig through my bag for an eraser or a pen—I can't decide which. I take out a box of paper clips and suddenly everything feels so fake I'm nearly dizzy. I have this disturbing idea that the entire classroom might just be set dressing.

At the front of the room, Denning is looking quietly defeated, and I feel sorrier than usual. I wonder what drives a person to become a high school Spanish teacher. Maybe she is in witness protection, or some vengeful god is punishing her for a past life. There are so many other career paths that don't involve daily humiliation.

"Who'd like to hand back the tests?" she asks miserably, preparing for our collective lack of response.

When I raise my hand, she looks surprised but smiles wanly. When it's a choice between me and anyone else, most teachers will fling themselves on the safety of the sure thing.

I make my way up and down the rows, sorting through papers.

When I get to Marshall, the smell of his hair makes me want to faint in some blissful, recreational way that would be good in a Victorian novel, but just seems totally impractical in real life.

I settle for breathing deeply as I flip through the sheaf of tests, looking for his name.

He hasn't failed it. He's missed a few points here and there for accent marks, forgotten that *poner* is irregular.

At the bottom, Mrs. Denning's prissy handwriting declares, *Nice work* ☺ *It's good to see you starting to apply yourself. If you still want some extra credit, see me after class.* ☺☺

I set the paper facedown in front of him and he doesn't look up. His hands are resting on the desktop, long and clean and still. I remember his palm on my thigh and wonder if it haunts him. If it even occurs to him.

Without stopping to consider the consequences, I lean closer, letting my breath wash over the back of his neck—a long, slow exhalation that sends a deep flush creeping all the way up to his hairline. His ears are burning.

I continue along the row of desks, leaving him staring at the blank side of his paper and blushing furiously.

In the space of less than one week, Autumn has become a different person. She deserves a movie montage, complete with some twitchy, fast-paced song by Mindless Self Indulgence or The Offspring. Her hair is shiny, her clothes preppy to a competitive degree. She even walks differently. But that's probably because she's wearing wedges instead of her Vans.

I find her waiting at my locker like a softer, pinker version of herself. The Pearl Perfection eye shadow makes her look harmless.

"Wow," I say, but it comes out sounding breathless.

She stands with her ankles crossed, twisting a lock of hair around one finger. Then she smiles her hard, sly smile and her face looks normal again. "I know, right?"

I'm admiring her newly unclumped eyelashes, adjusting her sideswept bangs to camouflage her rook piercing, when Maribeth shoves between us, smiling her sweetest, fakest smile.

The way she's blinking, fast and innocent, does not bode well. "Hi, new person. Waverly, I need to talk to you. I just saw the sketches CJ's been working on for the centerpieces, and they're not going to work."

I gesture with both hands like I'm presenting a game show contestant with a new car. "Maribeth, this is Autumn."

Maribeth turns to Autumn, studying her with deep concentration. "Okay . . ." Her voice is dubious, her eyebrows pegged at dramatic angles.

Autumn tucks her hair behind her ear and moves closer to me. The way she ducks her head makes it seem like she's using me as a buffer, which is something no one has ever done.

I'm the unnerving one—Maribeth Whitman's blank-faced vizier, high priestess of precalculus. Her quiet mercenary, her black cat. The girl who needs help remembering how to smile. I am Maribeth's ever-watchful familiar. She, beloved by multitudes. Me, beloved only by her.

But now Autumn is shoulder to shoulder with me, her back against the row of lockers, her arm touching mine.

Maribeth opens her eyes wide, her mouth an exaggerated O of delight. "Waverly, what is *this*? Making friends and influencing people? Are you sure you're okay? Is your motherboard functioning properly?"

Autumn makes a matching face. "Version update! Waverly's real people now!"

Maribeth is not amused. "*Where* did you find her, again?" she says to me. Like Autumn is from a foreign country, or at least not standing right there.

"She's on cross-country with me."

Maribeth's expression says, *And therefore . . . ?* It says, *So are a lot of other completely insignificant people, but none of them are standing here breathing my air, so what's the deal, Waverly? Enlighten me.*

"She does art," I say. "And we need someone to help with the centerpieces."

Maribeth studies me, then seems to soften. "Oh, so that'll be great, actually! I mean, we're still one short since Loring quit."

The way she says it is bright, like she's talking about an incident that has nothing to do with her. Like Loring's absence is voluntary. I wonder if it's what she actually believes.

"Perfect," I say. "Autumn can come over tonight."

"Perfect!" Maribeth responds. She might even mean it.

She twists her necklace around her finger, turning back to Autumn. "We're doing cut-paper lanterns with those little fake electric candles. Four-sided, maybe five. It would be good if they had a floral motif—no lilies."

Then she tosses her hair over her shoulder and leaves us standing at the open locker.

Autumn leans against the bank of metal doors, watching Maribeth disappear into the crowd. "What the fuck was *that*?"

I shrug and straighten my textbooks. I can't begin to count the times Maribeth has called me *alien* and *cyborg* and *genius* and *robot,* but this is the first time I've been embarrassed for someone else to hear her do it.

Autumn is looking at me now, waiting for clarity. Waiting for something.

I rake my bangs out of my eyes. "By the way, I probably should have asked. How do you feel about paper lanterns?"

"Pretty much like how I feel about steel wool or dwarf hamsters. So, when she breathes like that, does it mean she has something bitchy on her mind and she's just not saying it?"

I nod. "That's her judging sigh."

Autumn laughs the way that no one ever laughs when I talk—bright and uncomplicated, with her head thrown back.

It's not until we're halfway to the gym that something occurs to me. Maybe she wasn't shrinking close for protection after all, but stepping in front of me.

•

The meeting of the excessive confetti committee is the kind of thing that makes you want to put a pencil through your eye.

Everyone—by which I mean the grim cabal of Everyone Who Matters—is sitting on the cut-pile carpet at Maribeth's house, arguing politely over color schemes.

I try to remain focused on the intense appeal of paper streamers, but my thoughts keep wandering. I want to be home, in my bed, alone with my candle and the fascinating possibility of Marshall Holt.

I wonder if it's too soon, if he needs more time to recuperate. If the sensation of my breath on his neck today made him blush because he was responding to *me,* or if it was just the result of physiology and hormones—if any other girl could have gotten the same reaction. I wonder if he exists in the way I think he does, or if he's just something I've invented while I was busy trying to function normally. If he thinks of me at all. If the way he ran his thumb over my knee meant anything.

"Waverly, watch the edges—you're drawing them crooked," Maribeth says, and I lurch back to the task at hand.

We're cutting up poster board for her paper-lantern centerpieces, which is mind-numbing.

Across the circle, Autumn is sharing her X-acto knife with Hunter Pennington. She keeps swatting at him with her ruler and he's loving every second of it, offering her colored tissue paper and pretending to be wounded by her pretend disinterest.

I study Maribeth, trying to measure her reaction. In the glow of the recessed lighting she looks placid and pristine, but when I glance away and see her reflected in the glass door of the entertainment center, her expression is desolate.

The centerpieces are shaping up nicely. Autumn's pattern is good, easy enough for even the wrestling boys to cut out and assemble. My lanterns are neat, sliding together with precise tabs and notches. Palmer's look like angry, mutated beetles. Autumn's are delicate, verging on exquisite. I know that by the end of the night, Maribeth will figure out a way to make her do them all.

Autumn taps her bottom lip with her pen, surveying the collection of cutout shapes spread across Maribeth's carpet. "So, is the whole thing going to be a garden theme, or just the lamps?"

Palmer is the one who answers, looking bored and long-suffering. "It isn't final yet. We're still deciding."

She and Kendry are clearly distrustful, but they

haven't been outright nasty yet. After all, Autumn is here with Maribeth's blessing. Or at least, Maribeth's lack of objection.

Autumn opens her mouth, presumably to make the carefully planned suggestion I outlined for her last week, but before she can get a word in, Maribeth cuts her off.

"Oh, but you know what I was thinking?" Maribeth's tone implies she has just discovered a glorious unicorn. "We should have a school-wide vote, like we do for the homecoming court. That way, everyone will feel like the dance is *theirs* too."

The way she says it is offhand, speaking with casual authority, so magnanimous, but really, she's just trying to downplay the fact that we still haven't come up with a theme on our own. That *she* hasn't.

Autumn rolls her eyes, and not in a private way. And suddenly, I'm on high alert. I wonder if she even understands that her derisive faces are being broadcast to everyone.

"Or," Kendry says, giving Autumn a scathing look, "do you have a *better* idea?"

I nod discreetly, just once, to show she hasn't missed her opening. This is her window—her brief moment in time.

Autumn smiles beatifically. "I have a lot of better ideas. I could have a seizure and it would be a better idea. Look, you do not want to put the power in the hands of the people, okay? You're just going to get three hundred write-in votes for *My Dick*."

Whatever's supposed to be happening right now, it is not this.

The girls all look scandalized, but Hunter Pennington

and Chris Webb are snickering, punching each other in a way that suggests they would most definitely write in *My Dick*.

Maribeth opens her mouth to respond, but Autumn waves a languid hand. "Anyway, the theme is whatever. It's not like it matters."

Maribeth's eyebrows jump so dramatically they nearly take flight and I wince. "Excuse me? The *theme* is the unifying principle for the whole thing."

"I'm just saying, there'd be a better turnout at these things if they weren't always completely embarrassing. We could actually do something decent for once, like Cult Classics or Hollywood Heroes. That way the outfits would *be* the theme."

Maribeth sits up very straight, blinking innocently. "And showing up in costumes isn't embarrassing? I'm sorry, but I feel like I'm missing something."

Autumn charges on, completely undeterred by sarcasm or blatant hostility. "Think about it—if we do something with a really broad, dramatic theme, people will get to wear all kinds of dresses. The guys could choose their looks based on a hundred years of male leads, and they wouldn't need ties if they didn't want, or even jackets. I mean, it's not like Marlon Brando wore a cummerbund in *On the Waterfront*, okay?"

The girls are eyeing her with acute distrust, but on the other side of the circle, Hunter is nodding like what Autumn has to say is actually relevant, and some of the wrestling boys look more alert than they have at any point aside from Autumn's revelation that a school-wide vote could potentially involve their manly parts.

Maribeth, however, is deeply unimpressed. "Great, so they all dress exactly like they do every day? Excuse me, but what is the *point* then?"

"Oh, I don't know. Maybe the point is just that it's *fun* for once?"

I hold very still. It's actually kind of amazing how fast this has become the worst possible version of itself. Everyone else is diligently assembling their lanterns, like if they make eye contact, they might get sucked in.

CJ leans over the coffee table to whisper in my ear. "You look nice tonight," he says. "Like that girl in the movie. *Breakfast* whatever. If we do Autumn's theme, you should come as her."

"Holly Golightly," I tell him automatically, one eye still on the imminent disaster across from me.

Maribeth is sitting with her back very straight, clutching her composure by a thread. I wonder how much of her outrage is due to her sense that the dance-planning hierarchy has been violated, and how much is about the way Hunter keeps tugging on Autumn's ponytail.

Her gaze shifts to me, eyebrows raised delicately, telegraphing *Good work, Waverly. This plan turned out beautifully.* "What do *you* think, Waverly?"

She doesn't mean that. She means, *You think what I think, Waverly.*

"We could do something like Cherished Memories," I say, in an effort to get Autumn back on track.

"Or even something that *isn't* such a giant gaping cliché," Autumn says. Her smile is incandescent, and I have no earthly idea what she thinks she's doing.

I can't even tell if her performance is malicious, or if she's actually just trying to advocate for the dance she'd want to go to. But of one thing I am absolutely certain: her lack of cheerful acquiescence will not fly with Maribeth.

I adjust my face to look studious and helpful. "Or what about A Brief Moment in Time?" Because sometimes, you just have to scrap the original plan entirely and do what it takes to save lives.

For a moment, I think it's the wrong suggestion after all. The effort is, at best, too little too late.

Then Maribeth softens. She smiles. "That's good," she says. "No, that's really good. What if the favors were something with little clocks, or hourglasses, even?"

And like that, with the stamp of Maribeth's approval, our theme is finalized in less than five minutes.

I shoot a look at Autumn that's supposed to communicate my displeasure, but she isn't paying attention. She's gone back to her stack of centerpieces like nothing has happened, her hand resting on Hunter's arm. They're laughing together in short, muffled bursts.

When I ask her to come help me make some more lemonade, I lead her straight through the kitchen and out, dragging her into the vaulted entryway, away from the ugly little drama in the living room.

We stand facing each other by an extravagant arrangement of fake flowers.

"What?" she says. "Oh, come on. That was nothing—it was just a little tussle."

I'm alarmed at her notion that a blowout of such

proportions could be considered little. There is no such thing as *nothing* when it comes to Maribeth.

I can't even fully articulate the level of investment Maribeth feels for her various social projects, so instead, I lean around one of the faux-Doric columns and point in the direction of Hunter and the cheery little stencil party. "Off-limits, Autumn."

She shrugs, not looking particularly contrite. "I had to. She was about to cut me loose."

"And you think draping yourself over her intended boyfriend will keep you here?"

Autumn leans closer, her tone confidential. "Now it's a competition. She *has* to keep me around so she can win this shit in public. That girl is not the kind of person who's into victory by disqualification."

I raise my eyebrows. Autumn's assessment is both uncharitable and entirely accurate. "Do you want to at least dial back the antagonism? A little?"

"Look, right now, all I *want* is to go home, watch TMZ, and eat a goddamn Pop-Tart." She lets her head flop back and her shoulders slump. "Waverly, what are we doing here? This isn't even *fun*."

"I *know* it's not fun," I snap. "It's *never* fun." Which is a little bit of a lie because it wasn't always like this. It used to be fun. In seventh grade.

Autumn sighs, resting her elbows on the decorative half wall. "Look, whatever. Make my apologies to Queen Crowdsource. I'm going home."

She crouches and untangles her bag from the drift of

purses and shoes piled just inside the hall. No one can withstand the monotony of extracurricular event planning and sanctimonious good works, but being vindicated in my hatred of construction paper isn't as comforting as one would think. Even Autumn is less durable than she pretended.

"What are you doing tomorrow?" I say, although I've got nothing very tempting to offer. "We're all going shopping after cross-country. If you want."

"Sure, whatever." Autumn shoulders her bag and starts for the gleaming marble foyer. Then she stops and turns back. "CJ's right," she says. "About the dress. You should look for something in black or navy, with a low-cut back and a Sabrina neckline in the front."

"We're doing jewel tones. Maribeth already picked out the corsage colors and got the barrettes and everything."

I hate how compliant I sound, like letting Maribeth decide formal floral arrangements for me is some kind of compromise or concession, when really, I just don't care. For the privilege of not having to expend a single particle of my being on hothouse flowers, it's a sacrifice I'm willing to make.

Autumn smiles and shakes her head. "She wants jewel tones because she looks amazing in sapphire and turquoise. You need something more subtle. Something that looks totally conservative, and then, bang, they see you from a different angle and it's not. Also, you need a different date. CJ's really going to clash with your sense of intellectual superiority."

I laugh, even though I'm starting to feel claustrophobic.

I want to be home with my blankets and my candle. I want to be with Marshall.

Autumn stands in the doorway, just looking at me. She smiles and my throat constricts for no reason. Suddenly, I don't want anything but to run and run and run.

MARSHALL
Music Box

The first day back at school after being sick is always kind of weird, like you lost more time than you thought.

When I pulled into the parking lot, the building looked bigger than I remembered and for a second, the whole world seemed to be growing way too fast, spreading out and out.

But Ollie was there like always, swinging into step with me at the west entrance like he'd been waiting for me forever, totally sure I'd show up one of these days.

Heather wanted to know where I'd been, though, and if I felt okay and why I didn't call her. The thing is, I can't even picture her coming over to my house, sitting on the couch with me. Texting or flipping through a magazine while I coughed and slept and stared at the TV.

Or I can picture it, but it kind of makes my eyes hurt.

I feel better.

I feel see-through and like I've lost weight, but I'm better.

I'm behind in all my classes—the kind of behind you don't come back from, but after dinner, I spend a while getting caught up on the little stuff, all the review questions and worksheets I've been ignoring. Papers and reports are harder, but I half-ass an outline for partial credit and read some of *The Crucible* for English. History is kicking my ass, but in this cheap, lazy way where I'm basically letting it.

Now I'm sitting at my shitty little desk, staring at the assigned chapter for science, but not really seeing it.

I keep getting sidetracked by stupid things. I keep thinking about Annie's jewelry box. It was one of those white pressboard ones with a pink lining, and when you opened it, there was a little plastic ballerina in a lace skirt. The box played a song while the ballerina turned in a circle.

I'd sneak into her room, open the box. She hated when I messed with her stuff, but it was worth the chance of getting slapped just to see that ballerina turn.

It was like this little piece of quiet. This tiny, uncommon place I was in love with. Annie got rid of that thing like ten years ago. Nothing is really ever quiet anymore.

Finally, I turn out the light and get into bed. I'm tired, and not. My ribs feel sore, but the worst of the cough is gone, and I've been sleeping for days. It was a heavy, drugged sleep, and now it's like I can't remember how to do it when there isn't a dose and a half of NyQuil involved.

When I close my eyes, Waverly's there, flickering in the trashy movie theater of my mind. She doesn't belong there, but she shows up more and more—this thought I can't shut out. And let's face it, as guilty as it makes me feel, I don't really want to.

She's wearing this thin, silky shirt she wears sometimes. It's probably even made of real silk, which makes me want to touch it more. Her skin looks creamy next to it, like nice china or some kind of European doll that's hand-painted. Real, not-real. Right now, I don't even care.

We're inches apart, looking at each other, and then the picture changes. Out in the living room, my parents are going at it like people on one of those daytime talk shows. My pillow is lumpy under my head. My sheets smell like cigarettes and menthol cough drops, and I concentrate harder.

Waverly's on her back now, looking up at me.

When I undo the first button, the feeling roars through my chest, rushing in my blood. She bites her lip and her face is so open and so trusting that I want to reach for her and hold on like I'm drowning. Instead, I lean over, my fingers skimming her shirt, tugging at the buttons. I slip the top one from its hole and work my way down.

Her shirt opens to show the shape of her breasts, the lacy edge of a white bra. Her waist is narrow, and god, her skin. I touch the curve of her cheek and she smiles.

She says my name and says, "Kiss me."

When I bend my head to do it, she reaches for me. She puts her hand on the back of my neck, kisses me slowly, like she doesn't want to move too fast or wreck the moment. Like I'm the only person she wants to kiss.

WAVERLY

6.

The dark is populated by undefined shapes. It pitches around me. I can't tell if it's tiny or huge or something in between. I stand in the middle of it, unfixed in space.

The smell is familiar, the carpet is rough, and there's a low, constant sound that's going to drive me crazy if it doesn't stop. Then the full magnitude of the situation washes over me.

My voice comes out in a harsh, high-pitched whisper, almost a shriek. "Oh my God, tell me you are *not* doing that!"

Marshall sits up fast, slamming back against the wall. He yanks the blankets up to his chest in silhouette and for a second, there's just the sound of his breath, rasping in and out.

Then he swallows audibly in the dark. When he speaks, his voice cracks. *"Waverly?"*

I'm not a weak person.

I'm not fragile or tender—not easily embarrassed—but I can feel the mortification anyway, right there on my face.

I know, unequivocally, that I am not supposed to be

here. And maybe all those other times, I could just ignore it. I could get up in the morning and intellectualize about plastic lighters and blue T-shirts and leaves on my feet, tell myself it didn't matter or that the universe is vast. That it wasn't really real.

But this is horrible, undeniable—it's happening—and for a second, I just stand in the middle of the room, holding on to my own shoulders and feeling very small.

Marshall sits with his back against the wall and his knees up. We don't move. After a while, my eyes start to adjust to the dark.

"You can't be here," he whispers, and it's hard to tell if he actually means I *shouldn't* be here, or that I'm *not*.

I move toward the bed, shuffling my feet along the carpet, kicking scattered books and stray socks out of the way until I reach the corner of the mattress.

When I sit down, the blankets are warm and soft. They smell like Old Spice deodorant and his hair—a fragrant, smoky smell that makes my skin feel tight.

"How are you doing this?" he whispers, pressing his back against the wall, flinching away from me.

I slide closer, feeling for the headboard. When my hand brushes the top of his shoulder, he sucks in his breath. He's not wearing a shirt.

"What do you *want*, Waverly?"

And I stop moving. His voice is unsteady, unexpectedly sad.

We sit quietly in the dark, not moving, not touching. The mattress is squishy, sagging in the middle, and I've never felt this untethered before, never been on a boy's bed with him, never sat close together in the dark, in the middle of the night, in my pajamas, my hand still tingling hotly because I touched his bare shoulder.

"I want you to kiss me," I say, and it comes out all wrong—shy and faraway. I sound like I don't really mean it, but how something sounds doesn't always tell you a lot. It takes saying the words out loud to realize that I have never meant anything more in my whole life.

"I can't," he says.

"Why not?"

"Is that supposed to be a *joke*?" His voice cracks again, like he can't catch his breath. "Guys like me don't kiss girls like you."

For a second, I don't say anything. Then I lean in. Whisper it close to his ear. "But at night, we're not like us. We can do whatever we want."

He turns his face to the wall. "Yeah? Well, that's pathetic, then. It's cheap—some cheap, stupid fantasy." His arms are crossed like he can protect himself. His tone is bitter.

I, on the other hand, am perfectly content to take the fantasy.

I put my arms around his neck and kiss him.

The warmth of our colliding bodies is shocking, and for a second, the pressure of my mouth on his feels like too much, like at any second, my structural integrity will fail and I'll just implode.

Yes, I've been kissed—at formal dance after-parties and other social functions—long, uninteresting kisses with nothing fueling them, nothing attached. But this is the first time in my life that I've ever done the kissing.

Marshall sits and lets me do it. His mouth is soft and unresponsive, making it clear that I'm acting upon him, taking the initiative and the risk. Being rejected.

I pull away, dizzy and out of breath. And all those times I thought the way he looked at me might mean something . . . I was wrong.

Then he puts his hand on my arm and kisses me back.

It isn't like the kisses in movies or books. He doesn't grab me and slam me down on the bed, overcome with lust and frustration. Instead, he pulls me closer, moving slowly. His hands are big and warm, sliding up inside my pajama top. He tastes like toothpaste.

His chest is smooth and I shove him back against the wall, holding him there, kneeling over him. Then he moves so that the top of his thigh is pinned between my knees and I can't tell who is ravishing whom.

I have never in my life felt so electrified by anything as I am by the way his lips fit against mine, and when I can't take it anymore, I slide my mouth against his neck, then his chest, working my way down.

Right away, he catches me by the shoulders and pushes me back. "We shouldn't be doing this."

"Why not? Isn't this what you dream about?"

When he answers, his voice is harsh and plaintive. "*No.*"

He's lying, but he's also telling the truth. It doesn't matter if he likes me or doesn't like me, or if he's watched me in the hall once on some endless day and thought about touching me. None of that matters.

What matters is the realness, my hands on his bare arms, my body taking up space in a place that is supposed to be impossible. The fantasy is not supposed to turn into the reality.

There's hair on his stomach, but just a little, running down toward his boxers, getting denser. I follow it, letting my fingertips find the edge of his waistband. The muscles across his abdomen flutter and jerk as I touch his hipbones.

I've thought about this. In a hypothetical way, I've thought about it. Future Waverly takes her gear off for hypothetical future boy—in a mature, pseudo-adult world, maybe at college, because current Waverly has no time to go around perfecting her heavy-petting skills or wondering if she's ready. Current Waverly had only ever debated whether or not to allow CJ Borsen a chaste goodnight kiss.

Under my hands, Marshall's body feels rigid, like he's holding his breath.

I sit up, but don't take my hand away. "Do you want me to stop?"

"No," he says, lying flat on his back with his hands resting on my thighs. His voice sounds so guilty it's almost funny. *We shouldn't be doing this, but don't stop.*

I've never really touched a boy before—not like that. Never thought about it much, even when talk turned gleeful and dirty at sleepovers. The self-conscious erections of ninth-grade gym class, miserable in their basketball shorts, never had any bearing on *me*.

He's squeezing the tops of my thighs, gasping like he

can't catch his breath. Then he rolls away and sits up, grabbing me and pulling me hard against his chest.

His mouth on my neck is warm and sends a surge of electricity through my blood. And here comes the ravishing now, frantic, reverent. He's fumbling with my pajama bottoms, yanking them down off my hips, touching me, and I'm holding his face between my hands, wanting the warm toothpaste flavor of his mouth, wanting to kiss him, and not because I just want to kiss somebody.

Because I want to kiss *him*.

•

I have a problem.

Not astral projection. Not even the fact that I've implicitly agreed to a monogamous relationship with CJ Borsen, when the only person I can think about is Marshall Holt.

Never mind that Autumn Pickerel is turning out to be an engine of destruction, like I wound her up and set her loose, and now I kind of want to stand by while she wrecks the known world. Never mind that I have a regional meet and a trig test and last night was the first full night's sleep I've gotten in months.

I have a giant, colossal hickey on the side of my neck.

It's plum-red and shaped vaguely like Spain. It is large enough to have its own congressman. When the carotid artery throbs in my neck, it seems to be breathing.

I stare into the mirror above my dresser. There's no full-coverage makeup heavy enough for this. It's a battlefield of broken capillaries. It is a disaster.

I've always been more conceptual than not. It's completely normal for my nights to seem realer than my days.

I close my eyes, trying to find the thread. One night, just

over a week ago, I lit a candle, lay back. Woke covered in dead leaves. Since that night, there have been moments— usually when I'm heavily caffeinated, or starting to feel trapped in my own body—when I pull away from the whole situation. Ask myself, *How is this possible? How is this sane?*

The hickey's real, though, tender to the touch. Not some bizarrely vivid dream. Not a plastic lighter handed to me by a stranger. No, I unabashedly made out with Marshall Holt like my life depended on it. And it was exceptional.

I stand at my dresser, staring down my reflection like with the very force of my gaze, I could make her neat and orderly again. Or at least make the hickey go away.

No luck. The skin stays vividly contused.

At the bottom of my jewelry box, there's a glittery choker my grandma bought me for eighth-grade gradua- tion. It didn't suit my sharp corners or my general aesthetic, but now, the rhinestones twinkle up from the box as if to say, *Take us out and put us on. This is what we're here for.*

The choker is relentlessly ornate, covered in neo- Victorian filigree. When I fasten it around my throat, the girl looking back at me is suddenly earnest. She's fragile and innocent—subtle, like Autumn said. I look less like I'm hiding something than I ever have in my life.

The parade of passing periods is interminable.

I spend every ten-minute block dawdling at my locker, waiting for some kind of sign, but Marshall keeps his back to me.

If I could see his face, I'm almost sure I'd be able to tell what he's thinking. I'd have a sense of whether he was avoiding my eyes because he knows exactly what happened between us, or if the reason he's looking away is that he's a total stranger and there is no *us*.

But even at my most pragmatic, I know that's not the truth. Under the choker, the mark on my neck is dark like a brand.

And so I stare across the locker bay, waiting for the bell. And the whole time, Marshall keeps his face turned away, deep in conversation with Ollie Poe, ignoring me on a level that is close to extravagant.

Maribeth has, by all outward appearances, forgiven me for last night. She's graciously put aside the Autumn debacle, or at least decided to bottle up her displeasure and let it age for a later date. At my locker before trig, she gives me a quick once-over but doesn't mention the choker.

Instead, she hands me half of her Luna bar and spends the next five minutes regaling me with the hilarity of Palmer's insistence on finding the perfect pair of platform heels, coupled with her conviction that such a thing exists. We discuss the joys of colored tinsel, and even when my voice sounds shrill, I know that from a distance, I look remarkably carefree.

For lunch, we walk over to Little Szechuan, home of the seven-dollar combo meal. The board on the back wall boasts thirty-seven choices, all of which come in Styrofoam clamshells and outrageous portions.

Maribeth would normally veto Chinese, but when I suggested it, she just nodded gravely, like she was concerned about me. The day seems very bright, and I'm ravenous for something greasy and full of sodium. She doesn't say anything disparaging, even when her order arrives looking like it's been bathed in WD-40.

We're on our way back to school, clutching our coats against the wind, when she says, "Hey, you're still coming to the mall when you're done with your meet, right?" She slows down, then stops completely. "I was thinking Autumn could come too."

The sentence hangs in the air for one fleeting second before slipping away, getting lost. I don't know how to respond.

Maribeth's shrug is diffident and she looks away. "If she wants, I mean."

I nod, trying to look thoughtful, but privately, I'm impressed. When Autumn said Maribeth wouldn't take a victory by forfeit, she knew what she was talking about.

We're halfway across the east lawn now. The wind picks up, sending a flurry of cigarette butts and candy wrappers tumbling across the parking lot. The sky is a hard, uniform gray.

I step over a soggy french-fry sleeve and pain zings along the bottom of my foot. If the way my arches seem to be peeling themselves off the bone doesn't get better, I'll have to see one of the school trainers—but only as a last resort. Ever since she started collecting articles about how overexertion is ruining high school athletes, Molly Bruin, Sports Medicine Specialist, loves to bench people for *recuperation purposes*. There's no way it would end well.

Maribeth leans closer and gives me a conspiratorial smile. "So, how are things with *CJ*?"

"Good," I say, trying to sound bright and giddy. To sound like I think of him at all. "Really good."

I only mean to satisfy her curiosity, but as soon as I say it aloud, the exhilaration is real. The warm splash of adrenaline that hits my face is real. And I am back in the dark with Marshall Holt.

Twenty-four hours ago, I was a different girl. I didn't think about sex or boys or naked bodies, but now the proposition is inviting—a topic worthy of inquiry. I keep revisiting the way I kissed him, how reckless it felt. How I would do it again in a heartbeat. How I want to rip off his clothes with my teeth.

Maribeth's gaze is fixed intently on my face. "Oh my God, Waverly! You have a *see*-cret." She sings it like a jump-rope rhyme, eyes open wide, and even though I'm still wearing the choker, I cover my neck with my hand.

Out on the football field, the majorettes are practicing for regionals. They chant in unison and Maribeth chants with them to the tune of rampant school spirit. "Waverly's got a *see*-cret, yes-yes she *does*!"

"No, I don't."

She reaches over and slips her hand into mine. "Okay, you don't have to tell me right this second, but come on, did you think I wouldn't notice?"

The way she always wants to hold on makes me feel breathless, like we've fallen overboard and she's got me in a death grip, pulling me down to the ocean floor. I feel bad about lying, though, so I link my fingers with hers and squeeze back.

She leans into me, tipping her head to the cloudy sky. "Oh, my God! Are you completely freaking out right now?"

For a second, I can think of absolutely nothing to say. On the field, the majorettes are marching in their warm-ups and their mismatched winter hats. They look like windup toys.

"Waverly—Waverly, what is *wrong* with you? I mean, are you? Are you so excited you could die? Why don't you seem excited?"

The majorettes twirl in grim formation and I shake my head.

Can you please repeat the question?

We're out of seventh period early for the meet. In the locker room, Autumn ambles over like sharing my immediate space is the most natural thing in the world. Her sweater is possibly the pinkest thing I've ever witnessed, and I'm minorly relieved to see she hasn't gone back to wild hair and Cleopatra eye makeup. She's still dressing the part of the helpful committee member. I can't tell if her outfit is supposed to be ironic, or if this is really just what she thinks of Maribeth. What she thinks of me.

"You're high-class today," I tell her, nodding to her wide houndstooth headband.

She throws down her bag and her sketchbook, prying off her wedges and dropping them on the floor. "Same, times ninety-nine. You should wear more jewelry. It looks good."

Around us, everyone is hectic, racing back and forth with athletic tape and hairbrushes. Over in the corner, Palmer is doing yoga stretches with her eyes closed, reaching for the ceiling.

I run my fingers over the choker, picturing the bitten skin underneath. We aren't allowed to wear jewelry when we compete. The hickey is going to show eventually, ready or not.

When I take off the necklace, I don't make a production of it. Autumn doesn't say a word, but I can almost sense her working out how to approach the subject of my contused neck. I smile because smiling makes me look harmless and any second now, she's going to ask.

"Waverly."

The way she says it makes something prickle down my back. I press my fingers to the place above my collarbone. Take them away again.

"Waverly."

"What?" I sound tentative—confused—almost like I've been sleeping.

And Autumn hugs me hard, shaking me back and forth, then letting go to laugh and spin away from me.

"Waverly," she says. "You look *happy*. God help me, I think you're thawing out."

On the bus out to the Dove Creek course, we sit together, sharing her headphones while everyone around us shrieks and laughs.

The songs are unfamiliar but catchy, and we lean into

each other, bobbing our heads in time to the music. It's the kind of thing I used to do with Maribeth when we were younger, but for some reason, the experience stopped being satisfying. This is satisfying.

Autumn gazes out at the passing cars. She's not pumping me for details or gossip, not demanding to know how I wound up with a continent-sized hickey.

It's not until halfway across town that I understand why. She isn't avoiding the subject to be nice or polite. She comes from a remote region of the social world where making out like a wildebeest in heat is considered normal.

•

"You can't wear that," Autumn says.

The meet was essentially a disaster.

I finished fourth overall. My time would have been better if my feet didn't feel like they were being deconstructed with a boning knife. Autumn didn't come remotely close to placing.

Now, we're at Flora/Fauna in the mall and I'm facing my reflection in a floor-length satin travesty.

This is the fourth store we've been to, and with each failed expedition, I'm becoming more and more acclimated to the idea that Autumn has *ideas* about clothes. Thanks to her messy hair and her tendency toward T-shirts, I never considered that she might actually be fashionable, but her general apathy does not extend to the world outside of school. When it comes to formal dresses, Autumn is full of opinions.

My reflection gives her a hard, exasperated look.

She just stares back and counts off on her fingers. "Let us first consider the areas into which we must inquire.

One—who are you? Two—no. Three—seriously, *who are you?* Four—take it off."

"It's because of the corsages," I say, trying to keep my voice even. "They're these really gaudy orchid arrangements. I need something to go with fuchsia."

"I don't care. You are fighting every principle of color theory to accommodate a twenty-dollar flower with a safety pin through it. I'm not standing by while you humiliate yourself in that dress."

I shuffle into the changing room and shimmy out of the dress. The fabric is cool and slimy, and if I have to keep it on for one more second, I won't be able to resist the urge to claw it off my body.

When I come back out, the store is exactly as I left it. It has not miraculously burned down.

I yank a stretchy pink sheath off the rack and hold it up, already knowing there's no way I'd ever put it on. "Feelings on this one?"

Autumn is standing by Winter Outerwear with something dark draped over her arm. "I have a feeling it would look vaguely pornographic. Anyway, I've already got everything you need. It's here when you're ready, just waiting for you to set aside your wicked ways and come to Jesus."

The dress she presents me with is black, sleeveless, with a high boatneck in the front and an open back, just like she said. It looks nothing like anything Maribeth has ever dog-eared in a magazine, but as soon as I put it on, I know I'll never be able to consider anything else.

I look like me, but better. Waverly distilled. My shoulders

are precise and square, my back a smooth expanse—not too hard and not too soft, but just right.

Autumn smiles her Petal Pink smile, the smile of someone who has mastered the art of choosing lip color.

"There," she says sweetly, tenderly. "Isn't that better?"

Maribeth has come up next to her, holding a yellow satin train wreck I can only assume was meant for me. "It's kind of . . . plain," she says, giving me a worried little frown.

Autumn reaches over, sweeping my hair back from my forehead and examining the effect. "Is that another way of saying it doesn't make Waverly look like a demented figure skater with a glitter fetish? Because yeah, that is totally true."

Maribeth opens her mouth. Her cheeks are flushed and she eyes me with well-meaning distress, but her concern is slipping. For just a second, I can see the annoyance underneath.

She doesn't argue, though, because we both read the same article on rhetoric and brain activity for our civics project in ninth grade—outright disagreement provokes a threat response, and once that happens, you've lost your ability to persuade.

I change out of the dress and take it up to the register.

Once it's paid for and safely wrapped in tissue, I turn my attention back to Autumn. After all, someone needs to keep her from running amok or terrorizing the locals or brushing carelessly against Maribeth.

I follow her through the clearance section as she picks her way among fields of polyester and red price tags.

"Why are you even here?" Palmer says, coming up behind us. "If you're not going to try anything on?"

Autumn gives her a complacent look. "Think of it as a public service. Anyway, I'm making mine."

This kind of dorky DIY enthusiasm would ordinarily elicit an exchange of pitying glances, but Autumn has already proven herself gifted in the poster board arts, at least. Even Maribeth looks mildly impressed.

She leans on the clearance rack, fiddling with her necklace. "Well, what does it *look* like?"

Autumn smiles and turns away. "It's a secret."

I can tell they're dying to bully her into telling them more. Palmer and Maribeth do not believe in secrets among girls. Even the dirtiest, most sordid secrets are well-known facts when you get right down to it.

But Kendry comes out of the dressing room just then, in a catastrophe of rhinestones and fine, interwoven straps. "How much does this show?"

Autumn tilts her head, considering. "Everything. Well, wait—are we talking about abstract concepts, like taste and dignity? 'Cause yeah, I don't see that. But like, your boobs."

Kendry freezes in the crosshairs of the three-way mirror, arms clapped across her chest. I'm expecting some sort of blowout, but she's already in retreat, unzipping the dress, struggling out of it.

Palmer turns, flapping at Autumn with an aggressively patterned minidress. "What is *wrong* with you? God, you're a Gila monster!"

Autumn shrugs and does a lazy half turn—almost a dance move—hands raised above her head. "If she didn't want to hear she was hanging out everywhere, she shouldn't ask for other people's opinions when she's hanging out everywhere."

The look on her face should be chiseled on a Renaissance Madonna.

After the miserable parade of dresses, Kendry and Palmer head off to the outlet shops to look for shoes, and Autumn disappears to whatever magical land she inhabits when she's not playing student council with me, but Maribeth and I walk down to the food court.

I'm in the mood for some companionable silence, but she wants to discuss AP chemistry and dinner plans for homecoming and Palmer's latest conquest and subsequent breakup. Nothing is different between us, nothing has changed. I should feel flattered that she'd rather talk to me about these things than anyone else.

"Logan was pointless, anyway," she tells me, playing with her hair.

She speaks with authority, as though Palmer is no different from her, or from me, as though our needs and wants are identical. As though I have any opinion on any of Palmer's short-lived ex-boyfriends.

"He wasn't for us," Maribeth says gravely, and I know she's referring to the gaping discrepancy between the admirable goals of student government and the less admirable goals of boys who start on varsity lacrosse. Or maybe just his tendency to adjust his crotch in public.

She must see the disconnect somewhere in my face. She

leans closer, pitching her voice conspiratorially low. "So, what's Autumn's dress like?"

"I don't know. She didn't take me into her confidence."

"Oh, I thought you guys were like best friends now." She says it coolly, like she actually believes that friends are something you can acquire or exchange. That you can only have one at a time. That I could somehow just replace her with a stranger.

I look away and drink my smoothie, acutely aware that I'd rather be sitting in the food court drinking smoothies with Autumn. "No. We're on cross-country together, is all."

Maribeth nods, staring off toward the freestanding sunglasses shack and the herd of kids shrieking in the playland. Then she puts her hand on my arm and opens her eyes wide. "Well, are you at least going to tell me about your wild night of passion?"

"What are you talking about?"

"*Waverly,* you have a hickey! You should see your face right now. It is the face of wantonness and secrets! There is no *way* that you haven't been giving your android love to CJ, okay?"

I let my straw fall mid-sip. And I nod.

It's a stupid lie. An outrageous one, but *yes* is still exponentially less problematic than *no.*

If Maribeth decides to investigate, I'll be outed in a second, but I don't really think that will happen. She won't confront CJ directly—it would strike her as indecent. More likely she'll gossip about me to Hunter when they go to the movies together or meet for study sessions, or whatever it is they do.

Except that Hunter probably doesn't care much about hormonal head cases sucking on each other's necks when it's not him doing the sucking.

Except that Autumn is rapidly taking over Maribeth's life, and that includes hijacking her boyfriend.

MARSHALL
Numb and Hungry

Most of the time, I'm starving. In class, and at school, and late at night after everyone else is asleep. At lunch or Justin's house, I finish things other people don't want. Then I sit down at the table and it disappears completely.

Until my dad got sick, we never really did family meals. Now, every night is this brutal sit-down dinner, with cloth napkins and the kind of conversation that is basically guaranteed to not end well.

When he asks how school was, I don't even look up. His voice is flat.

"Why can't you be nice?" my mom says. "Why can't we have a normal meal for once?"

He taps his fork on the edge of his plate, like he's just doing it because he feels like it, but his hands are shaking. Some days, the nerves stuff isn't bad, and some days it is. Those days, everything else is worse too. "Because, in case you hadn't noticed, *honey*, the only way we ever know what's going on is to cross-examine him."

I wait for one of them to tell the truth—that they only focus on me so they don't have to focus on anything important. I know I'm supposed to be grateful. Our whole neighborhood is full of kids whose parents are total dead-beats, or who left them, the way Ollie's mom did, but mine aren't like that. With them, it's just this gross, messy despair that never goes away. It oozes out and fills the room. I can feel it getting all over me.

"Shane." Her voice gets high-pitched, and her chin starts to tremble. "Can't we just drop it and enjoy this? Please?"

I already know he's not going to apologize. He won't say something nice or change the subject. Instead, he'll shut down, dig in farther. He'll stare across the table at her like he's nowhere, and she'll be trying not to cry, her face red and her eyes full of tears, and I'll sit there, looking at my plate. I can feel it in my throat and it's like I can't swallow.

When I was little, I was the safe ground between them. They always argued, but they didn't like to do it in front of me. Even now, if I'm in the room with them, sometimes it stops things from turning into a complete nightmare.

And sometimes it doesn't.

It takes less than two minutes for the fight to get ugly. It's about me and high utility bills and Annie and Chowder and the car. It's about nothing and everything—all the little, stupid things that logical, grown-up people never fight about. Who left the milk on the wrong shelf in the refrigerator, who forgot to get the mail.

They never ask any of the real things, why the new immune suppressants aren't really working. What to do now. Whether it's stopped being intermittent and is officially chronic yet. Why they keep pretending they can stand being in the same room. Who has stopped loving who.

She spent two hours making dinner, like that might make up for the fact that he's been stuck at home for almost three weeks now. She keeps messing with the serving dishes, moving them around like it's possible to fix whatever parts of him are broken if she can just put things in the right order.

She leans across the table, reaching for my arm, but not touching it. "Mars, you're not eating."

"I'm not hungry," I say, even though I pretty much devoured lunch, and the rest of Ollie's pizza, and it wasn't even close to enough.

"Are you getting sick again?"

But even *sick* is like a dirty word. I can feel it taking up space in the kitchen. After this awful, empty silence that goes on forever, I get up from the table and scrape my plate, which is more than half full, and then she starts crying.

I shut myself in my room, which is small and dark and a shithole, but better than when I shared it with Justin. There's not much to do, so I get out my homework.

Out in the living room, the show goes on and on, like if they can stay focused on the little things, they won't have to remember that once, for no reason either of them can remember, they loved each other.

I scoot closer to my desk and open my English book. We just started a new unit—Literature of the Depression. I only get a few pages in before I have to stop. The introduction is full of pictures, kids whose whole lives were ruined by the dust bowl. Their faces are blank and sunburned, but their eyes scorch into me like they hate the guy with the camera. Like they can see me watching them.

It's too much to deal with. Like reading out loud in elementary school, feeling my voice getting hoarse and thick because a forest burned down or a dog died, and my teacher saying it's okay, keep going, it's just a story. Of not being allowed to stop.

Once, when I was twelve or thirteen, Annie told me that other people didn't feel things the same way I did. They don't get a stomachache from watching the news or feel like crying when other people are sad.

She said, "I don't know if you know this, but people are kind of numb, I think. They mostly think about themselves, even when they don't mean to."

Before, I'd always thought I was just like everyone else, only everyone else was better at ignoring it—that they were doing something where they turned it off, and I was just some sad abnormal failure, because I couldn't.

When Annie told me I wasn't normal, I was relieved. It meant that I was broken, but at least I wasn't failing. Then I started smoking pot all the time, and the nice thing about that was, I didn't have to feel anything if I didn't want to.

I need to finish the chapter for English. I need to stop being here. Out in the living room, things are stupid like always.

I put on my headphones and turn the volume up as loud as it goes.

WAVERLY

7.

The bedroom is dingy and cramped, with one window and no curtains. Its layout is vaguely familiar from the other night, but disorienting too. Everything seems smaller with the lights on. The carpet is an upsetting shade of burnt orange.

Marshall's sitting with his back to me, hunched over a little writing desk with a textbook open in front of him. He's eating Goldfish crackers out of the bag without looking away from the page. Close by, someone is shouting.

He's clearly used to it. He's got on big DJ-style headphones, which I can only assume are noise-canceling, because as soon as I touch his shoulder he jumps and drops his pen. When he whips around and yanks off the headphones, his eyes are all pupil.

"Sorry. I didn't mean to sneak up on you."

For a second, he sits perfectly still, staring up at me. Then his jaw gets tight and he closes his eyes. "How are you doing this?" he says, his breath catching in his throat.

"I don't know," I tell him, when what I really want to say is *Does it matter?*

And yes, I understand that it's supposed to, but it's a

line of questioning that stopped feeling very important right about the time I woke up with a giant, impossible hickey. I'm Waverly Camdenmar. I've spent my whole life memorizing unfathomable things. I'm ready to follow this rabbit hole all the way down.

One teaspoon of a neutron star weighs over a hundred million tons and giraffes only need to sleep twenty minutes a day. There's a star in the Centaurus constellation that's made of diamonds, and when it snows on Venus, it snows lead. I have a bruise on my throat the size and shape of Marshall Holt's mouth. If all those things are true, why does he seem so certain that *this* isn't?

Suddenly, it feels inevitable that he'll embrace the strangeness with me. He has to. Just let go and fall head-first, like his own personal version of compulsive running or insomnia or distant lonely moons.

"Maybe this is that soft, wobbly place where awake and asleep kind of blend together."

He stares up at me, shaking his head. "*No.* I mean, dreams can be weird, whatever. But they don't just *blend* with regular life. Things are either real or they're not, and if you can't tell the difference, what happens is you get locked up for having a breakdown. I've watched you disappear in front of me like a goddamn magician, and that isn't real. It can't just *happen.*"

"Why do people always do that?"

"Do what?"

"Say something can't be happening, when clearly it is?" When what I want to say is, *Your mouth is the first thing I have ever encountered that's more interesting than astrophysics.* I want to say, *You have savaged my neck. What does that mean? Does it mean anything that you savaged my neck?* "We've been defying rationality for a week and a half, and now you suddenly have a problem with it?"

"Yeah." His voice is flat, so carefully controlled it shakes. But sometimes that's the problem. The tighter you grip something, the more you betray the trembling inside. "I do. I mean, don't you get that it was different before?"

"Before. Before what?"

He looks away, shaking his head. "Look, when you're messed up, you can kind of just roll with whatever happens, but when you're normal, other things are supposed to stay normal too, or—or follow *rules.* I'm not messed up this time, okay?"

His tone is dogged, like he's proving something, but what he's saying is close to nonsensical. Things always follow rules. Just because you don't understand them doesn't mean they're not there.

He keeps going, pronouncing each word very clearly. "I'm not drunk, or tripping, or—or *delirious.* I'm sitting in my goddamn bedroom, trying to do my homework."

Under some other circumstance, I'd passively accept his objections. I'd nod and frown, avoid confrontation, because that's what people do—force myself to fit whatever mold the world demands. But now, in this room, my shape doesn't matter. I'm a completely different person than I am in the daytime.

"Marshall," I say, and I sound capable and brusque, like Jamie when our practice times are bad. "I get that this is out of your comfort zone—I do—but it's what's happening.

You're not allowed to stick your fingers in your ears and sing *lalala* anymore. We're past that."

He opens his mouth and I think he'll argue, even just to dispute the idea that something as pervasive and dependable as the laws of science could be called a comfort zone. But then his mouth snaps shut again. He drops his eyes to the desk and nods.

"Okay, then." I stand with my hands on the back of his chair. "Okay."

This is the first time I've really seen his room. It's like a museum display or an educational diorama—natural habitat of the North American stoner—with a scarred twin bed and a mismatched dresser. The rickety little desk and not much else. The closet yawns, spilling out undifferentiated clothes. His headphones are clearly the most expensive thing in the room.

I know I should do something, say something, but I have no idea what. I've spent most of my life following a set of helpful scripts and suddenly, none of them apply. How do you make conversation with someone when you've seen them kneeling on the bathroom floor? When their most private moments are yours to intrude upon at will? When they've had their hands up your shirt, and you are ninety percent sure you wouldn't mind if it happened again?

"What are you reading?" I say, leaning across him to examine the book.

"Nothing. Homework."

"I thought you hated school."

He flips the cover closed. "I don't hate American lit. I hate school."

The last time I was this close to him, it was a commotion of touching. His hands, picking apart the rigid panels of my exoskeleton. His mouth, finding mine with the certainty of a meteor.

"What do you *want*?" he says, and raises his eyes to mine.

A vacuum opens in my chest. It seems crucially important, suddenly, that he is the only person who ever asks me that.

"For you to kiss me."

I say it without blinking. I say it to his mouth and to his dark, steady gaze. The warmth of his body, the shape of his lips.

I keep waiting for him to stand and reach for me, but he just hunches over the desk. "Don't. Don't say things you don't mean."

I rest my elbows on the back of his chair, leaning close to his bare, blushing neck. "Marshall," I say. His name sounds strange coming out of my mouth. "I want to kiss you."

When he still doesn't move, I take his hand in both of mine, turning it carefully, then holding it against my collarbone. It's warm and pliable and he's shaking.

"Fuck," he whispers, unresisting.

The weight of his hand in mine is awful, and after a second, I drop it.

When he finally looks up, his expression is wide open, like I'm seeing him undressed. "Is there anyone you don't *lie* to?"

Like I am some sort of habitual and compulsive liar, like every word out of my mouth is malicious or false. As though I am not to be trusted. Whatever is taking place right now is not a sweet and tender moment. The silence that hangs between us is prickling and sharp. There is no moment.

"You," I say, looking someplace else. "I don't lie to *you*."

There's a certain thrill in being honest. I take a breath and keep going. Because precision matters. Because I don't get to do it much and what have I got to lose. "Or Autumn, I guess. I don't lie to her."

He shakes his head. "Who's Autumn?"

"Pickerel. She goes to school with us."

He laughs then—a sharp, staccato laugh. "You're kidding, right? *Autumn?* You do not hang out with Autumn."

"You don't know who I hang out with."

"No—no way. She's nobody. She is *way* too weird for someone like you."

And here we are again. No matter how hard I smile, how far I run, at the end of the day, it always comes back to the question of what I am.

I hug my elbows and shake my head. Autumn is not nobody, but a real, actual force of nature. She is so much more than just some run-of-the-mill *person*. She's Bette Davis and Dorothy Parker and Madonna. Autumn is Tyler Durden and Tony Soprano. Autumn is Cthulhu, Destroyer of Worlds.

I turn in an agitated little circle, pacing the room just so I have some space to breathe. When I sink onto his bed, the mattress is low and squishy. I settle myself into the saggy middle and lie back. "Maybe you don't know her very well."

"Are you serious right now? She was my best friend for like eight years. I went to all her birthday parties. You do *not* hang out with Autumn."

His voice is final, and suddenly I get it. He knows those things about her—knows she's bold and scary and surprising—and what he really means is, Autumn could never be those things to *me*.

I burrow into his pillow. The pressure against my face makes patterns on the inside of my eyelids. "Never mind. The point is, I'm not some rampant liar, okay?"

I hear the squeak of his chair, and then the bed sinks gently beside me.

When I lift my head, he's looking down at me. His gaze is dark and reflective, like well water or something by Kafka. It makes me feel nervous for no good reason.

After a second, he reaches over like he'll touch the side of my neck, but doesn't quite dare.

"Yeah. Thanks for that."

"I'm sorry. I didn't think it would—" His voice is heavy, too full of feelings. He leans closer, and when he does, it's like he's sucking all the air out of the room. I wait for him to kiss me and make the breathless feeling go away.

For a second, I'm sure he will. He'll fall toward me like gravity, press his mouth to mine, and I'll finally stop feeling like I'm waiting for disaster.

Then he shuts his eyes and turns away "Waverly," he says, and his voice is strange. Thick and unwieldy, like it's taking up physical space. "I like you."

I don't know what to say. He doesn't sound like he's lying, but the admission is too impossible to actually be true.

"Because of the other night?"

"No," he says, still not looking at me. "No. For a long time."

I stare at the ceiling, trying to see through the plank and plaster to the night sky above. "How long is long?"

"Remember last year?" He says it like the question conveys some highly specific meaning.

I remember many aspects of last year. It spanned, after all, an entire year.

Marshall is undaunted by things like complex chronology. He soldiers on, watching the carpet. "In history, Mosley—he was telling us all that slang from the 1920s and he talked about carrying a torch for someone. And I looked at you. Remember?"

The thing is, I do.

It wasn't real, college-track history, just a general requirements class I had to take before I could have the good one. Marshall sat at one of the group tables across from mine. Every time I glanced up from my notes, he'd be there, but not in a way that registered.

The memory is vague, casting him as some part of the background, not a real person. He was more like areas of texture and color, something you walk right by in a museum. Next to the Warhol and Pollock, so you're not taking away from the real art. He was the lesser-known contemporary.

But on the day of the Roaring Twenties slang expo, Mosley had given us the definitions, writing them out as he went—a disordered list rolling down the whiteboard, *all wet, the bee's knees, on the lam, dolled up, the cat's pajamas*. And there at the bottom, *carrying a torch*.

I'd looked up, and for a second, Marshall's eyes met

mine and all the texture and the flat, neutral fuzziness were gone. All I could think was how incredibly dark his eyes were. Then he rested his chin on his hand and his gaze slid past me. He wasn't looking away out of self-consciousness or embarrassment, but simply moving on—bored and slow, like I had stopped holding his interest.

"*How* long?" I say again. "How long have you liked me?"

That day, he was unsettlingly direct, but now he's looking at the floor. "I don't know. A really long time."

And whatever else he might be saying, by whatever scale he's measuring, I know that it's true. The sophomore history class was almost a year ago.

"*Why?*" It comes out sounding confrontational, when really I just want to understand.

I wasn't charming or interesting or exciting. I wasn't nice. Not the prettiest of the pretty girls or the perkiest of the pert. I was just . . . there, the same way he was.

Marshall does the strangest thing with his mouth, like he's trying not to wince. It's not the face you expect someone to make when they explain infatuation.

"I saw you in the hall one time," he mutters. "Messing with your sock. You had all these blisters, and your sock was, like, *stuck*. You were trying to peel it off. Your heel was a mess and I thought how I couldn't do that."

"Do what?"

"Keep going after the blisters pop."

I close my eyes, imagining—the bite of it, the metallic, satisfying sting. "It's not that hard. You just have to stop caring that it hurts."

"I can't," he says. He says it plainly, simply, as though it's something self-evident. As though it's nothing to be ashamed of.

"Maybe you're not trying hard enough."

"It was this other part of you," he whispers. "Not how you are in class. I knew I was the only one who saw, and saw that you were bleeding. I was just kind of in love with it."

"You can't be in love with someone you don't know."

"Not you," he says, and his whole face is red. "The moment. I was in love with that moment. How you peeled your sock off. It was just—it was like this private thing."

"So you had a crush on me because my foot was bleeding."

"It's not *like* that."

"Then what? Did you think it meant I needed help? Or that you knew me?"

"No." He laughs, a hoarse, humorless sound. "I mean, I'm not fucking *stupid*. I knew you were never going to be anything except a hangover girl."

I try several times to parse the phrase, but it stays very bizarre. "A what?"

He's still smiling, but in a bitter, painful way. Not looking at me. "Nothing. It's this thing Ollie made up. Just a girl you dedicate your hangover to. It's stupid."

I sit staring at him. I can't even figure out how to dedicate a conversation to someone who's in the same room. "You're telling me that I am the imaginary epicenter of your binge-drinking."

"It isn't *like* that," he says again. "It's just hard to explain."

I tilt my head, eyebrows raised. "Yeah? Well, I've got all night."

Marshall shifts uncomfortably, fidgeting with the blanket. "You get torn up about something, okay? And it doesn't really matter if it's a person, or something that happened, or just that no matter what, you're stuck with yourself. Sometimes, you need to get the fuck out of your head."

I sit against the wall with my knees pulled up. I want to reach for him and tell him he's a moron. There are so many ways to get free that don't involve substance abuse.

I am an expert at going farther longer.

He presses his hands against his face. "All I'm saying is, sometimes I'd use you as a reason. When you have a reason, getting wrecked is really easy. It feels good. You forget a lot of stuff. Then maybe you get sick, and that's okay too, because for a little, there's just that—that sick feeling. But when it's over, you're right back where you started, except you feel like shit everywhere instead of just your brain. Then you crawl in bed and curl up and wish things were different."

I'm suddenly convinced that he says *you* because it's easier than saying *I*. "So you associate me with feeling ter-rible."

"No." He's clenching and unclenching his jaw, chewing his bottom lip. "I associate you with wanting to feel better."

I'm inches away from him, and five or six thousand miles. We are side by side, and it's the little things that make me hungry. All the minor, stupid things I'd never admit to, like how seeing the pattern of his sleeve reproduced on his cheek once after history class last year made me want to kiss him.

The way he watches me is physical—a pressure on my skin. He is so tender, so immediate, and I am only good at wanting things from a safe distance.

I stand up and start to pace, because it feels like I will tear my way out of my own body if I don't start moving. Even the ratty texture of the carpet makes my feet sing out in pain, but I breathe deep and keep going.

Marshall scoots back against the wall. "Waverly," he says. "It's okay. Settle down."

Out in the living room, the voices have dropped to a confused mutter and then they spike again. Nothing is okay.

For a second, we freeze exactly where we are, listening to the shouting and pretending not to.

Then Marshall winces and starts picking at the bed-spread. "Well, that's awkward." He shivers, like he's trying to shrug off the whole thing. "Sorry. I don't know if you noticed yet, but it's pretty much shit here."

I pace back to the bed. Out in the hall, the melody changes keys. Marshall's father has been replaced by a girl's voice like a soprano flute or an angry clarinet. The pitch of her outrage cuts through the wall, perfectly audible.

I reach for Marshall's hand. When I lace my fingers with his, he flinches. "Is that your sister?"

He nods, pulling away, scrubbing his hand against the bed like he wants to wipe off my concern. "Annie. She's good at being mad."

"And you're not?"

He shakes his head. "I'm better at being sorry."

It seems impossible that anyone's reaction to chronic conflict would be sympathy, but I don't say so. His expression is deeply, inexplicably sincere. He just looks really sorry.

When he shrugs, it's apologetic. Defeated. "It's like, my mom can't let him just be a dick and be done with it. She can't let him go."

I scoot closer because I don't know what to say, and being close can sometimes feel the same as knowing the right words.

"It's scary," he says, glancing over with a tight, painful expression. "How much she loves him. How much she loves everyone. And I think I could be like that, if I wanted something bad enough. It's scary, knowing I'm just like her."

"What's she like?" But what I really mean is *What does that make you?*

He stares at the ceiling. His whole body is rigid, like he's waiting for someone to hit him.

"Okay, here," he says finally. "She's scared of spiders. I mean, crying-screaming terrified. But whenever she finds one in the house, she catches it in a water glass and takes it outside, because she can't stand to kill them."

I lean into him, shoulder to shoulder, when what I really want is to mash myself against him and grab whatever I can reach. He is so totally transparent, and I think maybe he's right. I can't picture him killing spiders.

For a second, he does nothing. Then he swallows hard and reaches for me, gentle when he puts his arms around me. It's not the kiss I asked for. It's not what I expected. I breathe out and let him pull me down onto the bed.

Marshall tucks his chin so he's talking into my hair. "Please, just tell me why—why me?"

It feels strange to lie so close to someone, to be so utterly aware of his heartbeat. I put my hand on his chest and close my eyes. Everything seems dense and perplexing, impossible to convey in words. I make a fist, winding my hand in his T-shirt, trying not to cling so hard it seems desperate.

The answer he's looking for doesn't exist. Not in a way that will satisfy. I am insubstantial. A tangled, vaporous creature that lives in my brain, almost wholly imaginary. I can be here with him as easily as I can inhabit a sonnet or an organic molecule, or crawl inside a math problem.

The way he's holding on to me is so tender it's appalling. I let myself sink farther into the softness and the stillness, whispering against his shirt, "Why did my blisters make you like me?"

He presses his mouth to my hair and it's the warmest thing I've ever felt. "I don't know. Because it was like a window to you, maybe. A way to see what was underneath."

His heart is thudding against my cheek. The rhythm of his pulse makes it hard to keep my eyes open.

"Maybe that's why," I say, finally. "Why I'm here and not in CJ Borsen's bedroom, or Maribeth's, or in Tunisia."

When what I really mean is that of all the sunny, well-meaning people who praise and reward my deceitfulness every single day—my talent for disguise, my carefully constructed face—he was the one who saw something true.

•

I wake to the shriek of my alarm and an ache that starts in my feet and pounds all the way up my legs. That can't be good.

On my bedside table, the candle still smells like smoke and spices, but sometime in the night, it's burned low enough to drown itself. The wick is sunk a millimeter deep, and I have to dig it out of the wax with a paper clip.

I ignore the pain. After all, that's what I'm good at. Everything is fine—totally doable, totally normal.

By third period, my feet hurt so much I can barely stand to put weight on them. My calves are starting to go numb. I skip trig to go see Molly Bruin in the training room.

"Do you have a minute?" I say, hovering in the doorway, trying to sound casual.

She adjusts her glasses and considers me, leaning back in her chair. "Sure, what's up? We don't see you in here much."

I try to find a way to phrase the magnitude of the situation. My tongue feels useless.

If I were talking to Marshall, it would be different. I'd

still be clenching my hands to keep them still. I'd want to look away, but at least I'd know the words. When I open my mouth, nothing comes out.

I stand in front of Molly's desk, gaping like a fish. Last night I said the easy part was not caring that it hurt, but there's nothing easy about this. If I were with Marshall right now, in the privacy of his room, maybe I could even tell him that. I shut my eyes and remember how it felt to be honest with someone.

"It's my feet," I mumble, as though Molly will be able to magically divine all meaning from one awkward sentence.

The look she gives me is appraising, like she's waiting for me to finish, but all she says is, "Okay, get your shoes off and hop up."

When I clamber onto the training table and offer her my foot, she probes the sole with her fingers, examining my heel and my arch. "You've definitely got swelling. Does this hurt?"

I nod as a familiar pain shoots up my calf. When she digs into my heel, I have to squeeze the edge of the table to keep from jerking away.

"How much have you been running?"

"A lot."

"More than Jamie works you guys for practice?"

"Yeah."

Molly takes a deep breath, like she's formulating her conclusion. Her diagnosis. "You're not going to like this, but you're going to have to take a break."

I shake my head. "We're in the middle of regionals." I can hear desperation in my voice, and I hate it. I hate the rising pitch. I hate that it makes me feel brittle like an egg. Crushable, smashable.

Molly sighs, leaning on the table and making a steeple with her fingers. "I need you to listen to me. Your feet are a tore-up mess."

I keep my palms flat on the vinyl. One breath, then another. I raise my head and smile my best student-council smile. "I can run through it, though. I mean, I know I can still hit my times."

"Waverly, you're not listening to me. If you keep running, it's going to get worse."

"And if I take a break, then what?"

"You rest, you ice. If everything looks good in two months, maybe I start *thinking* about okaying you for track in the spring."

The room is warm. The heat must be all the way up. I sit staring at a crumpled ball of athletic tape over by the trash cans.

"I'm sorry," Molly says. She sounds like she means it. "I know this is important to you."

I nod, just barely. I can't talk around the knot in my throat.

She reaches out and pats my arm, and then I understand. She thinks I'm looking shattered because I won't be able to compete, like I could actually give a shit.

The only thing that matters is the running. Without it, I have no place to put all my noise, no way to shut off my brain.

Without it, there's only the candle, and the candle just keeps getting smaller.

●

I can't run. This is the situation. I can't run and I can't concentrate, and I can't sleep.

Everything seems wildly unmanageable.

Crouched in the middle of my bed, nestled in a fortress of homework, I don't pull back the covers. I don't light the candle.

I want to see Marshall so badly I can taste it like metal. Unacceptable. Better to wait, let the thundering die down in my chest. Let the ache in my throat work itself out.

I sit with my chin tucked and my knees up, rereading all my notes on Poe, reminding myself that my single greatest asset is the ability to endure. And maybe every cell in my body feels like it's disintegrating? But it's not. Being forbidden from running does not make my heart stop or interfere with breathing. It's painful, but like most other painful things, it's survivable.

By morning, I'm seamless again. This is my life now.

I've been radically ahead in every class for weeks. Sometimes, though—just lately—my thesis statements don't make that much sense. It doesn't matter. If you establish a certain standard of work at the beginning of the year, you're golden. Teachers will grade on their first impressions for the rest of the semester.

Spanish II is quickly becoming the asymmetric center of my day, the enlarged hour that all other hours rotate around. It's nice just knowing that Marshall will be there. Comforting, like a smooth little rock you hold in your pocket so you have something to do with your hands.

All period, I frown studiously at my notebook, trying not to make it obvious that I'm acutely aware of him, and he sits impassively at the back of the room, trying not to make it obvious that he's looking at me.

Even the simple act of being near him is doing something to me. The person I was a week ago would never have gone to see Molly, no matter how bad the pain was. Under any other circumstance, I'd be gutting it out, trying not to limp through every practice, but my name would still be there at the top of the active roster.

Now, the damage is done, and here we sit in our respective seats, dutifully ignoring each other. Him, bored and sullen. Me, with my clean, helpful expression and my good posture and all my pens out. This is us in the daylight. And in the daylight, we are entirely different people.

In honor of Friday, or because we've run out of conversational exercises for the chapter, or possibly to celebrate the impending dance, Mrs. Denning has resorted to that bane of education: busywork. We are to practice our interpersonal skills, under the pretext of scholarship. We will perfect the delicate art of paying compliments in a language in which most of us do not demonstrate even the mildest level of proficiency.

She hands out numbered half sheets and we pass them down the rows.

The name I draw belongs to Laurel Bacard, and I try to think of things I could say that would be construed as both complimentary and accurate, using the unit vocabulary. I want to remark on the staggering intricacy of her highlights, but I have no idea how to say it in Spanish.

At the back of the room, Marshall is leaning into the aisle. He's turned away, whispering. It looks like he might be trading papers with Ollie Poe.

By the time I get out my binder, my hands are shaking a little. My heart is racing. I know the chemistry behind it. I drink coffee all day long. My heartbeat surges and plummets. My blood is high voltage, wired like the yard at a supermax.

I flip to a blank page and write,

I am a radio tower.

Then I invent five boring, incontestable things about Laurel, fold my paper in half, and give it to her. CJ is already reaching over my shoulder, passing a folded sheet up the row to me.

I don't know Marshall's handwriting. The particulars of his penmanship are not something I've looked into. It doesn't matter. There is no one else in the world who would have written the list of things in front of me.

It takes a while to sort through the verbs, even using my dictionary. I don't know the conjugations for half the future tenses.

After I've puzzled it all out, I sit staring at the paper. His compliments are decisive, dashed off in a fast, slanting scrawl. Next to them, in my own well-mannered handwriting, it says:

She makes me feel like things will get better.

She makes me want to be braver.

I try to be honest when I'm with her.

I try to be real.

I'm scared that without her,
I won't ever be this good again.

While other people raise their hands and share their compliments, I sit with a frantic buzzing in my ears. I want to shiver and laugh and dance around. My scalp is tingling. I smile without meaning to—a wide, uncalculated smile that hurts my face.

"Waverly," says Mrs. Denning. "You look like maybe you've gotten some nice compliments. Would you like to share some of them?"

And my smile, incandescent a second ago, is collapsing. None of the items on Marshall's list are the kind of thing you say out loud.

Frantically, I query my database for something normal. Grades are safe—grades are always safe. *"Era intelligente."*

"Go on," Mrs. Denning says.

"Ella corra muy rápido." My voice is bright and crisp. The sound hurts my ears.

Or maybe that's just the resentment, echoing inside me—how mad I get every time I'm rewarded for being the person people want and not the person I am.

Mrs. Denning clasps her hands, smiling like *isn't this fun?* "And one more, if you don't mind."

With a short, stabilizing breath, I raise my chin and recite, *"Ella está muy organizada."*

Which is when Marshall gets up and walks out of the room.

Mrs. Denning stares after him, her teacher's edition held against her chest. There's a frantic desire pounding inside me, an urge to go after him, pin him against a wall like a Gothic vampire, and compliment him back.

Mrs. Denning frowns and gives the class a searching look. "Is he not feeling well?"

No one says anything. Ollie Poe is scowling at his hands.

"Oliver, do you know if Marshall's all right?"

When Ollie looks up, his expression is open and kind of helpless. "He was out sick last week. Maybe he's not over it yet."

The remaining minutes seem to last forever.

When the bell finally rings, I feel it jangling in my teeth.

MARSHALL
Give It Up

My whole face feels hot and prickly. Even standing out in the empty language arts hall doesn't really help.

In my head, I can still hear Waverly. Her steady in-class voice, reciting some list of boring, factual things that have nothing to do with her, skipping over my feelings like she was grading them, drawing a line through them, crossing out every word, everything I thought was true.

If I feel stupid or rejected, though, it's my own fault for thinking what happens in the middle of the night has anything to do with real life. Of course she'd never read something so private to the world. That's not who she is. And even if she'd said the things I wrote, it wouldn't stop this feeling that everything is coming apart in my chest, like I have no idea which parts of my life are actually real. It wouldn't prove anything.

I start toward the parking lot with my hands in my pockets. I'm almost to the end of the hall and out the double doors, when behind me, there's a loud, skin-crawling whistle.

Autumn Pickerel is on me like a pit bull. She hits me hard between the shoulders and I flinch.

When I turn around, she's right there, hands on her hips, her toes almost touching mine. She's wearing this lace-covered dress with some kind of floppy, open-front sweater over it, and it's not exactly weird or anything, but it's weird for *her*, like she went out and bought this costume to make her look like everybody else.

"Where the fuck you been, Boo Radley?"

"Nowhere," I say, already backing toward the parking lot. "Around."

"Huh." Her hair is straighter than normal, and something weird is happening around her eyes, like she has about four times more lashes than the last time I saw her. "Does this mean you've finally figured out how to turn invisible just by putting up your hood and blowing off a science quiz?"

I laugh, but it comes out ugly. I don't know how to act fine when it's just me and her.

For six years of elementary school, it didn't matter that my best friend was a girl. And then we hit seventh grade and she wasn't anymore. The most obvious explanation would be that's just what happens—middle school makes people ditch their friends. But that wasn't why. Autumn has this way of looking at people. She finds the cracks and the weak spots. Then she tries to change it. The problem is, it's hard to be around someone who sees that far inside you when suddenly everything in there just feels bad.

She's standing almost close enough to trick me into thinking this is normal. Like I still know her. It's been three years since I've been to her house. Eight months, maybe, since we had a conversation, but there was a time in my life when I used to tell her everything.

"What are you doing out here?" she says, waving her stack of papers at me.

For a second, I almost just tell her the truth. But the truth is too awkward to explain. What would I say? That I walked out in the middle of class because Waverly wouldn't admit I exist because she *never* does?

"I needed a drink."

"Really." Autumn flicks her gaze to the double doors and the parking lot. "Would that drink be called *Cannabis indica,* by any chance?"

She's pretty much a genius at telling when I'm upset, and that's the real reason I don't look her in the eye anymore. After the thing with my dad, I could barely stand to be in the same room with her.

I shrug, jerking my head at her dress. Her sleek, preppy hair. "Is this like some kind of disguise?"

"Hey now," she says, holding up a stack of classroom handouts. "Thanks to this wholesome ensemble, I have been picked to make copies of random bullshit more in the last two weeks than I was ever allowed to be helpful in my whole life."

Which is probably even true. It's so stupid how people always just assume that Autumn isn't helpful. Sure, she's loud, or funny in a way that makes people nervous, but helpful is like her permanent condition—this bossy, overbearing thing she can't seem to stop herself from being.

"So?" she says finally, crossing her arms. "Should I be

on my way? I mean, since you clearly don't want to talk to me." She doesn't sound mad, just over it.

"Yeah, like my company's so great anyway. Besides, you've got plenty of other people to talk to these days, right? Fancier ones?"

I'm fishing now, angling for something true. Something meaningful. Something that makes the real world and the bizarre nighttime world actually line up.

"Waverly Camdenmar, you mean?" Autumn says it with one eyebrow raised. "Why don't you come to the dance and find out."

I look away and hope she doesn't see how hot my face is. "You are not serious right now."

"Hand to God," she says, and she even sounds like she means it. She gives me a look, crossing her arms. "Come on, don't you wonder what it's like, doing things for a change?"

I can't really argue with that, but I can't exactly picture it either. The idea, though—the idea seems . . . interesting. *Possible.* "I could take Heather."

Autumn scowls. "Really, Holt? I mean, really? A date is not even a thing you need. I don't have one, and I'm pretty sure they're going to let me in anyway."

But Autumn's the kind of person who can just show up anywhere and be okay there. I'm not even sure I can show up to my own life without getting wrecked first. Every day feels like some random event. Even with Heather, she was the one who picked me. *You look sad,* is what she said. I was standing against the pool table in her parents' basement at the end of last year. She leaned next to me so our hands were touching and then took me upstairs, grabbing at me the whole way because she was drunk enough to grab and it was what I needed. Or wanted. Sometimes it's hard to tell the difference.

Autumn is looking aggressively bored. "God, whatever. Just try not to get poor judgment all over the place."

And I understand that she's telling me something else, some kind of secret that I'm supposed to be able to decode.

We used to have a made-up language, but maybe it wasn't even ours. The thing about Autumn is, she knows how to make even the most normal words sound like something she invented. I'd thought that language belonged to us, but she was the one who made the meanings, so maybe I just happened to speak it once.

She smiles, and suddenly she looks so much like the person who used to draw me pictures of Deadpool and Batman and make fun of my Pokémon cards that it seems impossible I could have ever thought she was wearing a costume.

"Got to go," she says, flapping the stack of worksheets at me. "I'll see you at the ritual shaming, then?"

After she's gone, I go out to the baseball diamond and sit in the dugout, which was something I used to do back when my dad first got sick but after a while, it just got stupid. I haven't done it in forever.

The night after our parents told us about our dad, I went up to Gray Rock Canyon with Ollie and Hez and the Captain and we built a campfire and got annihilated.

It was bad, but only in this numb, blurry way where I was too messed up to care. The next morning was when it got awful.

We came down the canyon with the Captain riding the

brake, then stepping hard on the gas, and I spent pretty much the whole drive with my head between my knees.

We were halfway down this bad stretch of road that was all switchbacks when I really started feeling like I was going to lose it. My brain was full of smoke and my whole body was shaking.

I must have made some kind of losing-it noise, because right away, Ollie leaned across me and smacked the Captain's shoulder. "Justin, pull over. I think Marshall needs to get out of the car."

"Mars, if you puke back there, I will fucking destroy you."

I breathed in through my nose and out through my mouth and tried to tell him how it was just the road, just how thirsty I was. The taste of last night was in my throat now and everything felt like poison.

Ollie got up and started digging around in the Styrofoam cooler behind the seat, but all he could find was half a bottle of flat Coke.

"Hey, that's good," said Hez. "Coke's supposed to settle your stomach."

So I drank the Coke in little sips and tried to tell myself it was fine, it was okay—I was tired and hungover, but everything was under control.

It didn't matter.

My dad was still sick, he was still an asshole, the world was still ending, and even the Coke made me think of whiskey. Two minutes later, I was on the side of the road with my eyes closed and my hands braced on my knees. It wasn't one of the prettier moments in my life.

After, I felt better and worse. Now that I wasn't so

worried about keeping everything down, I was just left with the rest of it. A canyon was opening inside me. I tried telling myself the normal things—that I'd wake up tomorrow and feel fine, like none of this right now was even happening.

But my dad was going to be disabled, maybe for the rest of his life, and my mom would be pathetic and unhappy, maybe for the rest of hers, and I'd wake up tomorrow and I'd feel so much better and that was a lie. I would feel fucking awful. I would feel just like this and it was never going to be better.

When I finally looked up, Ollie was standing over me, squinting against the sun. "How you doin', Mars?"

And I was so sure he meant the gaping, hollow feeling in my chest and then I'd have to tell him about the non-divorce and how I couldn't fucking cope and my dad was sick and my parents were just going to keep doing the same ugly, stupid shit. And I couldn't stand to say any of that out loud.

"I'm fine," I said, and my voice sounded completely torn up. "Everything's fine."

Ollie stood over me, shaking his head. "What are you talking about? You just puked off two sips of Coke. Since when are you *fine*? They just want to know if you're ready to get back in the car."

He was holding out something rumpled and dripping, and it took me a second to figure out it was one of the Captain's work shirts. "That's Justin's."

"Fuck him," Ollie said, wringing it out and offering it again. "It's cold. Wipe your face. You'll feel better."

When I took the shirt, it smelled like the melted ice at the bottom of the cooler—wet Styrofoam and dirt. I wiped my face, then held it against my neck and sort of felt okay again.

When I finally got back into the Captain's Bronco, Ollie didn't look at me. He was all the way at the other end of the bench seat, wedged against the door, and at first I thought he was trying to keep his distance, but then he patted the seat and said, "If you want to lie down, you can."

I looked at the space between us and nodded. When I lay down and closed my eyes, everything stopped hurting so much. It was ridiculous how much better I felt when I wasn't trying to act okay.

I woke up when the Captain pulled into the driveway. I was lying across the whole seat with one arm pinned under me and the top of my head pressed against Ollie's leg.

Ollie was asleep against the door with his hand on my shoulder, and the weight of it was the exact maximum amount I could stand to be touched.

I'm sitting with my back against the cement and my feet up on the rail when Ollie comes around the corner of the dugout.

He stands over me, looking blank and backlit. "What. The fuck."

And I know he means me walking out in the middle of class, but the question is bigger than that. It's about everything backward or wrong. Me, wanting to feel like I matter. Like Waverly sees me. I don't know why I thought it would be different. This is real life.

"I don't know," I say, looking at my hands. "I really don't."

He sits down and takes out his cigarettes. "Denning wanted to know if you were dead."

I stare out at the baseball diamond, thinking about how my dad spent every Saturday the summer I was twelve trying to teach me to throw sliders. How much I hated it.

"No," I say when he offers me the pack. "Just needed a break."

I've been giving up smoking, but the habits are still there. I'm giving up smoking, except I still go out to the parking lot with Ollie every day. I keep half a pack of Camels in my jacket, and when things get bad, I run my fingers over the wrapper like any second I might flip the top back and knock one out.

I keep remembering why I started in the first place. Without a cigarette there, reminding me to breathe, it's hard to get enough air.

Next to me, Ollie flicks his lighter, then slams the top shut. "We going over to the Captain's this weekend? I've got some skunk, so if there's nothing else, we can just do that."

"I can't," I say. "I think I'm going to take Heather to that dance."

The look Ollie gives me would be hysterical if he weren't pointing it at me. I hate that he's embarrassed for me, and that he should be.

"Maybe it doesn't sound so bad," I say finally. "It could be fun."

For a minute, we don't say anything else and the lie just sits there, spreading out, getting bigger. I try to block it out with a picture of waves washing onto a beach, but it doesn't help.

"I might go too, then," Ollie says in a fake-casual voice.

"Wait, *what?*"

He shrugs and keeps playing with the lighter. "That freshman asked Little Ollie to go."

"So what's the problem?"

"He said yes, but I heard him tell that piece of shit Carter on C-team football that it's only because there's this other girl he wants to get with and he thinks he can hit it. Or whatever passes for hitting it with ninth graders. He's probably hoping that he'll get to touch a boob."

"Dude, you're spying on freshmen?"

He glares out at the infield. "I hate that he's such a little douchebag. And come on, are you telling me you don't think that's the most fucked-up thing?"

The truth is that I do, but I'm not really in a position to claim the moral high ground. Anyway, when it comes to being douchebags, sometimes people just are, and that's reality and you have to let them. The Captain is, just as a normal thing, and Ollie never seems too bent about that.

"Why do you even care? It's not like you know them."

Ollie frowns. "I just think if he has to go around being me, then I'm kind of obligated to keep an eye on him. She's a nice kid."

"Still."

"Oh yeah, I'm really going to take citizenship lessons from the person who is going with *Heather*."

"Fuck off."

"Why are you doing this?" Ollie says without looking up from his shoes. "Why do you even like her?"

I think about Heather in separate pieces. Her sticky

hair and her laugh and the stupid shit that comes sailing out every time she opens her mouth. "It's not that simple."

Ollie rolls his head to the side and gives me a look, like he's waiting for me to convince him of all the ways that nothing in my life is simple anymore.

I shrug and adjust my voice. "I don't know, she's just Heather. And yeah, sometimes she's annoying about stuff, or talks too loud, but it doesn't make her a bad person."

"Dude, what are you talking about? You don't like Heather. I mean, why do you like that chilly stuck-up bitch Camdenmar?"

I watch the chain-link diamonds in the fence. I want to ask how he knows, but that isn't the kind of question that you ask Ollie. He's always best with the quiet stuff. It's kind of his specialty.

I open my mouth, think of Waverly. She's sitting on my bed with her hand over mine, eyes down, half turned away. I close my mouth again.

I have no idea what words it would take to make him see. I can't explain that I can feel how nervous she is, just all the time. How it hums off her like a moth in a jar. It makes me want to save her, even when I know I can't and know she would never admit to needing it. I have dreams about holding on to her until the panic sound stops and she melts against me. The freak occurrence of her in my bed is the only part of my day that feels like it's worth anything. It's the part that doesn't suck.

I don't know how to tell him that and have him believe it, so I just look at him and shrug. "Maybe I'm tired of not wanting anything except to get stoned. With her, she's always trying to be better. I kind of just want . . . to be my better self."

"Is this why you quit smoking?" Ollie says.

"Yeah, maybe."

Without saying anything, Ollie swings his arm over my shoulders and after a second, I lean into him. We stay like that for a long time, heads together, not talking. I have an idea that Ollie's my brother if I could choose my own brother. That maybe that's enough. That right now, today, this is all I need.

WAVERLY

I spend the first fifty-seven minutes of dance-planning committee trying to look like I'm not about to drill an escape tunnel through my own eye socket.

We're in Maribeth's kitchen, arranged around the vast oval table, while she goes down her final checklist. The dance is in twenty-nine hours. The lingering responsibilities are many.

I'm in charge of calling the party supply store to check on the status of our metallic confetti delivery. Autumn will make sure the custom-printed homecoming banners are accounted for. Maribeth is in charge of DJ and catering, because she doesn't trust anyone else to do it. The wrestling contingent is notably absent. Their collective assignment is to stay out of the way. They can do this job from home.

Maribeth reaches for a celery stick and consults the all-knowing list. "That leaves the favors for Kendry when she gets back from debate, but maybe we should make her deal with the florist instead?"

"Oh?" says Autumn, looking innocent and kicking me under the table. "Should we?"

"Well," Maribeth tells her with a flat, factual expression that I hate. "I'm just saying, Kendry's strengths do not lean toward the organizational. I mean, don't you think that's true?"

"Kendry's not stupid," Autumn says. "It's just sorting a bunch of little hourglasses and plastic clocks into piles. I think she can probably handle counting to ten over and over."

"God, stop. I just mean, since she has so much on her plate already." The way Maribeth says it is wide-eyed. Earnest. Like she actually believes that she is being kind and not condescending.

Autumn leans back in her chair and makes a bored face at the ceiling. "Sometimes you are a raging, raging dickhead."

I take a breath and let it out, but it's just an automatic response. The truth is, I hope something blows up. The tasteful movie set of the kitchen, pink lemonade and granite countertops, gone in one fiery cataclysm.

But Maribeth simply pretends that Autumn hasn't said anything—her favorite trick—to act like a look or a word or a sentence doesn't *mean* anything, because she's so above it. I know better, though. In the dark territory that sits just under the surface of her china doll face, words and looks are the only things that matter.

With her pencil poised to cross off another item, she glances around. "So Kendry will take care of floral when she gets back from the tournament. And who are *you* calling, Autumn?"

"Vernon McVegetable's Magical Paper Emporium."

Maribeth sighs. Her mouth is dangerously thin. "Can you be serious, for like five minutes?"

Autumn leans her chin on her hand. "Seriously? I'm about to have an aneurism from boredom. Seriously." Then she turns to me like we are not sitting awkwardly around Maribeth's table, awkwardly planning Maribeth's dance. "Hey, do you want to come over to my place after this? We can listen to my mom's eighties vinyl really loud and eat something bad for us."

The question sits in the kitchen for longer than it should. I have never wanted anything more.

When I nod noncommittally, Maribeth grabs the vendor list away from Palmer and circles the number for the print shop. Her expression is impatient, and she will always do *some*thing, rather than not doing something.

As Palmer and Maribeth wrestle over the list, Autumn uncaps her marker and reaches for my hand. "Here, hold still."

With quick, graceful strokes, she draws a cascade of art deco flowers coursing down my arm, connected by a line of trailing ribbon.

The ink starts at the inside of my elbow and winds down to my wrist, where it narrows, terminating in a spray of tiny rosettes circling my pinky.

And this is the fundamental nature of the Pickerel Uncertainty Principle: the more accurately you try to predict Autumn's behavior, the less likely your predictions will be accurate.

Maribeth is coping the way she always does when the

situation looks like it might be ungovernable—by being passive-aggressive.

"Autumn, that is *so* creative of you! I just hope it comes off before the dance." She turns to me, bright and merciless. "Or are you thinking elbow gloves? You know, to balance out how your dress is that weird box shape. Oh, and Autumn—what's the name of the place you're going to call, again?"

Autumn plucks a carrot stick from the bowl and snaps it neatly between her teeth. Her gaze never leaves Maribeth. "It's called Go Fuck Yourself on a Pogo Stick. Kind of a weird name, but god*damn,* do they know how to put together an attractive banner."

In my notebook, I write:

Proposition: I don't want to disappoint anyone.

Material Implication: If I disappoint people, they will reject me.

Contradiction: I want to disappoint everyone.

Autumn's house is in one of the older neighborhoods, tucked at the end of a shady cul-de-sac, with a week's worth of unread newspapers in the driveway and drifts of leaves around the front steps. Inside, it's dim and sprawling, with an exhausting decorating scheme that must be how the world looked in the eighties.

We slink past garish artwork and loudly mismatched furniture, winding back toward her bedroom.

In her room, the walls are covered with pictures from celebrity gossip magazines, and there are inside-out clothes and colored pencils and little caches of sewing supplies all over the floor.

"Don't look in the corner," she says, shouldering past me.

I barely have time to make out something generally humanoid that looks like an old-fashioned sewing dummy, before she steps in front of it and throws a sheet over it.

"My dress for the dance. You can't see it yet."

Even with the dummy hidden, there's plenty to look at. The room is vast and disproportionately long, like it might have originally been a rec room. Every surface is cluttered with something unapologetically messy—paint, feathers, glue. There's a scarred drafting table against one wall and a brass floor lamp that looks like it might be an actual antique. The only place to sit is on the giant oak sleigh bed.

I wade through the mess, trying not to impale myself on any loose needles, and sink down on the edge of the mattress. "Are you really going to call the print shop for Maribeth, or should I just go ahead and do it?"

Autumn wades after me and takes a flying leap into the middle of the velvet comforter.

"You mean like make you do my work?" she says, draping herself over the curve of the footboard so that her head hangs off the edge. "No way. I wouldn't stick you with more bullshit just to torture her. She's got a real boner for paper products, though, that's for sure."

I sit watching her. I think she means it, but I'm not sure. "So you'd toe the line for her bureaucratic madness? Because I asked you to?"

Autumn lies sprawled over the footboard for a long time. Then she sits up, flipping her hair out of her face. "Waverly, I need to ask you a very important question."

"What?" I say, when in my head, I'm already paging through every invasive, revealing thing she might be about to interrogate me on.

"How can a person be seventeen years old and not know how friends work?"

And I laugh, because it's so horrible. It's true. Because she's the friend I wanted before I even knew that I wanted a friend.

The velvet bedspread is outrageously tacky and deliciously soft. Being the secret version of myself is easier in the giant repurposed rec room, with no audience but Autumn's secret dress, standing in the corner like a ghost.

"I don't exist the way you think I do," I say, and immediately I'm gripped by trepidation. I've said too much. She'll look closer, look harder. She'll see the jagged edges in me, the dark, unholy fascinations—spiders and nihilism, mutant cells and scalpels and sarcophagi.

Autumn just shrugs and tosses her head. "Does *any*one?"

"I don't know, you seem pretty authentic."

She stretches like a cat and rearranges herself to sit cross-legged. It's strange to be so easily assimilated into someone else's world. At school, I'm always sharing territory with people, but it never feels that way. We're inhabiting one another's vicinities, is all—shiny cars in shiny parking spaces.

"You have to pick your poison," she says. "I like to think I just went with the best possible alter ego for my talents and inclinations."

I've never heard anyone talk so easily about social artifice. Most of the time, Maribeth won't even acknowledge that's something we're still doing.

"Why did you defend Kendry today? You don't even like her."

The look Autumn gives me is sincerely bewildered. "God, *I* don't know. Because Maribeth was being totally disgusting and unfair when Kendry wasn't even around to hear it. Because it was the nice thing to do. I mean . . . haven't you ever just wanted to do something nice?"

But the thing is, I don't really think that I have. At least, not in the way she means—a genuine, empathetic way, beyond volunteer work or socially conscious committees. The spill wall is the only place I've ever been brave enough to comfort or stand up for anyone. It's the nicest version of myself that I have ever been.

"Not for someone who has, at any point, called me too freakish to be allowed," I say. "I mean, is principle a good enough reason to just ignore how she's treated you?"

Autumn reaches over and combs her fingers through my hair. "It's the only reason that matters."

The way she touches people never stops surprising me. It should feel aggressive or patronizing, but instead, it's just so easy.

"Your layers are looking kind of rough."

"I was supposed to get it cut last week. I forgot." Truth be told, I've been forgetting a lot of things.

"I could do it. It's cool, I'm really good."

Two weeks ago, I'd never have let her near me, but when she opens her desk and takes out the scissors, I get up and follow her, because the thing is, when Autumn says she's good at something, chances are, she is.

She leads me down a narrow hall into her bathroom, which is painted swimming-pool blue, and sits me on the edge of the tub. Then she takes a wooden step stool out of the linen closet and plunks it down behind me.

"Not going to chicken out, are you?"

"No. Are you going to disfigure me?"

"Like Audrey," she says, holding up the scissors. "I promise."

Her hand on my jaw is light and capable, turning me to look at her, studying my face.

When she squints, it's like she's seeing something intricate and far, the way she did the day she found my homecoming dress. Seeing the person I should be, instead of the one that I am.

When she makes the first cut, I feel lighter, like we are changing the shape of Waverly. Of everything.

I've never really understood this easy willingness to experiment or try new things, and it's startling now to realize that it's . . . fun. That a person can care about fashion or style or appearance just because they do—not resentfully, not because they have no other choice, but for the sheer enjoyment of it.

She works quickly, keeping her tongue tucked in the corner of her mouth and her hand on the crown of my head. I watch her as she goes, face angelic, scissors flashing.

This obvious familiarity with haircuts just reinforces how little I really know about her. She may be blunt and entertaining, but mostly, she's still unknown. She is my interesting endeavor, my latest area of study. And yes. Hopefully my friend.

Marshall's. The realization washes over me, so big it makes my face tingle. She is Marshall's friend. Suddenly, I'm intensely aware of what that means—of all the things she might be able to tell me.

"Autumn, do you know anything about—" But right away, it sticks in my throat, getting all jammed up against my teeth. I start over. "Boys. What do you know about boys?"

"They think with their nether parts and smell like Taco Bell?"

"But like, what do you think it means if you make out with someone and he gives you a tremendous hickey, and then later you kind of hold hands, but he doesn't kiss you anymore? I mean, is it possible for someone to be so into you that they just want to . . . cuddle?"

Autumn makes a vague humming noise and flicks my hair away from my face with the comb. "I think CJ Borsen needs to keep his tremendous hickeys to himself."

She says it sardonically, not how it would sound if Maribeth were offering similar wisdom. Autumn's judgment has less to do with wanting all acts of intimacy to be approved by committee, and more to do with her inherently low opinion of CJ.

"Oh, hey," she says, steadying my head with one hand as the scissors brush my temple. "Do you want to hear something weird, though?"

I nod cautiously. The question doesn't even make sense. I wait for whatever could qualify as weird in Autumn's unlikely universe.

She trims the last stray hairs, sweeping behind my ears with a casual index finger. Her touch is shocking, reminding me that this is happening in an utterly physical way, on an utterly physical plane. Afterward, I'll go home and look however Autumn made me look.

She gestures with the scissors, flicking them toward the sink. "So, do you have any idea who Marshall Holt is?—he's this complete pothead, but whatever. Anyway, he asked about you. Only, you know, without really asking."

And I stop breathing because my lungs are making everything too complicated. I'm half convinced this is some elaborate prank, a trick just to mess with me, but when I twist around and look up at her, she's not joking.

"Why—what did he want to know?"

"Just if I knew you. If we hung out at all."

I nod, then remember I'm supposed to be holding still. "Did he say why?"

Autumn shakes her head. "Not anything *actual*. I think he might kind of like you, is all."

I bite the inside of my lip as hard as I can, but my mouth keeps wanting to smile.

She raises her eyebrows and shakes a finger at me. "*Stop* making that face, right now. There are worse guys, believe me."

I immediately rearrange my expression so it doesn't look like anything. The other night, Marshall was so adamant that they were friends, but the two of them actually inhabiting the same space? I still have trouble picturing it. "So you hang out with him a lot, then?"

She rakes the comb through my hair so hard my scalp tingles. "Used to."

"Did you have a fight or something?"

"Oh, God, nothing like that." Autumn waves the scissors dismissively. "I moved, is all. My mom got promoted and decided it was time for a house with more than one bathroom. He probably would have ditched me eventually anyway, I guess. He's not really into arts and crafts and confrontation. I'm not really into getting so fucked up I can't stand. Plus, after that whole thing with his dad last year, he didn't really want to be around anyone for a while."

The way she says it is offhand, like the story is just *known*.

"What whole thing?"

The look she gives me is impatient, appalled at my social ignorance. "How his dad got MS? And it was this total shit storm that basically landed on top of this *other* shit storm, which was that his parents were finally getting divorced? But then his mom remembered that she's a giant codependent freak, so they'd probably better stay together after all. It was just ugly. Anyway, he kind of dropped off for a while."

I absorb this information, trying to look appropriate. What's the right expression again? The one you use when you hear about the misfortune of a stranger?

"So he dumped all his friends and just stopped talking to you?"

"Not like *that*. He just got kind of . . . what's that word when people disappear into themselves?"

I shake my head. "I don't think there is one."

"Well, there should be. Anyway, pretty much the only person he wanted to be around anymore was Ollie, probably because Ollie knows how to just shut up once in a while."

I close my eyes as she guides the scissors across my forehead, shaping my bangs. "That wasn't something you could do?"

"Oh, God, *never*. It's like, if there's a scab, I can't not pick it."

I clasp my hands, remembering that night in his room,

how plainly he talked to me, even when it was painful or embarrassing. And then, in class today. *I try to be honest with her. I try to be real.* Indisputable proof that on some level, he wants to tell someone all the things he carries around with him.

Autumn's using her comb to frame my face, holding my chin in her hand. "And completely not my business, I *know,* but he's been hanging around Heather McIntire again, which—gross. She always wants to discuss his finer *qualities* when we're supposed to be doing worksheets in English, when I can't even believe they're still *persisting* with that whole thing."

"What whole thing?"

Autumn shrugs, but there's something working around the corners of her mouth. Annoyance, maybe? Distaste? "Oh, just that whole doing-it-on-her-parents'-bed thing."

And if I'd ever thought I was so clinical or untouchable, I was wrong. I can actually feel the moment when comprehension reaches my heart. My mouth snaps shut.

I expect Autumn to correct my expression again, but she only laughs and shakes her head, like the way my eyes go horrified means something else.

"Yes, Virginia, he stuck his Rhode Island in her Delaware."

And I know I'm supposed to laugh—I know. I *try.* But all I can manage is a cough. I reach up, combing my fingers through my hair even though it sends loose clippings everywhere and she isn't done shaping the back.

"How do you know?" I say, after I've been quiet so long it's awkward.

"Um, because *high school*? I mean, it's not like it was a secret. Anyway, everybody's always doing it with somebody, right?"

Which is a pronouncement that makes very little sense. A state of sexual rampageousness is not inherent. I am never doing it with anybody.

"Anyway, he's just window-shopping in the masochism store again. That boy *needs* to be saved from himself."

She says it as though she has already done the due diligence and is now announcing her findings. I wonder if she's really that naive. No one can be saved from their own dysfunction by anybody else.

"Maybe he just likes her."

"Are you kidding? His shitty dating history is like the basis for every thirty-minute instructional video on how to be a sad, tragic figure. He doesn't *like*-like her, he just likes that she likes him. See? Shitty."

Her tone sends cold fingers creeping between my organs. Maybe he's the kind of person who just needs that much approval. Who would feel the same way about anyone, as long as they liked him.

Autumn stands over me with one foot in the tub and one foot out. "And God, we had this entire conversation about homecoming, like that's even his natural habitat. He said he was maybe going to ask her, which is *the* worst idea in the name of tiny baby herpes that I have ever, ever heard."

"She's pretty, though."

It's weird to hear the words coming out of my mouth with no forethought, no hesitation. Like I've ever considered Heather's aesthetic appeal in my life before this moment.

Autumn shrugs, making a neat side part with the comb. "Maybe if you're into that whole *yes, clearly* look. Anyway, sad but true, et cetera, blah blah blah. Not our problem. Here, check it out."

She guides me to the sink and presents me with my reflection, my new, pristine haircut. My face is so guileless. So innocent.

"If you want, I can teach you how to do your makeup. That cut would look good with a cat's-eye liner, and your dress needs something flashy to wake it up a little. How do you feel about false eyelashes?"

The question is immaterial. I am already grappling with one fully manifested feeling. I don't have room for another one.

I glance back at her, trying to look polite and curious without seeming too invested in the answer. "So, do you think he did it?"

"Did what?"

I rub the side of my neck. The mark is already fading. "Did he ask Heather?"

The look Autumn gives me is distracted, like my side part is so much more crucial to this moment than the pain in my throat. "Oh—shit, *probably*. I saw him talking to her after bio. She looked really happy."

WAVERLY

8.

When the house is dark and the whole neighborhood feels asleep, I light the candle. It's more than half gone, but I can't think about that now.

I swallow my restlessness, my prickly, twitchy impatience, and all my feelings.

Pull the covers over my head. Relax. Breathe. Count. Repeat.

The thing that Autumn told me doesn't matter. The thing that Autumn told me is not my business, not even a little.

Relax. Breathe. Count. Repeat.

When I open my eyes, Marshall is sitting on the floor of his room. He's got his back against the footboard of his bed and a textbook open in front of him. It's strange, seeing him so studious. So responsible, and on a Friday night. His desk lamp throws a warm glow over everything, but when he glances up, his eyes are guarded and he looks away.

Before Autumn's house, I was ready to fling myself at him and thank him for his compliments. Now the image of Heather McIntire keeps intruding, reminding me that once, or twice, or more times than I want to think about, he was naked with her. *Please don't be true,* a part of me whispers, the prayer of a raw, thumping heart. *Please don't be real.* But I know it is.

I pick my way over a mess of stray pens, open books, and loose, crumpled handouts, and sink down on the carpet. There's nothing but the narrow gap between us, half an inch of space. We sit side by side, looking straight ahead.

Finally, I lean sideways and rest my shoulder against his. "Are we not speaking, or are you just that into mitochondria?"

He shrugs, focusing intently on a diagram of cellular respiration.

I keep my gaze trained on the side of his face. "Quit being passive-aggressive and tell me what's wrong."

He's quiet a long time and even though it looks like he's ignoring me, I know him well enough by now to know that he's just trying to formulate what he wants to say. Finally, he takes a deep breath and clears his throat, still staring straight ahead. "Why'd you make up that bullshit list in Spanish?"

The question is ludicrous. Why did I avoid shaming him in public? Why did I go out of my way to protect his confessions, rather than rip the defensive coating off his heart and wave it around for everyone to enjoy?

"Did you really want me to say those things out loud?"

He shakes his head, looking down. "No. I don't know. I guess not." Then he closes his eyes. "Yes," he says. "Yes, I wanted you to say it out loud."

His tone is obstinate. It tells me, as if any further proof

were necessary, that he doesn't worry about his heart. His heart is there for public display and being ignored hurts worse than the chance that someone might get a good look at him.

I know I should explain—apologize, even—but I don't know the right way to say it. All my explanations sound like arguments. "You really think some busywork assignment matters? I mean, how can I say those things in class?"

He looks up, and suddenly it's like he's seeing inside me, seeing down to the bottom, how maybe I didn't keep quiet to protect him, but because the things he wrote showed too much of *me*. I didn't want to rip off my defensive coating. "Because they're *true*. I just want to know that you're there, and you see me, and it's true."

I kiss him, because it's the truest thing I can think of—a way to say everything without knowing how to say it. When he kisses back, the flavor of his mouth is unfamiliar, sweet and wistful.

"You don't taste like you've been smoking," I whisper against his chin.

He shakes his head. "I've kind of been quitting."

"How is it?"

"Hard."

I kiss him again, cradling the back of his neck, holding him against me. His breath feels good on my skin and our faces are impossibly close together. Better than anything I can conceive of having in the daytime. I touch his chest and pray that he doesn't take it as some kind of consolation prize.

He must not mind, because he hauls me onto the bed

and then we're rolling over and over in his sheets, and my God, all I want is to breathe his deodorant and his messy, shaggy hair and forget my life in huge, ravenous gasps.

He stops, trapping me between his elbows. Suddenly, I'm painfully aware of his body against mine. Painfully aware that he is close to undressed.

"That's a good haircut," he whispers, like he means it in some profound way I don't understand.

"Thanks," I whisper back, just as stupidly profound.

He's looking at me like this is a moment. Like I'm something special or perfect. I think Autumn might be an expert in everything.

Then he ducks his head, examining the trail of black marker snaking down my wrist. "What happened on your arm? What is that?"

"Autumn did it."

He looks down at me, not quite frowning. "You really are friends with her," he says finally. There's something strange in his voice. Curiosity? Wonder, maybe?

"I told you that already. I needed graffiti to prove it?"

"No, I mean . . . *friends*. She only draws on people she likes." He keeps touching the flowers. "*How* did you meet her, again?"

I don't want to get into the details. I'd have to explain that we met because Kendry and Palmer have the interpersonal skills of jackals. That she picked me, even though I did nothing to deserve it, and I don't know how to be normal or accessible or use my powers for good. "She joined one of the event committees a couple weeks ago. We're helping Maribeth with the homecoming dance."

"*Autumn* is," he says, like the very concept is impossible. "Isn't that stuff kind of . . . not her thing?"

"The weird part is, she's actually *good* at it. I mean, once she got over how incredibly boring it is."

"If you think it's so boring, why do it?"

And it's not that I'm lying, exactly, but my answer is starting to feel tired. "Maribeth really likes that kind of stuff and she's my best friend."

He doesn't argue, but his expression makes me feel defensive anyway.

"Look," I say. "She's the only one who's ever really okay with how I am. Everyone else, it's like they see a different person. This nice, obedient, well-adjusted girl who doesn't actually exist."

Marshall nods, still giving me that look of grave concern. "Did you ever think maybe you're *showing* them that?"

The question is frankly bizarre. "Of *course* I'm showing them that. That's the whole *point*. If I didn't, then it would just be one big advertisement for all the ways it's impossible to like me."

"How can you say that?"

"Because they *don't*." I only mean it in the flattest, most accurate sense, but it comes out sounding strangled.

"Whatever," he says. "Fuck them, then. *I* like you."

Which is irrefutable proof, as if any more was needed, that he still has no idea what I'm like. Waverly, unfiltered: brutal, calculating, morbid. Robot. He opens his mouth like he wants to say more, but it will just be one more demonstration of all the ways he still can't see, and I can't stand to hear it.

"Never mind," I say, cutting over him. "So, tell me about your big date. I heard you asked Heather McIntire to homecoming,"

I don't even sound spiteful—at least, not much—but his mouth snaps shut. His expression is so guilty I look away, trying to keep my eyes impassive, my mouth indifferent. Anyway, it's not like I have a right to be jealous. I'll be on the arm of CJ Borsen, who picked out the napkins for the refreshment table and who—excessive punctuation aside—is annoyingly perfect in every way.

Marshall nods. He's trying to look neutral, the same way I am, but the composure is so fake. "I asked her today."

All I can think is what Autumn said—he likes that she likes him. Maybe that's all that matters. Heather, there to make him feel real, to make it matter that he has fears or wants or feels things or takes up space.

"Because she likes you?" I say, almost whispering it.

He shakes his head. "Because you're going. And I've never been to one, and I thought it might be something to do. Look, I just figured, yeah, maybe I wanted to know what it's like, for once . . . doing things."

"Well, whatever you're expecting," I say, sounding more sardonic than I mean to. "You're going to be gravely disappointed."

Marshall just raises his eyebrows like he doesn't give a fuck about disappointment. He reaches for the sheet and yanks it over us like a fort, shielding us from the room.

"Tell me the good parts, then. Do you have some kind of special dress? I mean, that's what girls wear at these things, right?"

"I have a dress. I don't know about special. I thought guys weren't supposed to be interested in clothes."

"Come on," he says. "Just tell me."

"It's black, made of something slippery, satin or acetate. It's open at the back."

"How far?" He touches the space between my shoulder blades. "Here?"

I shake my head.

He slides his hand down to the middle of my back. "Here?"

I reach behind me and move his hand to the small of my back, almost to my butt. "Here."

He smiles and it looks completely involuntary, like the smile bypassed his brain and went straight to his mouth without him having to decide it was the right response. "God, that's hot."

We sit facing each other, with the sheet draped over us. Looking into his eyes is like looking into a metaphor, something by T. S. Eliot or Oscar Wilde. It's the ocular equivalent of every smart, cynical poem. Every book I've ever enjoyed in secret. I've spent my life wishing that gay dead men could be my boyfriend, and Marshall is right here, realer than any of them.

His smile is small and miserable and then gone. "I could tell her I'm not going with her."

"No, you couldn't. You'd feel bad."

"I'd do it anyway," he says, and I can already see the moment.

Heather, the dull, hurt look blooming on her face like a bruise, like he slapped the hopeful right off her.

And him, hating himself, but doing it anyway because he truly believes it's the necessary thing. Because he has some fantasy that I will become emotionally accessible overnight. That if he just calls off his date, I will magically figure out how to dismantle my own highly advanced insecurity system.

He's already looking past me, talking himself through it. The big, tearful blowup, the damage control. She'll cry, but only for a little. After a few minutes—a few days—she'll pull it together and ultimately forgive him. He's imagining a heartfelt resolution, like in movies or TV. Like I am not the most selfish person in the history of the world.

"Don't," I say, untangling us from the sheet. "It wouldn't be fair. And anyway, I'm not going to flake on *my* date, so what would be the point?"

It takes Marshall a second, but he nods. "Who are you going with?"

It's strange to think we've been sharing our nights for two weeks and this has never come up—my ostensible boyfriend. Major player in high school sports and politics, minor annoyance in the jagged, austere landscape of my life.

"CJ Borsen."

Marshall's expression is scandalized. "Oh come *on*. That guy sucks. Don't go with him."

"I told him I would. I can't just change my mind."

"You could," he says, staring out the window. The glass is made impenetrable by the lamp, reflecting the room back at us. "But you won't."

"No, I won't, because it's not a fair thing to do."

He doesn't answer, but the look he gives me is eloquent enough. This isn't fair either. I know that.

When I reach for him, he buries his face in my hair. "This is the best thing I've got right now, and it's not even real."

I close my eyes, breathing his skin, the realest, most important thing that's happened all day. "Don't ever say that I'm not real."

"This," he says. "*This* isn't real."

•

By Saturday, my arches are still breathtakingly painful. I've applied ice, heat, Tiger Balm. Gentle stretches, lots of rest. Doctor's orders. I've done everything I was supposed to, and nothing's changed. I have officially managed to damage myself in a way that is completely beyond my capacity to ignore.

When I get dressed for the dance, I do it like an acrobat, trying to stand without putting weight on my feet. The theory is notionally sound, but I'm defeated by the physics.

I apply my eyeliner the way Autumn showed me, a heavy black swoop that flares at the outside corners. The way it transforms my face reminds me of the day we browsed the drugstore together, how contrived that seems now. There is no conceivable way that Autumn has ever needed someone else to explain a neutral palette to her.

Her fashion expertise is nothing short of stellar. The dress she picked for me is darkly perfect, and my new haircut is the best thing that's ever happened—a style that looks good no matter whether it's wet, dirty, slept on, hanging in my face, or slicked back like a '50s greaser.

CJ picks me up at eight, with Hunter and Maribeth already in the backseat. The boys both tilt their heads in approval as I climb into the car, but Maribeth unbuckles and leans over the center console to stare at me. Her horror is deep, total, and apparently genuine.

"Oh, Waverly, you *cut* it! I thought you were growing it out."

I look at her, trying to see myself the way she must, these little twin dolls trapped in the center of her pupils. "Why would you think that?"

But I know. As far as she's concerned, we settled this weeks ago, the day she casually expressed her hatred of short hair on girls. She's had the final word, and that word was supposed to be law, and now here I am, running around messing up her neat little world.

My feet feel like something sharp and possibly scalding is stuck into the very center of my soles. I lean my head back and fight the impulse to slip off my stupid shiny heels. The whole way to the restaurant, I do calf stretches, pressing my toes against the vinyl floor mat and staring out at the street.

"I just can't believe you did that," Maribeth says. "What were you even thinking?"

And I don't say anything, because anything I say will be vicious.

I've slept six hours in two days, so when CJ guides me through the double doors and into the dance, at first I'm not even sure if what I'm seeing is real.

The gym is a festival of green. It looks like a chemical explosion, complete with colored streamers dripping from the rafters. We are stuck in the heart of a toxic tinsel disaster.

The rest of the dance planners are already here, clustered around the best table—at the edge of the dance floor, but not too close to the speakers. We weave our way over to them, Maribeth fluttering like a tropical bird, eager to flock decorously with Kendry and Palmer in their assorted jewel tones and their cattleya orchids and shiny barrettes.

Beside them, Autumn's outfit is almost too ludicrous to pull off.

Except, she's doing it.

She is *haute couture* and Hollywood Heroes and epic punk rock. She's come as Alex DeLarge from *A Clockwork Orange,* and also the most brutal Tinker Bell the world has ever seen, tricked out like some kind of psychopathic ballerina.

The material of her dress is nothing fancy—just plain white cotton—but the cut is shocking and whimsical, with a short, stiff skirt and brass zippers everywhere. The straps are styled like straps, but they're also suspenders. She's got the black bowler hat, the single false eyelash, and all of it's contrived, but none of it's wrong.

She is a fashion god.

"Oh, my brothers," I whisper, sliding into the empty seat beside her. There's almost always an empty spot beside her. This whole time, I've assumed it's because no one wants to get too close, like her lack of polish is somehow contagious. Now, though, I think maybe I was wrong all along, and really she's just been saving it for me. "Autumn, you look amazing."

She smiles and drops me a huge false-eyelashed wink. "They wouldn't let me bring in my swagger stick. They said it was a weapon."

From across the table, Hunter examines her with casual lewdness, openly appreciating her legs, the way her ultra-violent neckline accentuates her breasts.

Autumn is the new Maribeth. And not in that non-committal way that black is sometimes the new black. This is confrontational. It's daring—the social equivalent of Plaid Is the New Black. Fuchsia Is the New Black. Outrageous, sure, but what are you going to do? Everybody who's any-body is jumping on the plaid bandwagon.

"Sorry Hollywood Heroes didn't work out," I whisper. "It's hard to fight the inertia of poly-satin."

"Oh, who cares?" She sounds like she actually means it. "I'm wearing what I wanted to wear, and I fully intend to have the most fun that has ever been had at one of these things. So, slightly more than one tablespoon. Anyway, change of plans. My mom has this sales conference coming up in, like, Pittsburgh or wherever. I'm totally going to have a party, and it's going to be unruly and amazing and exactly how I want it."

When a fast song comes on, Autumn slides out of her chair and takes the floor, not sullen or slouching or any-thing I've come to expect from her. She moves to the music with her arms aloft, pirouetting through her own private *Swan Lake*. Her own irreverent ode to joy.

Halfway through the routine, people start to clap. She

maneuvers through the crowd like a beautiful, volatile gyroscope, impossibly graceful in her steel-toed boots. I wonder if they know she's making fun of them. I wonder how long it took her to learn her extensive selection of ironic Michael Jackson moves.

She flicks off her bowler hat, letting it tumble down her arm and into her palm, smooth and practiced, no hesitation. She drops the hat onto my head and smiles, batting her false eyelash.

I laugh. The hat is heavy and warm, slipping over my forehead. I want to hug her the way she hugged me that day in the locker room, to throw away all my carefully cultivated inhibitions and just plunge headlong into the chaos of her. The sheer, unspoiled wonder.

And right about then is when I see Marshall.

He's standing just inside the double doors, under a makeshift arch of silver and green balloons. He has on slacks and a dark button-down shirt and his hair is combed in a slick, deliberate way I don't recognize. It makes him look young and sort of wet.

The sensation is like someone sucked the air out of the room, and being breathless is strangely pleasant, until I notice Heather beside him. Her dress is a lurid shade of purple and, in a bold fashion move, is also encrusted with glitter. Her hand is resting on his arm.

The track switches over to a slow song and she reaches up, slipping her arms around his neck. It hurts in a way that I didn't know things ever hurt. Deep and without logic.

CJ sees me looking off at all the swaying couples and leans to whisper in my ear. "Would you like to dance?"

I let him lead me out into the middle of the gym, under all the fluttering, tumbling confetti.

It's probably supposed to be romantic, but it looks like someone planned a birthday party for the Green Goblin. I bet Marshall's into it anyway. He's biologically designed for flowers and soft things and all that sentimental stuff, which I know is supposed to be a secret, the way it's a secret that his heart hurts, a secret that getting insensible is his version of curling up on the floor and closing his eyes. His version of running the cross-country course at Basset at three in the morning until his feet bleed.

I want to think that Heather is just another part of that, warm mouth and clutching hands and numbness. The way she wants him is just so honest.

She likes him so much it's painful and I face front, staring at CJ's tie. It's subdued. Sensible. The kind of thing parents buy when they want their sons to grow up to be accountants.

He pulls me closer. His suit coat is lumpy with buttons. We turn slowly, swaying to the music, rocking in circles as Marshall and Heather wash into sight again and again.

She's leaning against him now, her cheek on his shoulder. His hands are long-fingered, clasped gently on her back, and I hate her. Not for resting her head in the place where mine should be, or even for liking him.

I hate her for existing in all the ways I don't. For knowing instinctively how to want him here and now, in front of everyone, without caring that everyone will know her desires and her secrets. I hate the way she never worries about anyone seeing her.

CJ is looking down at me, smiling in a solid, honest way. I lean my head against his chest and close my eyes.

When the music ends, I don't know what to do with my voice or my hands. I float back to our table and sink down next to Autumn. I think I might be shaking.

Marshall and Heather are still standing under the industrial fan, surrounded by confetti. She's got his shirt untucked and is sliding her hands up the back of his undershirt, reaching for someplace impermissible. *My* exclusive province, *my* territory. When she touches him, she is running her hands over *my* skin.

I look away, even though my first impulse is to make myself watch, to stare until the ache dissolves. Master the situation, move on.

I look away because if I don't, then . . . nothing. The wound will scab over, scar, go numb. It will cease to exist.

And so I look away, because there's a small but ferocious part of me that doesn't want to stop caring that Heather is getting her steadily degrading DNA all over him.

I fold my hands in my lap, chin high, back straight. Autumn is lining up silver plastic clocks on the tablecloth, making a tiny timepiece army.

She scrapes the clocks into a pile, then glances at me, leaning in like she might touch my hand. "Hey, what's wrong? Are you okay?"

But Maribeth flops down across from us before I can get the words out, starry-eyed and flushed. "Oh, no, don't worry. That's just Waverly's face." She reaches for my arm. "Here, come with me while I fix my hair."

Her voice is bright and strained and desolate. I can't

tell if it's over something real, imagined, or just the fact her whole extracurricular life has been building up to this fucking dance, and now that the moment is here, she doesn't know how to cope.

When she pulls me to my feet, I force a smile and follow her, tripping gaily along as she leads me through the crowd, holding hands like two little girls on their way into tangled thickets and dark woods. It's both gratifying and disappointing that my heartbreak face isn't much different from my everyday one. I feel utterly composed. And at the same time, like something inside me has cracked in half.

In the bathroom, Maribeth stands at the counter. "Here, can you pin this? No, not like that—just move it there and hide it under the edge."

I adjust the curls carefully. She could get someone else to do it, of course. Any one of them would be flattered, because one of the secrets of total social domination is to make your moment of vulnerability a premium. You trade on your need for people, bestowing it like a gift.

The gesture has a broad and cynical application, announcing that I am still the favorite. Announcing to me that I should be flattered.

Once you know the secrets, though—after all, you were the one who wrote them down—the language loses its meaning. The real reason she picked me is simply that I'm careful.

When her hair is arranged to her satisfaction, she turns and brushes my cheek with her thumb, wiping away a smudge under my eye.

"Aren't you having the best time?" Her smile is syrupy,

trying way too hard. "*So*, are you going to give CJ a kiss goodnight?"

She looks ferociously happy, and under that, she looks sad. I haven't seen Hunter in a while.

I want to let go of my tiny beaded bag and hug her, tell her it's okay. That even if Hunter never chooses her, despite all her demonstrations of organizational preeminence, someone will. I want to tell her about Marshall, but I don't.

This is just what it means to be friends with Maribeth. Never, at any point in my life, have I told her anything that qualified as a feeling. We are not allowed to see the dirty mechanisms of each other's inner workings.

Her world view doesn't encompass Sad-Waverly, and she'd try to fix it in the only way she knows how—by detailing all the ways I'm not built for anything so prosaic as affection.

She'd carefully explain the emotional limitations of species Camdenmar, prove beyond a shadow of a doubt that I am made of jumper wire and rare-earth metals. If I were really lucky, she'd move on to Marshall's fundamental composition next, take him apart and lay him out—drugs, report card, lack of healthy male aggression—like all the best things about him are not worth anything.

So I don't tell her, because a part of me is still strangely gratified by how it feels to ache for something instead of just waiting for it to be over so I can go home. But mostly, because I don't want anyone to see the way my mouth will tremble if I have to say his name.

Maribeth smooths her hair with a few drops of water, flicking her fingertips under the faucet. Her nails are painted a vibrant peacock green. "So, *Autumn* seems to be having a good time."

"I think she pretty much always has a good time."

Maribeth does this thing with her hands, like she's waving Autumn off. "She is just . . . too much."

I apply another layer of lipstick and wonder how a person ever knows what is officially too much.

When we leave the bathroom, we're both more composed, slick and hard as porcelain. Maribeth takes my hand again, tugging me toward the dance floor. She's got her finger hooked in my bracelet like a towline, but as we approach the refreshment table, she stops short. We stand caught in the eddies of dry, freezing air and confetti, green foil stars landing in our hair.

Autumn is luminous under the fractured light of the mirror ball, slow dancing with Hunter Pennington. His mouth is close to her ear. His hand on her waist is positioned a scant millimeter above someplace inappropriate.

Maribeth stands beside a giant bowl of pretzels, her finger still caught in my bracelet. I understand two things simultaneously—first, that she is desperately sad and second, that she would never, ever tell me that. At least, not in any way I'd know how to answer. I have a sinking feeling that this is the end of something. This is where I'll see her fall apart.

And then she collects herself. With a toss of her head, she leads me straight through the swaying crowd, back to the table, steering us to someplace we belong.

"*There* you are!" she says as we come up next to Kendry and Palmer, who are sitting with their heads very close together. Her tone implies that we have searched high and low and are now overjoyed to see them.

They jump apart, looking guilty, and I'm almost certain that the topic of interest was Maribeth and her philandering date.

The way she stands over them is imperious.

Palmer fidgets with a plastic hourglass. "God, so *Autumn* is really slutting it up, right?"

Maribeth shrugs like nothing has ever mattered less. "Well, I guess it's not even surprising. I mean, what do you expect?"

"Wait, what?" says Kendry. "Expect it why?"

"Well, it's just what I heard, but"—Maribeth's voice drops to a whisper—"last year she got caught behind Kroger's with the *janitor*."

Her expression is so gleeful—so hateful—it makes me flinch. This is Maribeth wounded. Not beaten or broken, but anguished enough to tear out someone's throat. I'm almost positive her supposed insider knowledge of Autumn's sex life is grounded in nothing. Still, it is an unfairness universally acknowledged that when it comes to gossip, objective truth has no bearing whatsoever.

"Oh my God," says Kendry, leaning across the table, wide-eyed. "What are you even *talking* about?"

"I'm serious, Kelsey Conroy used to work in the flower department. I can't believe you never heard that!"

"*Gross,*" Kendry and Palmer cry in delighted unison, while Maribeth looks at me expectantly.

I know her well enough to understand the only way to console her is by declaring my alliance. She wants me to prove that I'm still hers. I wonder if I am. If I ever really was. I don't know any of the words it would take for me to choose her, or why we have no idea how to be sad together.

Kendry and Palmer laugh behind their hands, the short, stifled laughs of people who know they're doing something naughty. I look away and tug the bottom of my dress. It's not even that short, but the bareness of my back makes me feel naked. I want Marshall Holt to see my spine, and no one else.

Another fast song comes on and the couples all break apart. The sudden change in sound track is too perky and upbeat to deal with. I push my chair back and cross the dance floor, winding between bodies, shuffling through twinkling drifts of confetti until I make it to the bleachers.

The custodial crew has covered the gap at the end of the stands with butcher paper to discourage closet drinkers and clandestine lovers, but their masking tape barrier is no match for my fingernails. It's dark under the bleachers and marginally quieter. I slide out of my shoes and sigh as my feet rest flat against the floor. The pain is sharp and immediate, but bearable. I close my eyes and lean back.

Out in the gym, the music is thumping, girls are dancing, couples are groping each other like drowning people. Somewhere in the dark, Autumn Pickerel is taking everything Maribeth wants.

I didn't do this. I didn't plan or design or wish it. I just made the larceny possible. I stood in the wings and watched it happen and now I'm left with that—that deep, filthy complicity.

When Marshall materializes out of the dark, there's a

cool, dreamy part of me that's completely unshocked. The sun is down, and with the sun down, nothing about the real world matters quite as much. Even the air feels softer.

My arches ache from faraway, pain thudding up my calves. I stand against the wall, cycling through all the words to describe his presence here—inarguable, impossible, insupportable—but his mouth is tentative and inviting. It's the only thing I want, and anyway, what's one more fantasy?

He ducks into the narrow gap and stands facing me. The metal folding supports are pressed against his back and his mouth is very close to mine.

"Hi," I say, so small and cautious I'm surprised he can even hear it over the music. My voice doesn't sound like mine.

He leans closer, and I close my eyes and hold my breath, nearly trembling at the weight of his body in my space. "Hi."

This is real. More than the lighter, more than a bruise on my neck—already fading—or some subjective, sentimental list to read aloud in class. This is the closest we have ever come in real life to acknowledging the impossible thread that exists between us. We're total strangers, and we are magicians with the intimate power to see inside each other, and we're missing all the small, crucial steps between those two things.

I have a disjointed daydream of kissing him, getting my special-occasion lipstick all over his mouth, and then I won't have to say it aloud, everyone will just know.

"How's the confetti?" he says. "Having a good time with the pretty people?"

He has me trapped against the wall, hands braced on either side of my head and I like him looming over me. I like him electrified and wide awake.

"That depends. Are you having a good time letting Heather grope you?"

"If I said no, would that make you happy?"

He stands with the insides of his shoes pressed against the outsides of my bare feet, waiting for me to say something. To tell him that *no* is the only word in the world that will make me happy, that I saw him with her and I hate it, that I *need* him to not want anyone else. But the scenario is impossible. Need is not in the Waverly vocabulary.

"So," I say, and I say it coolly, cruelly, like nothing in the world has ever mattered to me less than this. "I take it she still doesn't know that you're using her as your own personal razor blade?"

He flinches back and shakes his head. "What are you talking about?"

"I'm talking about your penchant for finding every toxic waste site and sharp edge in a thirty-mile radius."

"She's a person." But his voice is hoarse. He's not looking at me.

"Are you sure about that?"

Now he meets my eyes, chin up, jaw tight. "She's a *person.*"

He means it, but not in any way I need to be afraid of. His voice is hurt, not smitten. The way he's looking at me is like I'm the only beating heart in the world.

He's inches away, and it makes me think of sleep and

kissing. He smells like Heather's perfume, and who even cares? I want to climb him.

I move to press myself against him, but he pulls back. In the dark, his eyes are miserable.

"*What?*" I say, sounding ferocious, even to myself.

"Waverly, I love you."

And for a second, I stop breathing. They're just words. But they make something shudder under my skin. "No you don't. You love the idea of me."

For a second, I'm sure he'll let me go. He'll duck out from under the bleachers and walk away and that will be the end of it. Of everything.

Then he takes a breath and moves closer.

With his mouth against my ear, he slides his hand along the side of my face, cupping my cheek. "Waverly, I know it freaks you out, but I have the right to love you if I want."

"Stop," I whisper, because I'm starting to feel light-headed, like I might float away.

His hands are clamped on either side of my face now, holding me so that my chin is up and I can't look anywhere but him. "Why?" he says, with no heat, no rancor.

"Just *stop* it. I don't want to hear that."

He leans in so our foreheads are almost touching. "I don't care if you don't want to hear it. I want to *say* it."

I'm squeezing my tiny beaded purse with both hands. "Why are you telling me this?"

"Because I've never said it to anyone. Because I just want to be able to say it when I mean it."

"I'm not your girlfriend," I say.

He breathes out and lets his hands fall. His face is eminently readable. "I know that. Do you think I don't *know* that?"

"Why did you even come here tonight? Were you trying to *punish* me? To make me jealous?"

"No," he says, his lips barely moving.

"What, then? To make sure nothing *untoward* happened? To protect me from CJ fucking *Borsen*?"

He shakes his head, slow and real and honest. "Because I wanted to see you in that goddamn dress."

He is completely sincere. He can say some mundane, normal word like *dress* and mean it more than I have ever meant anything in my whole life.

I open my mouth again, but there are no words, no corresponding declaration. After a second, he turns and ducks back out into the crowd.

I am alone.

Over the PA speakers, the DJ is playing "Fade into You" by Mazzy Star.

The truth is, it's a very depressing song.

CJ takes me home at midnight. In the driveway, he kisses me and it's soft and unexciting. When he puts his hand on the back of my neck, I reach behind me for the door.

"I have to go."

"Let me walk you up."

"No, really. Thank you for dinner. I'll see you Monday."

"The food drive meeting is tomorrow."

"I'll see you tomorrow."

I get out of the car before he can reach for my hand or touch my face, and bolt for my house so fast that by the time I get to the porch, I'm almost running. My feet ache like fire in my slippery, shiny shoes.

In my room, I go straight to my nightstand and get out the candle. My hands are shaking and every time I flick Marshall's lighter, the flame goes out again, until I want to scream. The candle is a lumpy hockey puck, mostly melted. I measure the remaining height between my fingers—a slippery inch of comfort. It isn't enough.

When the wick finally catches, I stand over it, breathing in huge gasps, gulping down the smell. It reminds me so much of Marshall, I can half believe I'm already there. The smoke gives me something to fix on until I can find the part of me that exists beyond the dimensions of my room. That knows how to get to someplace I actually want to be.

When my heartbeat finally slows down, I yank off my dress and throw it in the corner. Autumn's version of me was stark—lovely, even—but I'm better in my pajamas, better without gash-red lips and huge, black-rimmed eyes.

In the dark I lie rigid, counting down, trying to reach the small, transcendent core that doesn't measure or calculate or obsess, exempt from matter and distance. *Be impermanent and soft,* I tell myself. *Just disappear.*

It takes a long time, because every number keeps turning itself into *Marshall, Marshall, Marshall.*

MARSHALL
Home

Razor blade.

I hate the words but I think them anyway, trying to get used to the shape.

Waverly's right. She's *always* fucking right. In the last six months, there've been so many times I used Heather because I could, for distraction or company or just to feel something else. I got so used to knowing that no matter what, she'd always just be there.

But I'm right too. Heather's a person. I can't keep jerking her around anymore.

I tell her in the parking lot, in case she'd rather get a ride from someone else and maybe salvage the evening, but after I finish my big ugly speech, she just opens the passenger door and gets in.

Ollie is MIA. He watched the little freshman with the kind of interest he doesn't usually have for anything, and when Little Ollie spent twenty minutes talking to every girl who wasn't her, then did a disappearing act, he pushed himself away from the wall.

He walked over to her through the crowd. Left me on

the dance floor with Heather. She slid her hand into mine, and when I didn't squeeze back, she held my arm instead. When she stood on her toes and tried to kiss me, I had to look away.

The whole way home, Heather sits with her head against the window, like she needs to get as far away from me as possible.

"I'm sorry," I say.

And she doesn't say anything. If she's crying, I can't hear it, and I don't look away from the road.

After a while, she digs around in her purse and lights a cigarette, but doesn't open the window. I'm nearly grinding my teeth with how bad I want one too, but I don't tell her to put it out. The smoke is everywhere and I want it with my whole body. I just stare straight ahead and keep wanting it.

When I pull up to her house, Heather drops the cigarette in the ashtray and takes one deep, shaky breath before she gets out.

"Good night," I say, and wonder if this is the last thing we'll ever say to each other.

"She's not going to pick you," Heather says suddenly, leaning back in through the passenger side. "Just so you know. She's not going to suddenly just *condescend* to be seen with you."

"What are you talking about?" I say, even though there's only one direction this could be heading.

"I *saw* you follow her, Marshall. I'm not a total idiot. What did you think was going to happen? Behind the bleachers like a total slut? God, have you *met* her?"

I recognize the girl that Heather sees. The one who never cracks.

But that girl isn't Waverly—at least, not *real* Waverly. Heather's only thinking about the lie. Waverly in the daytime.

The thing that hurts is something else completely. I said *love*. She didn't say it back.

Heather doesn't slam the door or make a big dramatic scene, even though she could probably pull off a decent exit. She just walks away, and I sit in her driveway, thinking about Waverly, how she's not my girlfriend, and what that means. How I'm one step closer to just accepting the terms of what we've got, the same way Heather spent the last six months accepting I was never going to hold her hand in public.

How even in that black dress, even in the dark, Waverly was the brightest thing in the gym.

I drive home with the window down and the radio off, just being quiet and alone. Just feeling the air against my face.

When I let myself inside and close the door too hard, Annie comes shuffling out into the hall. "What are you doing? Did you just get home?"

"Yeah."

She scrubs her eyes like she's trying to focus. "Why are you wearing that shirt?"

I look at the button-down. "There was this thing at school."

She squints and shakes her head. "A collared-shirt thing?"

"A dance, okay? There was a dance."

"Oh." Nothing for a long time. Then, "Do you have a girlfriend or something?"

"No."

For a minute, Annie doesn't do anything, just stands there, looking warm and drowsy. Chowder is huffing for my attention, butting the top of her head against my knee.

Finally, Annie nods and trudges back to her room. She mumbles something into her hand before she shuts the door. It sounds kind of like, "Have fun at your dance."

Then I'm standing in the hall in a collared shirt that I ironed myself. Badly.

I keep smelling Heather's lip gloss, tasting it when I breathe, this oily candy flavor, choking and slick.

I brush my teeth. A lot. In the shower, I scrub my face like I'm trying to wash it off.

In the mirror over the sink, I look younger than I'm used to. I can't stand how helpless, how pleading my eyes look. I cover my reflection with my hand so all I can see is my mouth.

Right away, I get an ugly flash of how my dad will act when he sees my handprint on the glass. He'll say, *what have you been doing in there?* Like I'm some degenerate. He'll want to know why I was putting my hands all over the mirror and I won't say anything, because the reason is too weird and stupid to explain.

I was covering my eyes so that I would stop looking at myself. Are you happy now?

I was covering my eyes, because I just got home from the kind of school function I swore I'd never go to. I spent most of it with my arm around a girl who doesn't know the first thing about me, while the only girl who actually matters was pressed up against someone else. This happy, confident guy with sports and activities and *lists*—these crazy lists of all the things he's going to do and be and accomplish.

He is the person I will never be.

That isn't some angry, defiant promise.

It's just the truth.

WAVERLY
9.

I open my eyes and nearly melt with relief. I'm in the only place I want to be, standing awkwardly in the corner by Marshall's desk and feeling like I've come home.

I hear him first, sense the magnetic tension as he approaches. But when he steps into the room, he moves right past me, padding across the carpet with a towel around his waist.

He'll see me in a second. He has to. His head is down, though. His eyes are on the floor, and the awkward moment when he doesn't look up just gets longer.

I stay where I am. He thinks he's alone, and maybe I've spent the last few weeks invading every corner of his life, but it's different now. He's let me see too much of him, offered more than I have any right to. He's not a stranger anymore.

At his dresser, he yanks open the top drawer. He's about to take the towel off, and once, I was in bed with him. I held him down in the dark, but this moment is not the same. It's private. Voyeuristic. When he gets out a pair of boxers, I back away, sliding furtively into the closet.

It's worse, standing in the dark like a contract killer or a movie monster. I keep my hands flat against the wall, like I might ambush whoever steps inside.

Marshall doesn't come near me, though. I can hear him out in his room, rustling around, getting ready for bed. Then he turns out the light.

In the safety of my hiding place, I stand against the wall, staring into the dark.

Out in the bedroom, his breathing has the cadence of someone wide awake, too careful.

He told me that he loved me. He has to see his grave mistake by now. Has to know that I am ice inside. I lean back and close my eyes.

After a while, his breathing loses its regimented sound. It evens out, and when it does, even the air seems softer, like the world has stopped standing guard.

I let myself relax. I don't move until the pain in my feet gets bad enough that it tingles all the way up my shins. Then I steel myself and tiptoe out of the closet.

In the dark, Marshall is a low shape under the blanket, silhouetted against the wall.

I sit by the head of his bed with my elbows on the mattress, watching him, watching his pale, fluttering eyelids and his mouth.

After a long time, I lie on the carpet beside his bed and pull my knees up. I fold my hands under my head and close my eyes until the sound of him breathing is the only true thing.

•   •   •

"Waverly."

I roll over, already resigned to my room and my bed and my frantic, shrieking alarm clock.

I'm not in my room, though. I'm still on the floor and Marshall is out of bed, crouching next to me and shaking me by the shoulder. "Hey, Waverly. What are you doing?"

I feel dazed, too stupefied to think clearly. I want to be tucked against his chest, warm and safe and far away from the grinding monotony of daylight. I turn my face into the floor and can almost feel it.

"Here," he says with his hand on my arm. "Sit up, sit up."

When I do it, though, nothing is fine or better. Nothing is okay. I'm still chilly and untouchable. Still me.

Marshall has me by the wrist, guiding me carefully into bed and climbing in after me so he's pressed against my back.

"Don't do that," he says into my hair. "Don't lie on the floor when you could be up here with me."

His body is warm. Inarguable. It feels better than any moment in any given day. I pull away and roll over. I don't deserve to be comforted.

"What?" he whispers. "What are you doing?"

I adjust my head on the pillow, trying to see his face in the dark. "Are you mad at me?"

He's lying on his back now, dimly illuminated by the light from the window. His silhouette looks up for a second, staring at the ceiling. Then he swallows and fumbles for my hand. "No."

"You should be, though." I squeeze my eyes shut tight for a second before I say it.

I mean for what I said, for how I acted behind the bleachers, but it doesn't really matter. I could apologize for every facet and fiber of my being, and it would still be just as true.

He doesn't say anything, just rolls over and pulls me against his chest, pulls me right where I want to be.

"I broke up with Heather," he whispers against the top of my head.

His breath on my scalp makes my heart leap and stutter. *"Why?"*

"Because I don't like her that way. And I like you. I don't want to be with anyone else."

For a long time, I just lie there in his bed. Safe. Perfectly still. "You wouldn't kiss me tonight."

He laughs a small, helpless laugh. It isn't really a laugh at all. "I didn't want to do it and still be pretending I was there for her. It was—it seemed gross. Or like . . . not the way I feel."

The weight of his voice is unbearable, so heavy I can feel it like a change in gravity, the force of it pressing on my body. My ribcage tightens and suddenly, every strange and wordless thing inside me is welling up.

He pulls me closer, squeezing tight. "Are you *crying*?"

I close my eyes, swallow down the lump in my throat. "No."

And because I'm in control of it—because I have stopped—it's not a lie.

He tried to give me something honest, something true. He said *love*, but there's a part of me that still insists in cool, clinical tones that he can't possibly mean it, and even if he did, I'm not mechanically designed to take it. My motherboard is only wired for analysis and calculation, no place to plug it in.

"I'm not good at being loved," I whisper. My voice is barely audible. "I'm good at being self-sufficient."

I'm touching his bare chest and his stomach now, tracing shapes with my finger.

"That feels good," he whispers back, and I don't know how to make him see.

He sighs as I draw the shape of my own private geography. My list of confessions:

Frigid

Insensitive

Narcissistic

Egocentric

Fine. I know he doesn't understand—can't read my secrets on his skin—but he pets my hair anyway. He pulls me closer, close enough that I can almost convince myself this is the only thing that exists.

"I wish you could put your hand on my heart and feel it," he whispers. "I wish you knew exactly how much I'm not going to hurt you."

I picture it—surgical, gory, distinctly unromantic—and stop tracing. Science Waverly, reaching into a gaping chest, lifting a bloody heart in one latex-gloved hand and fighting the urge to squeeze. I have never once worried about how much something will hurt.

He's drowsy now, sinking into sleep. His body softens, forming to my contours, filling in the jagged mountain range that constitutes my outline. He is molding himself around me, making a space for me that didn't exist before.

In the past, I've always thought that people's edges either lined up or didn't. Some days, I didn't even have to work that hard to overlook the fact that no one ever lined up with me.

I assumed it was a matter of time. One day I'd meet someone who counteracted my chemical structure. We would compete for supremacy, collide until one of us was forced to yield, or else go forth together, suspended in eternal stalemate.

But my model is inaccurate. The poets are wrong.

The opposite of ice isn't fire.

It's water.

The days are strange and the nights feel like some hyper-realistic dream I can't wake up from. The candle has shrunk to a sliver now. I cradle it in my hands like a holy relic. I don't light it, because I know that if I do, my window to Marshall just gets smaller.

I spend whole class periods staring at my textbooks, flipping through the pages, not comprehending. Marveling over the perfect blackness of the letters.

In every sleepless expanse of days, you come to a point where your brain stops processing information correctly. A chapter could be written in Cyrillic and you'd still get half-way down the page before you noticed.

You start to believe that you can see the future. You stop noticing that you've been staring into space for the last four minutes. Déjà vu is a daily condition. Everything seems recursive, winding back on itself. You look at the assignment on the board and are sure that you've already done it.

In the west hall bathroom, secrets keep appearing—proliferating, overlapping. Sometimes I don't know what to say. The confessions are too heartbreaking, familiar and foreign at the same time.

There's this one:

> *I've stopped wearing makeup to school*
> *because when you cry all the time, it's too*
> *much work to keep redoing your eyeliner.*

And this:

> *When someone says I'm pretty,*
> *I always think they're lying.*
> *I think they must just feel sorry*
> *because of how ugly I am.*

Girls worry about their popularity, their weight, their goodness and intelligence and worth. Their stupid secret crushes.

By the sink in the corner, someone has printed the message, enigmatic, but oddly affecting:

> *I used to think I didn't deserve this.*
> *Now I know that I do.*

I want to tell the confessor and the world that I understand the feeling, but instead, I don't write anything.

Near the paper towel dispenser, someone has written:

I got dumped at the homecoming dance
by a boy I wasn't even dating,
for a girl who doesn't even want him.
No loss, right?

I uncap my pen, put it to the wall. Maybe it's Heather's secret, maybe not. Maybe it doesn't matter.

For Heather or Maribeth or every heartbroken girl whose chosen boy has passed them over for someone else, someone who doesn't have the common decency to appreciate what they've got, I write:

I'm sorry.

Every day, someone else's heart spills out a tiny, unvarnished truth, like the very substance of our lives is determined by whether or not we're loved.

There are eleven hundred boys in this school and plenty of them look all right, they sound all right. They buzz around the hallways, indistinct, while girls gaze and pine and lust after them.

Those girls are lucky, and sometimes I even want to tell them that, ink it on the wall in blood or sear it into the latex paint. They have a place to be honest.

In trigonometry, I open my notebook. In the margin, in pencil, I write:

He is the lighthouse; everyone else is just boats.

MARSHALL
Damage

I stop waiting. I rake the leaves, do the dishes and the grocery shopping. Laundry, homework, disappearing act. Whatever needs doing.

I don't sleep in the middle of the bed anymore on the chance Waverly might appear out of the dark and get in next to me. I wake myself up reaching for her. When I roll over, there's nothing there.

In the locker bay during passing periods, Ollie never asks why I don't go out back to smoke anymore. He seems strange lately, or like a stranger, but I can't tell which one of us is different. Sometimes it seems like we both are.

We're standing at our locker after lunch when the little freshman shuffles by and smiles at him.

Ollie smiles back, a small, offhand smile, and waves. Once, like it's no big deal.

"So you're friends with her now?"

He shakes his head. "I walked her home from the dance, is all."

"Are you *high*? I mean, you don't like her, right?" For a

question, it sounds more like an argument, and I elbow him harder than I mean to. "Do you *like* her?"

"Mars, she's a kid." He's looking down toward the line for the vending machines, where Little Ollie is panting around after some ninth-grade volleyball players in their microscopic uniforms. "I just wanted her to be okay."

I nod, but it's that slow, uncertain kind of nod. I don't know what makes Ollie the official chaperone of fourteen-year-old girls all of a sudden. I always figured that was me, wanting so badly to make sure everyone was okay. That I was the only one.

I just assumed he was different, somehow. Bored and over it, putting up with me when I was too daydreamy and weird for everybody else. I know it's not the truth. He just got ruined is all, the same as I did.

Once, in seventh grade, Jason Costello pegged him in the face with a basketball, which wasn't even really an event. Someone was *always* getting pegged in the face, usually if you were skinny or short or fat or bad at sports.

It wasn't like it hadn't happened before. Jason maybe hit him harder than usual, but for whatever reason, Ollie wound up with a gusher of a bloody nose.

Everyone would have stared anyway because of the blood, but the bad thing was that Ollie started crying. It was this basic rule of middle school that if someone messed with you, you were supposed to just take it like a psychopath. Only Ollie wasn't one.

The popular guys all started laughing at him, calling him a fag. Everyone else mostly stood around looking at the floor. The whole class, there in this big, wobbly circle that wasn't even really on purpose. And Ollie, standing in the middle, shaggy and skinny—we were both so fucking skinny—with his hands up to his face and blood running between his fingers and I knew I wasn't supposed to help him, but it was so much worse to stand and watch.

In middle school, you were supposed to pile on with everyone else when someone was weak. You were supposed to smash until you hit bone. What you were never supposed to do was step into the circle.

But I couldn't help it, because it was Ollie, who always sat with me on field trips even though I got carsick pretty much any time we had to be on the bus for more than half an hour. And because I knew he wasn't crying over how much it hurt. His mom had left three weeks ago and his dad had checked out so hard it was like he was a missing person even when he was in the room. Jason and the bloody nose and the basketball were just the last tiny cut.

So I stepped into the circle, because it was the only thing I knew how to do, and when we'd gone to the museum for social studies, Ollie had spent the whole ride talking to me about marmosets while I stared out the window and tried not to focus on the telephone poles. I stepped into the circle because it could have been me.

The whole time I was getting called a queer, standing there with my hand on his shoulder, handing him paper towels, I knew I was exactly where I was supposed to be.

I think now that somehow those things destroy us. That day in the gym made us meaner or worse, instead of helping us. We weren't even doing anything wrong.

I wonder suddenly if there's a part of Ollie that would still rather be the kid with the bloody nose, sobbing over how people treat each other, than Ollie stoned and bored and staring at the floor like the whole world can just fuck off.

"Hey," he says, hitting me with his elbow and pointing to something stuck in the side of my locker door. "What's that?"

I pull out a folded piece of paper, and for a second, I have this completely stupid idea that maybe it's from Waverly, but as soon as I open it, I recognize Autumn's writing. The note isn't a note, but a drawing of a girl with short, messy hair and huge vintage-looking eyes. Behind her, a shining gangster city looms Batman-style, like the cities Autumn used to draw for the stories I made up. At the top of the page is a movie marquee, inviting me to a party at her house, in honor of the Golden Age of Hollywood.

Across the bay, Waverly is standing in a little cluster with her friends, digging around in her book bag. I shove the invitation in my pocket.

I keep thinking about that first night in my room. How Waverly climbed into my bed, without a reason or an invitation, without thinking twice. Her hair was damp, like she'd just washed it, and smelled like flowers.

I hate wanting anything this much.

Next to me, Ollie sighs and knocks his shoulder against mine.

"You're inspecting Camdenmar again," he says. "If you keep trying to take her pants off with your eyes, one of these days, people are going to notice."

I nod but don't stop. I spend the rest of the passing period watching her across the linoleum. It's not so far. Eleven steps would get me there. It's barely a distance at all. And at the same time, it's so fucking far that I will never make it.

WAVERLY

The weather is frigid now. The week is long and gray and vacant.

I'm changing. I can feel it like a continental drift. My territories are shifting. If I just let go, I could stop being me, stop holding on so hard, guarding my borders like a country under siege.

I'm scared to disturb the balance, though—that delicate equilibrium. Marshall and I can only exist in the narrow spaces where I'm not me and he is not him.

So I do my homework. I focus on how to survive without cross-country. An earlier Waverly would have called life without motion impossible, but I'm finding the rhythm of it. I'm learning to exist without the numb, faceless miles— the daily expanse of parks and city blocks, until I'm too wrung out to feel my bones.

I spend my afternoons in the library or the student council room with Maribeth. In the evenings, I lounge on Autumn's bed while she makes plans and invitations for her Autumn-themed party. I don't mention Marshall to anyone. I don't look at him. I wish for him on every penny and star and eyelash.

This preternatural self-control doesn't last, though. It can't. On a foggy, drizzly Tuesday night, my resolve begins to weaken. I do homework until my eyes blur. Until I can't stand myself anymore. I've finished one problem set, two four-page papers, a Spanish handout, and there's nothing left. Since the dance, I've kept the candle far back in my desk drawer. Now, I sit with my hands tucked tight between my knees and try to ignore it, but it's like starving for something that's right in front of you. I might be made of wires, but I'm not made of stone.

It isn't even nine yet, but I turn out the light and get into bed.

The days are so much colder and night comes early now, but it's still strange to be sitting in the dark before the neighbors' lights go out. This is the earliest I've been in bed since I was seven, but the only place I want to be right now is the one where I get to be the person I am when I'm with Marshall.

With the candle lit, the little pool of wax scorching next to me in its glass dish, I force myself to lie still.

It's so hard to focus, though, to just dissolve. I feel made of amphetamines.

I keep my eyes shut anyway, yank hard on the power cord to my brain—count and count and count.

I get there in the end.

WAVERLY
10.

In Marshall's bedroom, the light's still on. He's sprawled on his bed with the covers wadded up at his feet and a textbook open on his chest.

He's not the boy he was when I met him, high and tripping and insensible in a bathtub on a school night. The floor is covered in what looks like an entire semester of American lit. The shaggy yellow dog is curled in the middle of it, watching me with its tail thumping fitfully.

As soon as Marshall looks up and sees me, he smiles and moves over, offering me a spot on the bed. I sit down on the floor instead, with my legs stuck out in front of me and my elbows locked. My feet hurt so much the nerves feel like someone's been working on them with a grater.

"What's wrong?" he says, like I've given him some kind of sign.

But I'm not brave enough tell him. The candle is barely even a solid thing anymore. It will not last the night. This is the last time I'll see him as the girl I don't know how to be in the daytime—my strange, secret self—and I didn't spend it on some existential emergency or special occasion. Just an ordinary weeknight, because I couldn't stand my own brain.

There are no words. Nothing is fine, nothing is okay. Without a way to bring me here, I'll go back to who I am when everyone's looking—Daytime Waverly, with a 4.0 and a stare like bulletproof glass. I'll be the girl with all the answers, bobbing along comfortably in the wake of Maribeth Whitman, and he'll still be the boy who said he loved me once. Said he *loves* me. What does that mean?

He doesn't even know me.

I flop sideways and rest my cheek on the dog's yellow back, smelling the warm, comfortable smell. Animal, and animal shampoo.

"What's wrong?" he says again, rolling onto his stomach, his hair hanging in his face and his mouth against the edge of the mattress.

"I'm off the meet roster for cross-country," I say. And even though it's true, it sounds like such a lie. "I messed up my feet and now I'm not allowed to train. It's just for the rest of the season." I press my face into the dog's fur, closing my eyes. "It's not that big of a deal."

I wait for Marshall to call me out, tell me to try again. He doesn't say anything. Instead, he leans over the edge of the mattress and rests his hand on the top of my head. After what feels like a full minute goes by and I don't move, he tugs at the collar of my pajama top. "Here, come here."

I give the dog a farewell pat and climb up next to Marshall, ready for him to come at me like a car crash, kiss me sloppily into oblivion.

Instead he puts his arms around me and hugs me hard.

His shoulder feels just right under my cheek and I close my eyes. I could lean against him and have that be all I need for the rest of the semester. The rest of the year. I could fall asleep here, settle in until spring. Hibernation sounds good. It sounds like a sweet, impossible dream.

He presses his mouth against my cheek and I nuzzle closer, savoring the scrape of his jaw. I love how his skin is rougher than it looks. I want to bite him as hard as I can, which is the literal embodiment of everything wrong with us. The last thing he needs is someone who wants to savage him.

He holds me tight, rocking me like something fragile. "What can I do?"

I force myself to relax my grip. I'm clinging to him like I need the consolation. Like I can't take care of myself. "Nothing. There's not anything."

"Lie down," he says. He says it like he knows what he's talking about.

I let him turn me facedown on the bed and kneel over me, running his hand up the back of my calf. The pain is deep, zinging through my heel and all the way along my arch. I gasp and press my face into the mattress.

"Does that hurt?"

"Yes," I whisper. "But keep doing it."

He moves carefully, touching the tender places, making the pain flare sharp and insistent. His fingers are precise, finding the spots where the muscle has started to twist in on itself. I lie facedown and let him do it. When he slides his thumb along my arch, tears gather in the corners of my eyes.

"You're like the little mermaid," he says softly.

I snort into the bed. *"Ariel?"*

"No, the real one. The one who kept dancing even though it hurt. How she never let it show. And everyone just thought she was all right."

"It was easy for her, though. I mean, wasn't she a mute?"

His hands are warm, cradling the length of my foot. "You kind of are too," he whispers.

I don't answer, just scrape my face against the sheet to get rid of the tears.

"I used to think about this," he says, kneading my arch with his thumbs, making tiny arrows shoot up my calf. "I used to dream about it."

"The moment I finally managed to half cripple myself through a combination of ill-fitting shoes and overzealous training? You should open a psychic hotline."

"No. I just mean I would wish for things."

I pull my foot away and roll onto my back. "Like what?"

He ducks his head. "It's embarrassing."

"Tell me anyway. I like embarrassing things."

"I know you do," he says. "Which is totally screwed up."

And I laugh, because it's better to hear him say that and know he means it than to hear anyone else in the world call me good and sweet and tenderhearted, and realize they don't know anything about me.

Marshall rests a hand on my ankle. "I always wanted to—not protect you? But just . . . take care of you." He smiles awkwardly, looking down. "It's okay if you laugh. I know how stupid that sounds. I didn't know you yet, is all."

I sit up and take his hand, spreading his fingers, holding

them in front of my face, studying them. "It's not stupid," I say, touching his palm and then each knuckle. "It's sweet."

When what I should have told him is, it's true.

"You're acting weird," he says. "Weirder than normal."

I close my eyes and roll away, burrowing into the bed, which is the best, most satisfying bed in the world. "Everything is terrible," I whisper, winding myself in his blankets.

For a second, Marshall doesn't say anything. Then he tugs gently on the hem of my pajama shirt. "Do you want to tell me about it?"

I sigh and put the pillow over my face. "What's to tell? I can't run, I can't sleep. I don't know what to do with my own *thoughts* most of the time. Every day is the most boring thing I've ever sat through. Oh, and I think I might actually hate my best friend, so there's that."

I say the last part fast, muffled by feathers. He just reaches over and takes the pillow away.

"How can you hate your friend?" he says. "That doesn't even make sense."

"It does, *kind* of. Just in a really dysfunctional way that's hard to explain."

"Try," he says, but he is so unguarded. So perfectly earnest. No matter how much he thinks he'll understand, he won't.

"Maribeth is just *mean*." I'm startled at how raw my voice sounds. "She's self-centered, and condescending, even when she's supposed to be nice or—or *helping*."

Marshall's watching me, shaking his head. I *need* him to see. My daytime life is made of all these tiny, ugly moments that render even the most pedestrian interactions vicious, and it will take the very worst parts to make him understand.

"Alyssa Barrity's mom died last year."

"Yeah, I remember."

"Well, Maribeth was a peer counselor that quarter, and she was assigned to Alyssa, and that's how I know Alyssa had sex with Anthony Dean."

Marshall is looking at me like I've just told him that Alyssa went to the store and bought nail polish and gum. "So?"

"So, it's supposed to be *confidential*. Anyway, Maribeth might have still . . . like, given her a pass on account of bereavement. But then Alyssa did it again with Nathan Schuster a couple weeks later."

Maribeth told everyone. But in this grave, tragic way, where it sounded like she was really worried, but the other meaning was clear. It was her way of saying, Alyssa Barrity is a dirty, dirty slut and she deserves to be ostracized.

Marshall is sitting with elbows on his knees, trying to get his face under control. "That's so shitty, though. It's not *Maribeth's* business what someone else does. And I mean, maybe Alyssa didn't even want to, maybe she was like numbing out—or just needing someone to *be* there with her."

"Yeah," I say. The spill wall means knowing the complicated sadness of people better than I ever have. "Yeah, maybe that's why."

The way he's watching me makes me feel guilty without knowing why. "Did you say those things about her too?"

"No, but I didn't do anything to stop it."

"That's messed up, though. I mean, that's really fucking cruel. Is that actually how girls *are*?"

"Marshall, it's how *people* are. I mean, are you telling me that guys belong to some kind of honorable brotherhood?"

He shakes his head. He's smiling, but not like anything is particularly wonderful. "No, just that when they're shitty, it's completely different shit."

I nod. It's strange to truly recognize that he has his own collection of painful memories and moments, beyond casual self-destruction and loving me. "Like what?"

"Just, things. I don't know how to explain it. They just remind you there's only one way you're really allowed to be." He closes his eyes and he's still smiling, but now it looks tired. "You know those really bloody, torturey movies, like *House of 1000 Corpses*?"

"Marshall, please." My custom figure of Captain Spaulding sits serenely on my shelf of horrors, just before Coffin Baby, just after Blade from *Puppet Master.*

"Okay, so there's this part where they're down in some underground lab with all these surgical tools and this guy is lying on a table, and he's all mangled and coughing up blood."

"And then Denise comes in and she's wearing that little Alice in Wonderland dress and the camera pans back to show how Jerry's leg is all mutilated and surgically altered?"

Marshall winces and makes a sound like *ughhh*. "Yeah, that part."

I'm laughing suddenly—not in a light, amused way, but breathless, covering my mouth with my hand.

"It's not *funny*," he says.

"No, I know—I know. I'm sorry. I've seen it a lot, is all."

He looks away, shaking his head. "Of course. Of course you have. It's probably a secret documentary of your life. Forget it."

I lie back, studying him. He looks so mortified, so truly embarrassed. "No, say what you were going to. I won't laugh anymore."

"It was on at Justin's one night, and when it got to that part, I started feeling *bad,* like I couldn't get enough air. I just needed to find someplace I could breathe."

I reach up and run my fingers down the side of his arm. His skin is prickling with goose bumps like the memory is a chilly one.

He pulls away, turning so he's practically talking into his own shoulder. "I got as far as the kitchen before I had to sit down. Justin—God, he's such a dick. He's, like, standing over me, pushing me with his foot and him and Hez are just laughing and laughing. I mean, Jesus, it was like a year ago and everybody *still* gives me shit about it."

I touch his forehead, the side of his face. "All of them? Even Ollie?"

He lets his knee knock against my arm, smiling his weird, painful smile. "No. Ollie never does."

"You're lucky, having a friend like him."

Marshall gazes down at me, and his face is gentle. "It's not luck, Waverly. I mean yeah, to find someone who really *gets* you, maybe that's luck, but if you treat people like they matter, they remember it."

I nod, hiding my face in the sheets so I won't have to tell him how hard that is, treating people like anything.

"Why are you friends with Maribeth?" he says, and his voice is so tender. Just so, so sorry.

"Because she understands me." Because Maribeth Whitman has always been there, ready to explain and to help, to look past the pleasing pastel mask I wear every day, and recognize the sharp-edged monster I am inside.

Marshall ducks under the sheet to lie next to me. "No she doesn't. The way you talk about her makes it sound like she treats you like a robot."

"Well, yeah."

"That's bullshit," he says. "That's not who you are."

He says it like he knows that for a fact, like he knows so much, and I lie very still, staring back at him.

"I'm not telling you who to be," he says. "I'm just saying that what Maribeth treats you like is not what you are. She doesn't see everything."

"And you do?"

He laughs, shaking his head. "No—no one does. But at least I fucking *know* that."

He reaches for me, pulling me closer.

"You don't have to have lots of friends," he says. "As long as the ones you do have are good."

If I had to pick only a few, the candidates would be him and Autumn. That's it. There's no one else. The knowledge leaves me lonely and strangely content at the same time.

"You're cold," he says, running his hand down my arm.

"I'm always cold."

He rolls out of bed. I want to grab him and pull him back to me, but he crosses the room and tugs his Pink Floyd hoodie off the back of the chair.

He bundles me into it, putting my hands through the sleeves, closing the front carefully and yanking the zipper up. Then he grabs me around the waist and pulls me down onto the mattress. Wish You Were Here.

"I think about you in class," he says. His mouth looks soft, like something I never knew I needed. "I think about kissing you. It makes the day go faster."

"Where do you kiss me?"

"Here." He bends so his mouth brushes my cheek, just lightly. "And here." He tugs the hoodie off my shoulder and kisses my neck, my bashfully lowered chin, my collarbone.

Every time he says another syllable, his breath hits my skin, making tiny shivers ripple up my back. My heart is beating so hard it seems to fill the room. I think I'll choke on the sonic vibration.

He lays me back, leaning over me on his hands, staring into my face until I'm so claustrophobic I have to look away.

With my face to the wall, I squeeze my eyes closed and make fists. "Are you trying to tell me that you want to fuck me?"

He takes my chin and turns me back to look at him. "No."

"So, you're saying you *don't* want to fuck me."

With his hands braced on either side of my head, he

leans closer, looking down at me. "I want to have sex with you."

"Right now?"

"Someday."

"Because all seventeen-year-old boys are completely obsessed with sex?"

"Because I *like* you," he says. "Because that's how much I like you."

I start to twist away, but he stops me, holding my face in his hands before he lets me pull free and hide my eyes against his shoulder.

"How can you do that?" I whisper.

"Do what?"

"Just *say* things—say how you feel."

He shrugs. "I don't know. I guess I figure I'm going to regret it either way. Might as well."

"That is the saddest thing I've ever heard."

He laughs softly in my hair. "Maybe. But it's better than not being able to say it at all. Waverly, you're the most important thing that's ever happened to me."

I smile against his neck. "I'm not a thing."

He pulls the sheet over us, making a tent. The light from the lamp on his desk is buttery and warm, glowing through the sheet like a halo.

I reach for him, grabbing him by the back of his neck. Kissing Marshall Holt is the highlight of my life.

I let my hand drift against his stomach, feeling the muscles twitch and flutter at my touch. The pads of my fingers skimming his hip bone, his bare chest, the perfect, ghostly line of his rib cage. My pulse, which used to limit itself so unimaginatively to my major arteries, is everywhere now, banging frantically in my entire body, but its changing epicenter is wherever his mouth lands, lighting me from within. It's the only thing that keeps me from caring that I can no longer tell the difference between awake and asleep.

•

The candle is gone—nothing but a lump of scorched wax in a cheap glass dish, wickless now, burned oily black on top.

I sit on the edge of the bed in my pajamas, holding the remains, and even when my dad pokes his head in to warn me I'm going to be late for school, I can't seem to make myself move. I sit with my aching feet tucked under me, the dish in my hands, thinking how far the distance is between my standard, ordinary day, and anything that matters.

•

The world is different now, but on the surface, nothing's changed.

I try, with varying degrees of success, not to think about him. Not to even think his name. I keep remembering at the most arbitrary times that once he was mine, if only in the barest sense.

We skipped all the things that normal people share— the shows we watch, the songs we like or hate. Favorite colors, numbers, foods, a hundred getting-to-know-yous that never happened. Instead, the things I know about him are true in a way I can't explain. They are a kind of closeness I never thought I'd have with anyone.

I want to travel back in time—back to when I was young enough to think the real world was just something I had to sit through until I could be alone. Back to when my dreams felt like the realest thing about me.

Being alone isn't enough anymore.

At school, I watch him in the halls. He and Ollie are so effortless together, always knocking into each other, bumping shoulders.

He knows how to be touchable, how to let people near him. In the daylight, I can barely stand to breathe other people's air. When Maribeth reaches over to fix my hair, I have to dig my nails into my hand to keep from twisting away.

•

It's chilly out, and gray. I can't remember if it's Wednesday, Thursday, Friday. Time is elastic and hard to understand.

I refer to my calendar every two seconds. Forget what it said. Look again. One morning, I came to school and it seemed like every third girl was dressed as a cat. It took me most of first period to figure out that I wasn't dreaming or hallucinating. It was just Halloween.

Wednesday, Thursday, Friday? It can't be Saturday, because I'm in English class. We're discussing the evolution of the mystery story, or at least, Mr. Hoffmeyer is. I'm drawing torture devices in my notebook, propping my head up with my hand.

Hoffmeyer has just started making bullet points about gothic imagery when I glance up in time to see Marshall pass the long windows that look out into the language arts hall.

There's a tight look around his eyes, and he doesn't turn toward the bathrooms or the drinking fountain, cafeteria, library, counseling office. He chooses the other direction, toward the door to the back parking lot.

I want to get up and run after him. I want to remind myself that the world doesn't work that way. I don't have any contingency plan for this. I don't have any right to him.

But I remember how he touched me, his hands cradling my feet, finding the places where they hurt. He didn't ask or hesitate or waste time wondering if he had a right to. He was ready to do whatever it took to make me feel better, because I needed help, even if I wouldn't say so. I close my notebook and raise my hand.

"Waverly, thank you," says Mr. Hoffmeyer, pointing energetically. "Do you want to tell us which early work touched off Poe's short-story career?"

"No, I'd like to be excused."

As soon as I step through the doors, the wind is ferocious. Marshall is already halfway across the practice fields, receding purposefully into the distance toward the baseball diamond.

I stand on the steps of the west entrance, watching. If he turns or glances back, he'll see me here. But he doesn't.

His silhouette is dark against the sky, getting smaller.

The scenario is already playing out in my head—the sequence of events if I were to follow him, crunching out toward the bleachers across the dead lawn. Crossing the baseball diamond, then sinking down next to him on the bench in the dugout, feeling the cold cement, realizing too late that I should have brought a jacket.

It's not hard to imagine us there. When I blink against the bright, chilly daylight, I can already picture it. The two of us hunched close together on the bench, my hand in his, foreheads nearly touching. Without the candle, grimy, secret places like the dugout are the only way to be *us* now, but I'm already cataloging all the ways it wouldn't be the same. Instead, I'd be the person I was behind the bleachers, not the one he actually needs. That cold, unyielding girl, hazardous and distant, polished to a high gleam. Always saying the worst, most thoughtless things.

He'd just be the place that I escape to.

What we had is over. For the time it lasted, we were perfect how we were, but it's done. I'm not going to ruin the memory by polluting it with who I am the rest of the time.

Marshall is gone now, disappeared into the dugout.

After a long time, when my ears are windburned and my fingers freezing, I turn and go back inside, where the halls smell like floor cleaner and the heat is on full blast.

I should go to class, learn my literary symbolism. Tend my notes like everything is normal.

Instead, I flatten down my windblown hair and head for the west hall bathroom, because there, at least I understand myself—my place in the world—and when the confessions are anonymous, every voice looks just like every other.

Standing in front of the spill wall, I count up the number-one-fan secrets—all the different brands of admiration, aspiration, envy.

I admire: this athlete, rock star, movie star, porn star, fashion icon, fictional character.

I want to be: Taylor Swift, Bella Swan, Katniss Everdeen, Rihanna.

The names are different, but I want these things too. I want to be William Shakespeare and Galileo and Robert

Frost. I want to be Sappho. I want to be Jane Austen. I want to be Holden Caulfield and Marilyn Monroe and Joan of Arc. I'm sad to think they came before me in history, they made their mark without me. But they were there. They happened.

I close my eyes and rest my cheek against the wall. It's cool, lumpy with so many layers of paint. I imagine the snarl of confessions transferred in reverse, leaking onto my skin, printed on my face for everyone to see. They're waiting for a connection, intimate contact with whatever it is they find remarkable. Beautiful.

I write the answer with my forehead pressed against the wall, clutching the pen like a torch or a sword, like I will never let it go:

Your gods don't know you exist.
And that's okay.

MARSHALL
Surrender

In the guidance center, I spend way too long hovering in the doorway. My hands are freezing.

The Trunchbull's at her desk, flipping through a course catalog for one of the state schools. Finally, she looks up and raises her eyebrows. "I don't remember getting a performance alert for you, having the office send you three separate reminders, and then pulling up your schedule so I can tell your homeroom teacher to nag you every day until you made an appointment."

"Yeah. Sorry." I can't tell if I'm apologizing for always making things hard, or just for being here now when I don't have an appointment and she's probably busy anyway.

I could still leave. I don't have to be here or talk to her. I don't have to say anything at all. I just spent forty-five minutes shivering in the dugout, trying to figure out how to breathe, which is shitty, but totally familiar. I've done it before. I could just keep doing that.

Then she closes her catalog. "Better come in and tell me what's on your mind."

I slouch into her office and sit down. I don't know what to say.

This hopeless feeling has been sitting in me for so long I've almost gotten used to it. The words for it are impossible, like trying to explain your own heartbeat.

On the corner of her desk, there's a bunch of applications for the peer counselor program and I stare at them. The forms are green half sheets, cut crooked, with a bad cartoon of the Henry Morgan bobcat on them. It's wearing a letter jacket and grinning like a total asshole.

There are vintage superhero postcards lined up against Trunch's window and her cork board is covered with clippings about rescue pit bulls that got adopted and photos of abandoned buildings filled with plants and flowers. I can't tell if it's real, or if she just puts them up to make people like me feel like we belong here. I stare at all the green, growing up through rotting floors and covering the cracks.

Trunch scoots closer to the desk. "Marshall," she says, "I don't know exactly what's going on with you right now, but I can tell you one thing. Toughing it out is not a strategy."

She sounds so much like Ollie it's ridiculous—this raspy, cranky lady who's older than my parents and has a laugh like gravel going down a slide.

I know I'm supposed to be better, or at least figure out a way to keep the weak parts from showing. There's an ache in my chest. My throat hurts, and for a minute, I just sit there, trying to get it under control.

"Okay, fine," she says. "How about this? Theresa Denning came to see me. She seemed to think you might be going through a rough patch." Awkward pause. "I gave your mom a call."

This conversation is the last thing I want. I hold my breath and clench my jaw.

Her voice is softer now, but her face doesn't change. "We talked about your dad."

"Yeah, well, things have been like that for a while. I'm over it. It's not a big deal."

"You could still talk about it if you want."

But I don't even know where to start. Talk about what? About how we don't understand anything about each other? About the way he's never been close to a good father *ever,* not even when I was little? About the fact that for one magical week six months ago, they almost got divorced and their kids were ready to throw them a party?

I can feel every fiber in the carpet under my shoes, the pressure of my clothes on my skin, the dust particles in the air. "What am I supposed to say?"

"Whatever you feel like."

It sounds so simple, but the words won't come. There's all this chaos and noise I carry around with me every day. I could talk to Ollie, but I don't. I did talk to Waverly, but that's kind of like talking to a ghost. The weight inside me just keeps getting worse. Something has to change.

I take a breath, staring at the floor with my chin down and my hands fidgeting, tearing an add/drop form into little strips. I start, because if I don't, then everything just stays the same.

When I make it to the end, Trunch sits there with her hands folded and doesn't say anything.

"Something's wrong with me, right?"

She scoots forward in her chair, her elbows planted on the desk. "How do you mean?"

"Just, all of it. How messed up and sad I get. Not being able to breathe. Like, doesn't this mean I'm supposed to be in counseling or something?"

She tilts her head and gives me the kind of shrug that says *yes, Holt, probably.* "It might help."

"But you're not telling me I have to."

"Marshall, I know you. I know if I push, you won't argue. You'll just disappear." She says it quietly, and for a second, she looks so unbelievably sorry. "I'd rather have you here in my office every day until graduation than tell you to go figure it out and then watch you slide out of sight."

Her gaze is so heavy I can hardly stand it. For once in my life, Waverly's restlessness makes sense, pacing around my room like she needs to climb out of her own skin. I want to get away from my body, to peel off everything that's touching me. Even the weight of the air is too much.

Trunch is still looking at me, kind and steady. "I'm here every day until at least four."

I'm not going to waste her time. I'm not. But it makes me feel better knowing I could.

When I take a flyer off the peer counselor pile and fold it carefully in half, she raises her eyebrows, but doesn't comment or tell me to put it back.

I tuck it in my pocket and look away. "It's not for me."

She pushes back her chair and walks me to the door. "If it was, though? That wouldn't be the worst idea I've ever heard."

WAVERLY

Morning is bright and wickedly cold.

I'd go hide out in the athletics wing, except the locker room isn't really my home anymore. The cafeteria feels almost entirely imaginary.

I need a donut. Now. I need the refined carbohydrates and the sugar and the illusion that I'm doing something rational and normal. At the café cart, I buy myself a custard-filled bismarck and a coffee laced with two shots of espresso.

Then I wind my way over to the tables by the window, where Maribeth is perched demurely on the edge of her chair with her activities binder out, going over her list of action items for the food drive. Her hair catches the weak November sunlight in perfect soft focus. She looks like a Hallmark angel.

Kendry is cozied up next to her, much closer than I ever sit to anyone if I can help it. She's wearing a plain gray blouse that must be new.

When they see me coming, Kendry and Palmer both sit very straight, like they've just been caught whispering, but Maribeth only smiles, waving me over. When she makes room, though, it's Palmer's backpack she pushes out of the way and not her own.

"Waverly, thank God. I need you to look at these donation numbers for the food drive and see if they make sense. Also, the events calendar is a disaster and we need to organize groups for door-to-door. And are we still on for Autumn's party Friday or what?"

I nod, standing over the table. She says it like Autumn has never offended her, usurped her boy. Been the lurid epicenter of Kroger-janitor rumors that may or may not have originated solely with Maribeth. I know I should sit down, but I can't figure out how, when Kendry is already in my spot.

"Are you going to just keep standing there?" Kendry says. "You look deranged."

There's a sharp, insistent bell ringing someplace faraway. It echoes in my ears, clanging, clanging. I set down my coffee, trying to figure out what's wrong with Kendry's hair and why she sounds like someone slipped her five or six valium. Ordinarily, she does not use the word *deranged*.

"And you look like someone's insecure mom," I say, plunking down my books and sinking into the empty chair. It comes out sounding harsher than I mean it to.

She scowls but doesn't answer. She's got on some strange, nude lip gloss, which doesn't make sense. Her coloring is way too warm.

"Oh, God," says Palmer, staring at my donut. "Are you really going to eat that? Do you have any idea how much saturated fat is in that?"

I pick up the donut between my thumb and forefinger

and study it. "Yes, I'm going to eat this." Then I take a big, savage bite. I chew slowly, without looking at her.

She sighs, dropping her chin into her hand. "That's so unfair. I guess if I had your skeleton genes, though, I wouldn't worry either."

I don't say anything. I continue to eat my donut.

All three of them are looking at me now. Belatedly, I realize that I've missed a crucial cue. Here's where I commiserate, cite my frantic metabolism, say something suitably self-deprecating, complain about my nonexistent chest or my bony knees.

They're all sitting there, waiting for me to deride myself, to show some solidarity, Waverly.

"You don't have to do that," I say.

Kendry makes a bored, dismissive noise, rolling her eyes. "Do *what*?"

"Be so mean about herself. She doesn't have to keep saying those things just because someone fucking *made up* this arbitrary idea of what's attractive or—or *good* before we even got here."

And I know that's not true. She *does* have to, because the penalty for not doing it is judgment, rejection. Maybe even banishment.

But I wish it weren't.

I turn to Palmer, resisting the urge to grab her arm and squeeze until she hears me. "Saying that shit doesn't help anything, okay? It's destructive and pointless, and it's just going to make you feel worse."

This is the longest, most truthful thing I've said to

anyone in days. I sink back in my chair, trying to convince my fingers to stop mashing the donut.

"God," Kendry says. "Calm yourself. It's not like she's *hurting* anything."

"Did you even listen to any of the words I just said? It's *exactly* like that."

Kendry gives me that bland, unfocused look again. Her face is slack, mouth slightly ajar, and suddenly it clicks. Straight hair, boring blouse, colorless makeup. She's not *trying* to sound incapacitated or like she has a concussion. She's trying to sound like someone who's simply too far above it to be bothered with vocal inflection.

She's trying to sound like me.

For the last three years—maybe longer—I've been defined by the path of my orbit within our tiny solar system. Not the gorgeous, molten sun, but an icy planet, stark and miraculous. My lack of habitability has never mattered. Despite my noxious atmosphere and frozen seas, I've always been Maribeth's clear favorite.

I know I should assert my supremacy, put Kendry in her place, but the only thing going through my head is, *This? Really? Is this what I look like to you?*

The donut tastes like empty calories and heaven. I stare out the window at the sky and the gently aging housing development across the street. The parking lot looks like a traffic report, gridlock that goes on for miles.

What is the point? Autumn asked me once.

And here's the thing. I have absolutely no idea.

WAVERLY

Maribeth picks me up for the party at nine in her tidy, perky Civic. Even the upholstery smells wholesome, like vanilla air freshener.

"We need to talk," she says without looking at me.

Her voice is businesslike and I brace myself.

The evening is chilly and wet. She's going to ask why I've been so remote. So secretive. So increasingly incomprehensible. Why I spent the afternoon at Autumn's last Tuesday, instead of in the library with her.

She takes a deep breath, keeping both hands responsibly on the wheel. "You have to figure out what's going on with you and CJ. You're completely leading him on and I don't think it's fair."

And every excuse and explanation dies on my lips. I have no idea how to tell her that on any given day, CJ Borsen is the absolute last thing I think about.

At Autumn's house, the party is in full swing. Her living room is packed with two-thirds of the junior class.

People will usually show up anywhere if there's alcohol involved, but even by the standards of free liquor, the turnout is impressive. I dig around in a plastic cooler for a beer and try not to make eye contact with CJ, who is already hovering intently. Maribeth must have promised him she'd take care of me. Just one of her many services—the efficient and professional handling of Waverly Camdenmar.

He finally corners me in the living room beside a giant rubber plant that is either real or fake. I have an overwhelming impulse to touch it.

"Hey," he says.

"Hey," I say, running my fingers over the leaves.

"So, I hear you may not actually like me." His voice is confusingly cheerful, like he's going out of his way to be bluff and hearty. Or maybe he always sounds that way and I just never noticed.

"Of course I do. You're not Jeffrey Dahmer." The plant feels cool and slick. I still have no idea whether or not it's real.

He shakes his head. "You don't like me the way I *want* you to."

The sentiment is accurate, but mysterious. No one ever likes us the way we want them to.

"I'm sorry." It feels slightly dishonest, but I say it anyway. I owe him that much.

He nods, watching like he still expects something else—like I could conceivably give him more.

I look away and drink my beer. "I guess I wasn't really in the market for a boyfriend. I should have been clearer about that. I'm sorry."

"It's okay," he says. He even looks like he means it. "It's my fault too. I think I had this imaginary version of you in my head. And you're just . . . you're not like I thought you'd be."

I gaze up at him, trying not to squint. Every version of me is imaginary.

"I guess I thought you'd have a wild streak or some kind of secret bad-girl thing or something." He smiles like he wants to shrug. "But you're pretty much exactly how you look."

In a way, it's a compliment. An affirmation. It supports everything I've worked so hard to cultivate. And still, something in my chest just sinks and sinks.

It's not as though I imagined this going differently. His assessment conjures up the things I write in the margins every day. All these scraps of stifled, pent-up wisdom. *Girl with dark hair behaves herself.*

Now he's talking about what a good rapport we have and always staying friends, like our friendship is profound or valuable. Like it ever actually existed.

I keep nodding, slowly, thoughtfully. I sip my beer, remembering the outrageous lie that I wrote next to the flagpole problem in my trig notes, just this afternoon.

Girl cut from marble needs no one, when it should have said, *I have been so lonely for so long that I have almost stopped breathing.*

MARSHALL
Implosion

For the longest time, I thought Waverly was somehow better than me. Smart and strong and perfect—this superhuman creature I'd never be. Now I think that maybe she's just different.

It never seemed weird before, running so long the skin peels off your feet, but that's pretty grim when you actually think about it. Concerning. Like maybe I'm not the only one who doesn't know where to put my feelings.

School is okay. I don't go to see Trunch every day, but I go. It's just nice—having a place where everything shuts up for a while. Better than the dugout in November, at least.

She doesn't talk much, mostly sits and listens while I ramble at my shoes. The best times are when she has a lot of paperwork, because then she just lets me hang out in the corner and I don't have to talk either.

On Friday, I sit with my chair tipped back and my feet on the radiator. "My brother's coming over for dinner."

"Are you looking forward to that?"

I don't know what to say.

All semester, all I wanted was for him to share this.

Now that he's finally going to, I want to start smashing things. No one talks about the way he's spent the last four months pretending our parents don't exist. They just keep going through the motions and fucking each other up and acting like it doesn't matter. Justin has never once tried to be part of it, and now suddenly he gets to just show up and everyone acts so grateful, like he's the good son?

When I tried to talk to Annie about it, she just shrugged. "It's *dinner*. It's not a big deal."

"So that means we have to just act like everything's so great and perfect? Oh, wait, I remember—whenever things get stupid around here, you get to *leave*!"

We were in the kitchen. I was getting myself breakfast while she put away the dishes, and she slammed the cupboard so hard the glasses rattled. "Leave? Do you think, if things were different, that I wouldn't be halfway across the fucking *continent* right now? But this is the situation, Marshall. This is *it*. We might as well get used to it."

Then she went back to sorting forks and I stared into the cupboard, trying to decide between shredded wheat and cornflakes like there was even an answer.

No matter how hard I try, I can't figure out how to make myself be like her. She rolls her eyes or tells them all to knock it off, then goes on with her life like nothing happened. And I don't *want* to be like Justin, hard and disgusted and over it. All I want is for things to actually get better.

Trunch always says the same thing. *Your family is your family, but they're not your responsibility.*

That's easier to agree with than it is to believe, though.

By the time I get outside, it's starting to drizzle. Ollie's waiting for me by the bus stop, smoking and staring at the sky. "I was starting to think maybe you ditched me," he says, stubbing out the cigarette and dropping it in his shirt pocket.

He hasn't mentioned it, but since I started quitting he tries not to do it in front of me, like he doesn't want to make it any harder.

I shove my hands in my coat. Autumn's party flyer is still there, crumpled up with the shocking-green peer counselor form from Trunch's office.

The sky is so low and wet it's almost on top of us. Ollie trudges along next to me with his coat collar up and his head down. We're almost across the parking lot when I stop.

"What?" he says, squinting at me through the misty drizzle.

I don't say anything, just offer him the form.

He looks at me like I've just handed him a loaded gun or a hedgehog. Like I have lost my mind. "What the fuck is this?"

The form is crumpled and kind of linty, and maybe I don't know how to be like Justin, but I know how to actually look at people. I know my best friend, even if the person he is isn't the one he wants to be.

No matter what, Ollie's always just been there for me, as much as I would let him. He cares so much about what's fair and right. He thinks the feelings of little freshman girls are maybe actually important, and if Maribeth fucking Whitman can do it, then the office ladies should be falling all over themselves for someone like him.

"Just read it," I say, and leave out the part about him being basically the best person I have ever met.

He's watching me. Not the usual bored stare, but very careful, like I might be making fun of him. "Are you serious right now? You are *not* serious."

I shrug and throw my arm over his shoulders, lean into him, pull him close. "It's who you are anyway. They just made a job for it."

For Justin's stupid special dinner, my mom makes fried chicken because it's his favorite. The scene in the kitchen is bad. All the raw, oozing joints and the shaking, browning, spattering.

She talks to herself the whole time, reading recipes aloud, hoping that the roads are good, that they won't ice over. Outside, it's raining.

It's familiar and awful eating with Justin. He takes over the table like he never left, all elbows and arms, and everyone else just acts so bright and happy, like he never spent the last four months avoiding us. Like we should be so grateful that he's sitting here now.

"What's new at the shop?" my dad says while my mom hands out plates. He sounds way too interested in oil changes, and that's how I know it's not a real question. "Seems like you've been pretty busy."

My mom just smiles weakly and scoops more corn onto my plate while I think about what it means to be in someone's arms.

In someone's arms.

Before Waverly, I never thought about it much. There was only ever my tongue in someone's mouth. Only my leg hooked over, my hand sliding under. In someone's arms, there is you. You're there in the shelter of them—safe, inside. Everything else . . . is not.

"I'm just saying," my dad says in a voice that implies he is not *just* saying anything. "Maybe you should see about cutting back your hours, if it's so demanding."

Justin stares at him across the table. Then he leans forward and slams his hands down on his placemat. "You want to turn this into some passive-aggressive bullshit? Great! I'm not your problem anymore, and how I fucking live my life is none of your business."

"Says the freeloading slacker."

They're both red in the face, both edging toward explosion, and Justin has always been the loud one, the angry one. Now, though, he keeps both hands flat on the table and closes his eyes like he might be counting.

My dad is building up to something, getting good and mean. "Isn't this shit exactly *like* you! Acting like you're so goddamn busy, or maybe just too good to waste your time on us. Not so wonderful when you were flunking out of trade school. Not when you were asking me to drop four thousand dollars on some HVAC certificate that never materialized."

The shot is so cheap that I feel it in my gut. We all know school has never been easy for Justin, not even when we were little. And still, maybe he would have picked something to get good at if our dad wasn't always up his ass about picking something.

"I don't have to sit here for this," Justin says. His voice is flat, horribly even.

I'm so sure that in a second, we'll be treated to the version I know. The Justin who's always been a junior copy of our dad. He's going to get nasty, get cruel or sarcastic. He's going to break something.

Instead, without saying anything, he shoves back his chair. He looks from me to Annie—this hard, complicated look, like *we're* somehow the ones letting him down. Then he walks out of the kitchen and out of the house.

We hear his car start up, go screeching down the driveway, and then it gets quiet. Out the window, it's still raining.

I sit and wait for everyone to sigh in relief, like now we can stop playing this ugly *Leave It to Beaver* game and go back to our stupid, screwed-up lives. I'll finish the creamed corn, put my plate in the sink, go over to Autumn's and get numb. Or maybe not—maybe I'll just skip it. I'll stop by Ollie's instead, and we'll drive around and listen to the radio and be really careful not to talk about why I never let him come over anymore.

Annie will lock herself in her room, or meet some friends for study group. We'll escape into the little secret hideouts that we made, and leave the two of them to cry and shout and fuck each other up some more.

I sit with my head down and wait for someone to act like anything at all has happened. The problem, though, is that they can't. That would make it real. We'd have to admit that all the chaos and the noise is just this thing we do. We need it, because if no one's yelling or crying, then there's nothing left to hold on to.

We all sit there, busy with our forks, like it's not sickening to eat this way. I shove a gooey lump of scalloped potatoes around on my plate, whisper *"Razor blade."*

My dad is going in for another dinner roll, but he freezes midreach. "Something on your mind, Marshall?"

"No," I say, trying to look as blank as he does.

Waverly, wrapped around me like she could shield me with her body.

At the other end of the table, my mom is concentrating on her salad. Her eyes are red and shiny the way they get, but she's acting like everything is totally, stupidly fine.

My dad's still watching like he can see through me, peel back the layers between me and him and start digging around in my bones. He looks so disgusted and I can already tell we're going to do the thing—that thing where he tells me I'm pathetic. That at least Justin stands up for himself or knows how to act like a man.

"Then you'd better adjust your attitude, because right now, it looks like you've got something you want to say."

I know he's baiting me, still jonesing for the explosion that never happened. The only thing that can shut him up now is a fight.

"Please." There's a knot in my throat, but my voice isn't shaking. "Please just stop."

"Excuse me?"

I put down my fork and look up. "Stop acting like we're the ones doing this to you. Stop pretending you ever once acted like you could stand to be in the same room with any of us, or like Annie somehow owes it to the goddamn family to put her life on hold. That's not what this is."

He stares hard at me, but doesn't answer. He might be all about the sneering and the shouting, but when it comes to saying how he *really* feels, my dad would always rather say nothing.

"No one has a problem here but you," I say. "We're just trying to get through this, the same as you. So quit acting like we're some kind of huge pain in your ass, because we're not the ones making your life shitty."

I feel dizzy, almost. Out of breath, even though I haven't moved from the table. My blood has turned to acid, flooding my body. At the same time, I can hardly feel my hands.

He's staring back at me, brutal and cold, and under that, hurt.

"You don't deserve this," I say. "It sucks, and it's not fair. But we don't deserve it either."

For a second I think he might hit me, even though he hasn't even spanked me since I was a little kid. His face is red. His hands are clenched in fists.

"So just *stop*," I say, and this time I don't say please.

My mom puts her head down on her arms and starts to cry like someone just died, but I don't move.

Suddenly, I have a horrible feeling that I'm saying the thing everyone's secretly been thinking. That me and Annie and my mom, and even Justin, became *We* five or ten years ago, maybe from the beginning, and on the other side, there's just him and no one else.

"Give me the car keys," I say to Annie without looking at her.

My mom looks up, wet-faced. "Where are you going?"

I shake my head, still looking at my dad. "Away."

I don't say that I'm sorry for this, or tell him that I hate it, that I don't even want to be saying it—there's really no way to make peace now. He's the one who set the terms.

It's him or us, and now that I'm actually honest, I realize I've known that for years. He hasn't left any of us a choice.

WAVERLY

The party is never, ever going to end.

After an interminable debate with Maribeth over whether or not I've ruined everything by neglecting to give my heart to CJ, I escape into the hall, and then the aggressively outdated dining area, milling around with everyone else, bumping from room to room. This is where I live now.

Autumn has outdone herself when it comes to homemade movie posters and colored lights, but everything else is just like any other party.

The beer tastes thin and bitter. It's cold, though, and that's appropriate and fitting, because I am cold. I drink it fast, like penance, and go get another.

Time is stretched. It's relative—a perceptual miracle. I've never liked the dumb, despondent haze of being drunk, but I love how the minutes pass in quick, untethered jerks. I wonder if Einstein ever had occasion to notice, if he devoted any calculation or causal hypothesis to the temporal properties of beer.

Autumn is camped out in the kitchen, sitting on the

counter by the stove, swinging her feet and drinking something offensively blue and fittingly unidentifiable through a
twisty straw.

"Waverly!" she screams in mock delight. She's wearing
a beaded dress and combat boots. She looks beautiful. Her
wide-eyed rapture is half ironic and half because she is actually that glad to see me. "I have a present for you!"

My blood alcohol level is telling me now that sure, I'll
do this. I'll flirt and smile and act coy and careless and ef-
fervescent like everyone else. I lean against the stove and
raise my beer can. "Is it a pony?"

Autumn shakes her head, twirling the twisty straw
between her fingers and smiling wickedly. Her teeth are
stained a pale, venomous blue. "It's better. Come on, I put
it in my mom's office for safekeeping."

She leads me through the house, thundering like a god-
dess in her black boots. Her hand fits neatly in mine, her
way of saying without saying that we are together in this,
whatever this is. She drags me along, pulling me close, but
sends me down the last darkened hall alone—a scene befit-
ting a horror movie.

I shuffle toward the office, wondering what she could
possibly have put aside for me. A homemade Hadron col-
lider, complete with hand-stenciled electromagnets and
glitter-covered compressors. The preserved skin of some
obscure eldritch horror. I can wear it as a costume—make
my surface match my inside.

I push the door open and stop.

Marshall Holt is standing under a confusing piece of

contemporary art, with his shaggy hair and his slacker hoodie and his deep, uncomplicated wanting. My whole body feels warm.

"Waverly," he says. That's all. Just three aching syllables.

My heart starts beating faster before I even reach him. He looks immaculate and defenseless against the statement painting—three circles and a huge smudgy triangle. This is Autumn's present to me. The wish I'd blow out birthday candles for. "What are you doing here?"

He doesn't answer, just offers me a piece of heavy paper. It's a pencil drawing of Audrey Hepburn, backed by a fantastical city, overgrown with stylized art deco vines like the ones that Autumn drew coursing down my arm. In the middle, directly below Audrey's pearl-wrapped throat, it says:

Merry Christmas, Marshall Holt

"This is bad," I whisper and as soon as I say it, I know that it's the truth.

His eyes are wary, terribly unsure. "What is?"

But for a second, I can only shake my head. The truth is that I'm dangerous. The brutal sum of everything that made it so impossible to be gentle with him behind the bleachers or follow him to the dugout.

Every way I break it down, failure is inevitable. The limited amount I have to give won't be enough. I'll disappoint, be found insufficient. And when I finally ruin the last vestiges of what I have with him? Then I'll just have nothing.

"This. *This* is bad. We can't be here, Marshall. *I* can't."

"Hey, I'm sorry," he says, taking back the invitation,

shoving it in his pocket. "I just—I was having a bad night. You haven't been around at all and I really wanted to see you."

"And then what?" I say, holding perfectly still. The need to reach for him is fierce, and I am terrified to touch anything for fear that it will break.

"I don't know," he says. "Go somewhere, do anything you want. Coffee, the park, the goddamn *grocery* store. I'll drive you around Fullerton Heights to look at bulldozers or abandoned warehouses, I'll take you to see one of your psychopathic splatter flicks."

I look away and squeeze my beer can hard enough to make dents. My heart is slowing down again. "No you won't."

He shakes his head. "Don't tell me what I'd do. You know I'll do whatever you want."

"*Shouldn't,* I mean. You'd hate it. You shouldn't do things you hate just because it's what I like."

My voice is empty. Sad. I think that I have never in my life felt quite this sad. Instead, I've spent years feeling brittle and angry. All I wanted was to make out with Travis Bickle, Tyler Durden, someone who wanted to watch the world burn. Marshall is the complete opposite of a psychopath. We are not a symbiotic species.

He shrugs. "I'd take you anyway."

The gaping ache in him is tangible, there in his face and his voice, worse than ever. He needs me to be here in a real, honest way. A way that there's no going back from. Alcohol is humming in every capillary in my body. My skin feels tingly.

Magically, we've moved closer. I can already feel the magnetic charge between us. Too definite, too intimate. And still, I find myself crashing toward him. My hand is a discrete entity, floating a millimeter from his cheek.

Then, just as I reach for him, someone behind me lets out a harsh, incredulous breath.

We stop, caught in a rapidly decaying orbit, my hand already veering away.

Kendry is standing in the doorway. "Oh, wow," she says. Her shirt is hanging off one shoulder, and her weirdly nude lip gloss has migrated halfway across her face. "*Wow.*"

Marshall and I jerk apart like we've been electrocuted, and Kendry doubles over, covering her mouth with her hands so it's just her wide, gleeful eyes staring up at me. "Waverly, Jesus! I knew you didn't get out much, but god-*damn.*"

From out in the hall, people are already trickling in, crowding into the doorway, anxious to see what the commotion is about.

Kendry is shrieking now, howling with mirth. "Give her two beers and she'll throw herself at anyone!"

Everyone is poised, breathless—watching us, waiting for the next delicious thing. The sensation of their eyes is in my blood like ice.

Then, like a lecture slide changing over, Autumn is there, grabbing Kendry, turning her by the shoulders. "You're one to talk, Drunky McGlitter-Face."

Kendry gives a high-pitched little squeak, then hiccups once, but her laughter cuts off abruptly.

Beside me, Marshall is standing with his hand held out

like he wants to reach for me, but I don't reach back. My defenses are cracking now, too fragile to withstand any but the most quarantined environment.

Autumn's standing with her hand on Kendry's shoulder, waiting to see what I'll do, but it's Maribeth who breaks the silence. "Waverly."

She says it without inflection. Without articles or verbs. She doesn't have to say anything else.

I stare back at her, trying to remember that we are standing in front of fifteen people, all crowding up behind each other in the doorway. A wasteland opens inside me at the thought of being seen. Not my skin or my naked body, but the true, inarguable shape of me.

This is not supposed to happen, not in front of Maribeth, not to the boy with the quiet voice and the bleeding heart. Love is a sparking, arcing power surge that shorts out everything and I am shivering with it, desperate to get someplace where everyone will stop looking at me. Someplace safe.

"Take me home," I say, reaching for her.

The words are all wrong. Even as I say them, I understand that home is not a place I can get to from here. It's not my room, it's Marshall's, but to choose him now would mean giving up . . . everything. My seamless facade, all the stupid little conventions that define my life. Admitting weakness, admitting need.

It would mean giving up myself, and more than that, giving up Maribeth. There is no room in her carefully ordered world for a Waverly who longs to be more than a machine.

She reaches back clumsily, catching hold, tugging me closer. Her palm is warm and sweaty. The brass key on her necklace of romantic aspirations is long gone. She barely glances at Marshall. "Waverly, I'm in the middle of King's Cup. You should come play. Anyway, we're *way* too drunk."

I do a quick check, comparing the proposed state against my actual condition. I still have access to basic chemistry, and the formula for distance. I plow through all the presidents in order, conjugate *destruir,* run a diagnostic on Hamlet's third soliloquy. *Thus conscience does make cowards of us all.* I'm nearly paralyzed by the ferocity of my heartbeat.

Autumn is the one who breaks the silence, appearing in front of me with the dignity of an iceberg. "What is your problem? You're acting like a possessed person. Seriously, are you having a stroke, because I will call an ambulance!"

Marshall glances at her, shaking his head. "It's fine," he says, and the edge in his voice twists hard against something in my throat.

We stand in the office, arrayed in frank disorder, and through it all, Maribeth just looks at me. The shape of her mouth is studious. Inevitable. I jerk my hand away and head for the door, pushing hard at the crowd until they part. I walk out in a daze, propelled by the force of my own adrenaline.

Marshall catches me in the mudroom. I'm already struggling into my coat.

"Where are you going?"

"Home."

"I'm giving you a ride."

And part of me leaps at the promise of being alone in the dark with him. It's immediately overwritten by the panicked loop that circles in my brain. *I can't, I can't, I can't.* That voice is louder than any other thought, and I have finally found something that Waverly is simply incapable of.

I grab my purse and slam my empty can down on the bench, then start for the door.

"You can't walk home," he says behind me. His voice is low and even. "Your feet are too messed up. Just let me give you a ride."

I whip around, nearly toppling into the coat rack before I right myself. "Don't tell me what to do."

The look he gives me is inappropriately kind. "Go outside while I find my coat. I'll be there in two minutes."

I stand at the top of Autumn's driveway. I could start walking. I could leave, but I know I'll only get a block before Marshall catches up with me. He'll pull up next to me and say *get in,* and I'll do it, because he'll be right.

But even the introduction of stone-cold logic won't be enough to power off my red alert. The emergency siren has been activated, blaring in time to the warning light that flashes in my head. The hull is breached. All nonessential sectors are on lockdown. It's so hard to love someone when you have to do it in the open. The second you expose a thing to air, it has already begun to oxidize.

When Marshall comes out a minute later, head down, hands in his pockets, I'm still standing at the curb.

He leads the way to a rust-speckled car, unlocks the

passenger door, and I get in. The interior is shabby and smells like smoke and exhaust and him. He flops down in the driver's seat and turns the key. The engine sputters and coughs before it evens out.

"This isn't okay," he says.

I lean against the window, feeling drunk—but only in the tingling numbness of my lips, the pressure behind my eyes. The rest of me is immovable and stiff.

He takes a breath before he continues. "I'm serious, Waverly. I can't keep doing this. I want something that's an actual life."

"You have a life."

"No, what I have is you, and then a whole bunch of other shit."

It's hazardous, though, being that much to someone. When you're the yardstick that everything else is measured against, eventually, you just fail.

"Every morning, I wake up alone," he says.

"So do I."

He keeps going like I haven't said anything. "I wake up and everything I had before is gone."

I nod with my forehead pressed against the glass.

"No," he says. "You don't *have* that. I go to school every day and I watch you float around someplace I can never get to. You don't *lose* anything. You just go back to your real life and I'm not there."

I close my eyes and think of everything I have. The transcripts and the course times and the clubs, performances, activities, all worth so much on paper, the currency for a better, brighter life. They're quantifiable, measurable, valuable, but they're not *mine*. They're a collection of accomplishments designed to prove that I'm good and capable, but all they really mean is that I'm not a failure. Not a total loss, and that's scientifically invalid. You can't define anything by what it's not.

I thought the two of us together would be enough, that we'd just stay safe in the blurry territory of nighttime and it would all be fine. But there is no escaping the reality—I run on jet fuel and pistons. Even here in the privacy of his car, I am not reachable.

"You don't have to keep working so hard to love me," I say, and my voice sounds strangely clipped. Professional. "It's okay if you don't."

"God *damn* it, would you stop acting like you're defective or something? There's nothing wrong with you."

The pronouncement is so ridiculous, though. I laugh—a tiny digital laugh. He has no idea.

"There's nothing *wrong* with you," he says again. "You're freaked out, and whatever, that's fine, but Jesus Christ! This isn't something that's only happening to *you*."

We hit the intersection at Jackson just as the light turns red. Marshall leans back, banging his head softly against the seat, pressing his fingers against his eyelids.

"You know me, Waverly. You know all this stuff about me, all this weak, ugly stuff. Do you think that's *easy*? You're pretty much the only person who's ever really known what I'm like, and it fucking destroys me that it's not good enough."

I don't have the language necessary to explain how wrong he is. There are no words for the substance of him, how overwhelmingly *enough* he is. The separation between what's in my head and what might come out of my mouth has never been so insurmountably huge.

"Why can't you just tell me I'm not good enough?"

"Stop it."

He turns to face me, and for the first time tonight, he sounds angry. "*No*. I want to hear you say it, and then I'll get over it and I'll move on or disappear or whatever. But I want you to tell me to my face."

I tug at the bottom of my jacket, looking out at the empty street and wet, shiny pavement.

"I can live without you," he says. "I've been doing it my whole life."

His voice is flat. It makes my skin hurt and I don't say anything. When the light changes, he accelerates without looking over.

The road flashes dizzying and wet under the streetlights, shining like the sea.

Marshall swallows hard, like he's swallowing against something barbed. "Everything is better when you're there, but I won't keep wrecking myself over you if you don't feel the same way. I'm tired of this." His voice is low, uninflected. He does sound tired.

The air outside is hazy with tiny particles of water, too small to be rain. We're less than a block from my house, from the life that no longer seems adequate. I don't know how to ask for what I want. I don't know how to be okay with wanting something.

Marshall has no built-in sense of shame when it comes to expressing his desires.

He pulls up to the curb and doesn't kill the engine. "I want my lighter back."

"Fine. Give me a minute. It's in my room."

When I come back out, he's still idling at the curb, staring out over the neat suburban extravagance of my neighborhood.

I toss the lighter onto the passenger seat. It shines under the dome light, small and ordinary. Cheap. "Does this mean we're breaking up?"

"No." He turns and gives me a long, unreadable look. It's cold and flat, and shuts me out completely. "To break up, you have to have been *together* at some point."

•

I can't sleep.

This is nothing new.

The nights are long and monotonous, and bleed into the days. The weekend passes like a bad dream.

Monday comes and I make a performance art of punctuality. I arrive at every single class and meeting and activity exactly on time.

Then Tuesday. Tuesday can fuck itself.

Together. The word is neon, glowing in front of me, and a month ago, I didn't know the meaning.

Marshall, always breathless, always waiting for me, and I was so rabidly protective of it because it was mine. Mine. Mine and no one else's.

Now it's nonexistent.

On Wednesday, I go down to the west hall bathroom on my office hour to look at secrets, maybe occupy myself for a while with someone else's problems. It's been days since I visited the west hall bathroom. Days since it even occurred to me to worry about anyone else's business.

Maintenance has painted over the wall.

It was bound to happen, but I hadn't really considered that secrets could just disappear. Not now, when I need them.

The new color is a whiter white than the other three walls. When I stand very close, I think I can still see a few pale ghosts in outline under the paint.

What gives me the authority to offer anyone sage advice, anyway?

On Thursday night, I pierce my ears.

I sterilize the needle using a lighter and a cotton ball soaked in rubbing alcohol. For the first one, I numb it with an ice cube, holding it there until the skin feels rubbery and like I'm touching someone else. After the initial resistance, the needle goes in easily.

In the mirror, the girl's eyes fill with tears, but her expression doesn't change.

The second one, I don't bother with the ice. My reflection stares at me. Her face turns red, and then goes back to normal.

I sit on the porch in my rabbit-print pajamas, with my bedspread wrapped around my shoulders like a cape, and watch the sun rise.

MARSHALL
Heartbreak

I feel like I'm going to throw up.

At first I thought it was nothing—just some twenty-four-hour thing, then a forty-eight-hour thing. But it doesn't go away.

My dad moves around the house like a ghost. We don't look at each other. We pretend the blowup at the dinner table never even happened.

All the things I want are hard to find the words for. That night—that ugly night at Autumn's—Waverly was close enough to touch, and now she's nowhere and I'm not even sure we were ever real at all. I have a disposable lighter and a memory of what it felt like to have someone see inside me and be okay with the mess there. I want to know I didn't make this up.

Autumn finds me out by the baseball diamond, sitting on the cement half wall behind the dugout. I'm supposed to be in Spanish, but I'm already so far behind that there's not really any point. What's another day?

She scrapes her boots on the edge of the pavement like

someone getting ready to walk into a house and flops down next to me.

"Hey," she says, like this is totally normal and I am always on the dugout wall instead of in class and she is always sitting down next to me.

The wind is dry and brutal. It cuts through my clothes to the skin, and that's good, because when all I can feel is cold, I don't have to feel everything else.

Autumn settles herself on the wall, pulling off her mittens. Then she sticks her hand in the pocket of my coat and starts digging around. After a second, she makes a triumphant noise and holds up my cigarettes.

I haven't smoked since before homecoming, but I still carry them around. It's reassuring, knowing that if things get bad enough, I have them. I can take them out, lean close to the flame and maybe remember how to breathe.

"Help yourself," I say with my elbows braced on my knees.

Autumn lights one and takes a couple drags. Then she scrubs it out on the wall and makes a face. "God—*vile*. How old are these?"

I stare out at the packed dirt and it kills me that of all the words in the English language, she says *vile*, because it's something Waverly would say.

Autumn shoves the cigarette back in the pack, and then starts fishing around in my coat again, easy like that, like we never stopped being best friends.

She leans back and kicks her feet up on the rail, flipping through my wallet. She counts my cash—seven dollars—bends the corners on my coffee-cart punch card, thumbs past my driver's license. "Nice photo. *Hi, I smoke crack.*"

"Look, can I help you with something? Otherwise, I'm not really in the mood."

She ignores me and starts lining up the stuff from my pockets in a wobbly row—spearmint gum, Rolaids, the red plastic lighter, the crumpled drawing telling me to come to her party. The vile and ancient cigarettes.

I want to mess up the line before she can figure out the pattern. I think if she keeps looking, she'll know everything about me. She's already smoothing out the drawing, touching the lighter and some month-old gas station receipts. She stares at the Rolaids a long time.

"Do you want to talk about anything, Holt? Maybe your life choices? Or your feelings?"

I close my eyes against the sun. There's an ache in my throat, but I already know I won't cry in front of her. I can't even cry when I'm alone. "Autumn, go away."

"Hey, are you okay?" Her voice sounds awkward, and when I open my eyes again, she's got this strange, worried expression that doesn't look like her at all, but maybe that's not even the truth. Nobody knows what Autumn really looks like.

"No," I say. It's weird to say it out loud, to have someone in my everyday real life ask me that like they care. I lean my head back, staring at the sky. "I hate school. I hate home, and my brother, and how my parents act. I hate November, and how everyone in this whole stupid place treats each other. I miss Waverly."

Even saying it hurts my chest. I've never said her name out loud to anyone besides . . . Waverly.

"I know," Autumn says. She leans in a little so our shoulders are touching, just barely. She doesn't say anything else.

The wind gusts across the infield in a storm of dust and gravel.

I've been looking at Waverly's face and her neck and her hair pretty much since the first time I saw her, but it's so much harder knowing what's underneath. The best parts are the hidden ones. The way she always knows all the literary symbols in a short story, and her real, true smile when she talks about strategies and inventions and ideas. How being cold is just the surface and her real smile and her real voice are so much warmer. The invisible parts are the ones I miss the most.

"She was so much better than normal life," I say. "She made *me* better."

Autumn glances over and shakes her head. "Don't. That's not how it works. Nobody makes you be anything. You just *are* that, whether you like it or not."

She doesn't sound angry, but like she's explaining the world.

"That, then," I say, looking at the empty baseball diamond. "That's what I meant. Just that when I was with her, I was *allowed* to be better."

WAVERLY

It's after three a.m. when the family room door creaks open. My mom has padded downstairs on little cat feet and is standing over me.

"Waverly," she says. "We need to have a talk."

I look up from my American Gothic nest on the floor, a bloody dissection of theme and imagery. The phrase *we need to talk* is one I hate more than anything, but in my mother's factual cadence, it sounds different than when Maribeth says it.

"Is there anything you want to tell me?" She's using her therapy voice, the one she keeps for cracking people open and digging around in their private dirt.

"No," I say, closing the book with my finger between the pages to keep my place.

"I noticed you haven't really been training for cross-country lately."

"I can't right now," I say, biting my cheek to keep the tears where they belong. "My feet are overworked, so I have to take a break." Molly's words, coming out of my mouth, making the problem sound small and manageable.

"Oh," she says. Then, with the most invisible compression of her mouth, "That must be hard."

I nod, sinking my teeth deeper into my cheek. It's strange, spending so much time with Marshall has made it harder to be my normal self. Harder to lie.

My mom is watching me closely. "I don't think you've been sleeping," she says.

Her gaze is shrewd. No matter how flaky or disconnected she might seem, you'd have to get up pretty early to slip something past her. Fortunately for me, my median rising hour is four a.m.

"I sleep," I say, keeping my eyes on the mess of sticky notes and index cards. "There's just a lot of stuff due for school right now, so I'm really busy."

"If you don't feel comfortable discussing this with me, we can make an appointment for you to see Gary."

Gary. Her med-school buddy with the bad psychiatrist jokes and the worse neckties. He's come to dinner a few times. His fingernails are always spotless.

"I'm fine," I say.

For a second, my mom sways on the spot, like she might turn abruptly and go back to bed. Then she pulls her robe around her and sits down next to me, surveying my index cards. The scene strikes me as ludicrous suddenly, hilarious and compulsive, like I'm seeing us from above. We are not the gregarious mother-daughter team of primetime television.

For a minute or two, I just sit there with her, feeling the comfortable hum. There's a familiar frequency to her silences that makes all my own silences and idiosyncrasies okay. My mom knows more about neurobiology and has fewer criteria for "normal" than anyone I've ever met.

"Mom," I say to my color-coded grid of gothic trivia. "You love Dad, right?"

The way a person avoids a question can tell you a lot about the answer. There are all kinds of ways to deflect uncomfortable inquiry. *How can you even ask that?* or *Why, Waverly—what a horrible thing to say!*

Instead, she considers it. She looks exceptionally solemn, sitting there beside me, cross-legged with her hands in her lap.

"Yes," she says finally. "Yes, very much."

I know the story of how they met in the psychology department at Stanford and the longer story of how he came to the library every week to see her—how it took four months for her to agree to go out with him, because she was in the middle of a research project on eating behaviors in rats, and inflexibly certain that she would never date a person who wore oxblood loafers and listened to new wave.

They were both abrasively intelligent, though, both ironic—the only creatures capable of occupying one another's space long-term. I've always understood the *why,* but the mechanism behind it is mysterious.

"How?" I say, horribly aware that this is not a question most people need to ask.

She looks away, touching her hair. It makes her seem very young, suddenly. "He understands me—how I am. If I forget to come up for air, he reminds me. If I get too literal or too focused, he doesn't take it personally. I'm better at loving him than anyone else, because he never makes me guess what he needs. And because he lets me."

"He just accepts you the way you are?"

"*Oh,*" she says, hands flying up in surprise. "Oh, no. He enjoys me, but he doesn't treat everything about me as a permanent condition. I think that would be a mistake. I don't always know when to make room, you know? That's good for designing research or figuring out a problem, but once you throw another person in the mix, it's not okay anymore."

But the phenomenon she's describing is the hardest thing to master—the fact that who you need to be changes based on who is in the room, and still, it's all actually just you. For the first time in my life, I've known what it's like to feel ecstatic about someone—not the right way, but my way. I thought he made me a different person altogether, but maybe I was always holding those pieces inside me, waiting for a chance to use them.

"The part where we enjoy each other is important," my mother says, still touching her hair. She's not looking at me. "But there are so many other considerations. You try to be a good partner and you fail. You try again. After a while, you teach each other how you need to be treated."

And therein lies the problem. I've spent most of my post-grade-school life learning by mimicry, emulation, analysis. I know how to recognize the significance of a tone or a gesture, but I've never really had a sense of how to treat people. Everyone around me acts like it's simple—this orderly series of steps that doesn't need documentation. Until now, my saving grace has always been Maribeth prodding me in the back, curating my words like a ventriloquist, providing the script, the list of appropriate expressions. I might be preternaturally skilled at strategy and subtext, but I've never known how to navigate the tangled landscape of emotions without someone else pointing me in the right direction.

•

Coffee is the only thing keeping me alive. It roars through my veins with the force of a thousand volts, the Hollywood horror experiment, born on an operating table, powered by insanity and lightning. If someone touched a match to the back of my neck, I'd go off in a flash of black powder and sulfur.

There are too many people, and all their faces seem to bleed together. Every day, I search for Marshall, but he keeps not being there.

Every passing period, I stand at my locker. If Marshall would just spend two seconds in the same place as me, I could figure out what's happening. If he looks at me, then I'll know this isn't permanent. If he just *looks* at me, then I'll be all right.

For the first time in a week, I straggle back to the west hall bathroom. The wall is still blank, white from floor to ceiling, except for one declarative statement written in five-inch letters, in black marker.

Waverly Camdenmar slums with poor white trash

The code of the spill wall has been broken. The wall is

for honesty, anonymity. It's for secrets and confessions, not for personal attacks. I stand by the row of sinks and look at it, just feeling it. The shock, the confusion. The brutal indignity of my name on the wall.

It's nothing, compared to sticking a needle through my earlobe, but the sentence echoes in my bones. It glows in front of me, taking up residence inside my chest, radioactive. When my anonymous detractor says *trash,* she's talking about Marshall.

•

The graffiti is vicious in a way I can barely comprehend. I've just always assumed that no one knew me well enough to actually hate me.

"What's wrong?" Maribeth says after second period, reaching out to pat my hair. "You're all scowly." Then she drops her hand and gives me a concerned little frown. "You haven't been in the west bathroom yet, have you?"

I shrug, making my face inscrutable. "It's okay, I saw."

"What do you think?"

"That someone has very little imagination."

But that's not exactly true, and I have a small, persistent theory I can't get rid of.

It's funny. I used to think that when people were curt with Maribeth, or cautious, or casually avoided her, they were doing it because they were jealous. Their resentment for her was the price of politics, and once she found her calling, there was just so much to envy—her easy, gleaming beauty and her confidence. Her absolute conviction that whatever she wants is not only attainable, but somehow due to her. Her position on power has always been that if you can take something, then it's rightfully yours.

I'm not naive, though. It's been a long time since I was ingenuous enough to actually believe that was the reason. There are a hundred girls who lost their friends or boyfriends or their cherished extracurriculars to her. Girls who quit clubs or threw away favorite shirts, and who might, even now, be resentful enough to want some kind of retribution.

Loring, or Mallory Silva, who ran the food drive last year, or any of the other battered casualties. Anyone who's ever been hurt and is still too cowed to come for Maribeth in the daylight. To any of them, I might make a compelling target instead. It could be anyone.

In fact, of all the girls in school, there's only one I can think of who it definitely *wouldn't* be.

If Autumn wanted to hurt me, she'd burn me down like Genghis Khan. She'd set me on fire, but she'd do it to my face. She doesn't write her disdain anonymously on walls. She torches whole villages.

I haven't talked to her since her party. Haven't run into her, haven't seen her. Now that I'm off the meet roster, we don't even intersect in the locker rooms anymore. I keep thinking that if I could just *talk* to her, she'd be able to help, but she isn't there in my field of rotation anymore. She isn't anywhere.

It seems that when I lost Marshall, I lost her too.

When I finally track her down, she's standing in the senior locker bay by the art wing, talking to a pair of expensively bohemian girls with assorted facial piercings. I take her arm and pull her unceremoniously into the empty ceramics room.

"Why did you stick me in that room with Marshall Holt?" I say, trying to sound cool or indifferent, like my world has not recently been shattered.

Autumn leans against one of the art cabinets and twirls her hair around a languid finger. "Are you saying his brand of understated charm and basic decency doesn't light your fire? Because you are so full of shit."

My throat tightens—it aches—the muscle memory of how it felt to be ambushed there in her mother's office. Asked to act human without warning. When her eyes drift over me, I feel practically imaginary.

"Why are you avoiding me?" I say finally.

Autumn crosses her arms over her chest. "Because you're fucking *infuriating*, okay? You are the most frustrating person I've ever met."

I should feel sadder than I do. I should want to fix it, to take it back. All I can think is that for the time it lasted, it was nice, having someone on my side. "Infuriating how?"

"Don't act stupid. It doesn't look good on you."

"I just want you to tell me what I did to you."

She regards me with her hands on her head and her hair raked back from her face. Her eyebrows are knit. Her mouth is open. "To me," she says finally, letting her hands fall. "What you did to *me*. Waverly, you didn't do shit to me."

She bends over one of the long worktables and unzips her bag. She takes out her sketchbook and slams it down in front of me. "Look, I'm not completely oblivious, okay?"

When she shoves the book at me, I take it and flip back the cover. A few pages in is a sketch of me in a gray blouse I used to wear all the time last year. I'm in the foreground, bent over my desk with my face half turned away. Behind me, Marshall Holt is sitting with his chin on his fist and his gaze fixed on me. The darkest part of the picture is his eyes.

In another, we're standing in the locker bay with our backs to each other, each pretending so diligently, so *obviously,* to be intent on our own little worlds. She's drawn a faint, flowing line between us, a ribbon that connects us even when we're facing away from each other.

More sketches of classrooms, desks and hallways, of me and Marshall. It doesn't matter who the primary focus of the picture is. He is always looking at me.

But we are far from Autumn's only subject.

Here, I see the wastoid kids clustered together at the city bus stop, leaning against each other, making a circle that shuts out the school and the world.

Kendry in the locker room, staring at herself in the full-length mirror. Her back is to the viewer but her reflection shows half of her expression. Anguished.

Hunter and CJ, royally surveying the junior hall. CJ laughs in awkward capitulation, while Hunter leers at a passing sophomore. The lecherous expression on his face is only half joking.

And Maribeth. Maribeth bright, and Maribeth bossy, and the little worried frown she gets when she can't remember where she left her keys. Maribeth with her winter hat, rosy-cheeked coming in from the cold. She has been rendered in loving detail.

Autumn has captured us, collected us like butterflies, preserving, cataloging. She's pinned down every single one of us.

When I look up from the sketchbook, she's watching me.

Her arms are crossed. Her mouth is strange, like she might be biting the inside of her lip. "Marshall Holt is the best guy I know."

I nod, waiting to see if this line of discussion leads to something else, or if we're just saying facts now.

"He's spent one entire, tragic year being totally in love with you."

Love lands in my chest with a thunk. I know I must look like every close-up shot of every lascivious camp counselor who ever walked into a barn or darkened farmhouse to receive a pitchfork to the heart. The hapless victim. The plunge and the stagger. They never know enough to just fall down.

Autumn reaches for me like she's going to take my face between her hands, but at the last minute, she chickens out, shaking her head and smiling a grim, helpless smile. "Then it changed. You started looking back at him."

So that's it.

My feelings are not a secret, not the buried treasure I thought they were. It's horrible to know that after all this, I really am that obvious. That transparent.

"I just wanted to give him something good," Autumn says. "I wanted you to be worth it."

But the unfortunate conclusion is that I wasn't. I'm not.

Most people would find this surprising, I suppose. But I can't work up the necessary energy. Ulterior motives honestly make more sense than the alternative, and the truth is, I would have done it too. The careful study, the tinkering. The most gratifying goal of any undertaking is figuring out how to fix a problem.

"So all that time you spent with me was just a test, then? The clubs and activities, being completely obsessed with Maribeth?"

For the first time, Autumn looks at me in real confusion. "*You're* the one who's obsessed with Maribeth. I was just getting to know you. I was trying to take an interest in your hobbies."

What can I say? The girl spots dysfunction from a mile out.

"Look, I know it's not my business or anything—and also, when have I ever cared that something wasn't my business—but what happened with you guys?"

I hug myself and look away. The answer to that is too complicated to fathom, and so I keep it simple. "He said I was the only thing good in his life."

There's an inevitability to telling the truth—people never react the way you need them to. I know that if she smiles or squeals or tells me how romantic that is, I will have to scream. I will have to start demolishing buildings.

But Autumn only frowns, looking pensive. "Well, that . . . is a lot of pressure?"

I nod, picking apart the ways it's true. Pressure to be soft, to be accessible. Everything he wants or needs at any given moment. Instead, I held him at arm's length until I couldn't. I was the only kind of close that I could stand to be. Everything and nothing. Safe. I did exactly what I was always going to do, right from the start.

"Was it because of Maribeth and all them?" Autumn's voice is gentler now. "Because of your friends?"

"No," I say in a tight whisper, remembering the time in eighth grade when we went on the ecology trip.

I collected seven caterpillars and put them in a jar. I was going to feed them milkweed leaves and watch them change. Maribeth made a big scene about it and laughed at me for being so childish. Then Kyle Norton thought it would be really funny to kill them.

"It's because of how people act when they know what you want." It feels like too much truth to say out loud and I close my eyes. "They look at you, they hold it over you. They take it away if they can. It's like they can see inside you."

"God, you are such a pussy."

She's says it so easily, so disdainfully, and I just shrug.

"No, seriously. You know that's *normal,* wanting things, right? It's what makes people interesting."

Autumn perches herself on the edge of one of the art tables. "I didn't like you," she says, like it's no big deal to just say that to someone. "I figured he was looking for something else to smash himself to pieces on."

I feel paper thin, like I'm all used up. "What changed?"

"That first week of cross-country, everyone was bitching about how much we had to run for conditioning, and you didn't. We were doing those stupid distance relays, and when your group came into the checkpoint, you were way ahead, and you had this *look* on your face. You were just so . . . happy," she says. "It was the only time I'd ever seen you look happy."

She's watching me, her lip caught delicately between her teeth like she feels sorry for me. I hate that she feels sorry for me.

"I wasn't trying to hurt you," she says. "I didn't know you guys already had some weird secret thing. Waverly, I didn't *know*."

She's telling the truth, but it doesn't matter. The damage is done. Marshall hasn't looked in my direction for days.

"I don't know what to do," I whisper.

Autumn looks so bright and warm against the gray backdrop of the cabinets. She doesn't say anything. Suddenly, she reaches out and grabs my hand, pulling me close. She pins my wrist in the crook of her elbow and uncaps one of her felt-tip pens. For one desperate second, I want to pull away. I'm so sure she's going to write something hateful, mark me like a brand.

Instead, she shoves up my sleeve and scrawls a number down the inside of my arm. She does it with a flourish, printing the last digit in my palm like a jewel.

She doesn't add a name or a signifier, doesn't say anything else. She just drops the pen in her bag, scoops up her book, and walks out.

．

I text Marshall, and after half an hour, when there's no response, I text him again.

My phone sits on the bed, and I sit staring at it.

When the silence goes on so long I think I'll go crazy, I hold my breath and call the number. It's one in the morning and I'm not really surprised when no one picks up. The line rings for what seems like a year before it goes to voice mail.

He hasn't bothered to record his own outgoing message and I sit listening to the robot monotone recite the number I have reached. For a second, I consider the possibility that Autumn has given me a fake number, but that seems unlikely. A total stranger would have at least taken pity on my dismal series of texts. They would have responded, if only to explain to me that I have the wrong person.

When the tone sounds, I take a deep breath. My heart is beating in my throat and I close my eyes before I speak.

"Hi." That's a good place to start, right? "It's me. I

was just thinking. I wanted to see how you were doing. Anyway."

The ache in my throat gets worse.

I hang up before I get the chance to find out whether or not my voice will break.

MARSHALL
The Wall

It's weird to live in a house with a person you just unloaded all your feelings at. To walk up and down the same creaky floor and open doors that you know they've opened too, to breathe the same air.

My dad is nowhere. It's not like he's avoiding me, exactly. He just hasn't spoken to me or looked at me or been in the same room since the night of the full-scale meltdown. Or else I haven't done any of that. Sometimes it's hard to tell.

I come in late and go to bed early. I lie in my room with the blanket over my face, holding the phone against my ear.

Waverly's voice, crisp and capable. *Hi.*

I listen to it over and over. Every time she says *Hi,* I hold on tighter, waiting for her to say all the things I need her to.

This time. This time will be different, and she'll tell me she misses me, say she wants this—wants me—without squirming around or rolling her eyes, without me having to beg for it.

The last word hits my stomach like a fist. *Anyway.*

Then I hit replay and the whole thing starts over.

. . .

When I open my eyes, I'm pretty sure I haven't really slept. I must have, though, because my phone is mashed awkwardly under my head and the blankets are on the floor.

It's morning. But only just. The room is gray with a weak, murky light creeping in around the shade, but that isn't what woke me up. I lie very still, listening to muffled voices and synthesizer piano.

As soon as I roll over, I have this crazy idea that maybe it's Waverly, maybe she's come back and everything will be like it was. But even if I hadn't told her I was done, or she could show up when the sun was already rising, she wouldn't be out in the living room, watching TV with the volume turned down to *inaudible*.

I shuffle down the hall and then stand in the doorway, blinking at my dad. He looks tired and rumpled, like maybe his night was about as good as mine.

I recognize the scene on TV. It's the middle of *The Wall*, at the part in the hotel room, and Pink is wrecking everything, smashing the furniture, ripping down the blinds. Screaming into the flat black sky. My dad is staring at the TV like he can't see me standing there.

"Marshall," he says finally, and he sounds so, so tired. "Just come in here."

I still don't say anything, but I go to sit on the edge of the couch with my shoulders hunched and my hands wedged between my knees. The house is freezing.

"I know this isn't easy," he says, not looking away from the screen.

I stare at the floor. The music has switched to "Is There Anybody Out There?" and I don't like the part where Pink shaves off his eyebrows. Every time he nicks himself, I feel a little queasy. My dad is breathing very slowly, choosing his words, but I already know where this is going. He's going to start explaining in detail how life isn't for quitters.

"Whatever," I say, so careful not to look at him.

"It's not easy," he says again. "Not for me, or for your mother, or Annie. I just—I shouldn't expect it to be different for you."

As sentences go, it's not even fully coherent. I have no clue why he would *ever* have thought this is easy for me. I sit there, waiting for him to tell me how I'd better start sucking it up.

Instead, he leans back in the chair, in the gray morning light, watching me. "I don't want you thinking this is who I meant to be," he says.

The truth, though, is that I never thought that. I never thought he did a goddamn thing on purpose, and that's what makes it worse. If you're doing something on purpose, you can stop.

"Believe me, if I thought you had some kind of strategy or plan, it would not be this." I only mean it in the literal way, but I sound like a real asshole.

He hears it too, because he glances up. "Don't."

"Don't *what*?"

"Don't be like me," he says. "Don't be like Justin." The words are heavy.

"Why not? That's who survives, right?" I wrap my arms around myself and shiver even though I don't want to, thinking how Justin is probably asleep right now. Justin is missing this, avoiding it. Getting rested up for another glorious day as the Captain.

"Because it's not you," my dad says. His voice sounds empty. "That was never supposed to be you."

The way he's looking at me is gentle, like he forgives me. And that, more than his shitty way of communicating or the fact that he's sitting here in the living room at six in the morning, when all my mom wants is for him to be huddled in bed with her—huddled in their failing marriage—makes me want to just start breaking things.

The room gets colder and the scene on TV switches to drug coma and "Comfortably Numb," shining winter gray on my dad's face. He looks so tired. So done.

I keep trying to find reasons it's us out here in the living room, freezing and silent, watching this movie that's one long music video about how much it sucks being a kid. How much it sucks trying to figure out how to have feelings and still act like a man.

Fuck him for acting like I'm the one who's defective. For treating me like every time I do what I think is right, I'm failing. Like *I'm* the one who needs him to forgive me, to tell me it's okay to be the person I already am.

It's not until he heaves himself up out of the chair and reaches for my shoulder that I understand. He's not saying those things. I'm the one who's thinking that. Who thinks that. He's just working on his own private shit and then giving me a choice. Asking me to forgive him. Asking if I can.

I wonder how long he's known that every impulse I have is telling me to forgive everyone all the time. I wonder what he must have been like when he was my age. If he used to feel it too.

WAVERLY

11.

Every minute, I have to check my surroundings to make sure that the floor is still under me, that the air is still breathable, that all my limbs are still attached.

I spend the days with my head buried in my nonexistent notes. I have tried every candle in our house and none of them will bring me back to him.

In the west hall bathroom, the graffiti is still there, looking huge and defamatory. It's been over a week now, and still no one else has added their confessions. The epic shaming of Waverly Camdenmar intimidates all other secrets.

Every passing period, I make my ritual pilgrimage to the wall, waiting for the warning bell to ring, my next class to start.

I'm killing the window between chemistry and Spanish, trying not to hope for anything—that today will be one of the days that Marshall comes to class. It's honestly a relief when he doesn't show up. It's easier.

I'm staring at the graffiti when Maribeth comes in alone, looking impeccable. She stops right behind me but doesn't say anything. I can smell the sweet, self-righteous smell of her perfume.

As I study the words, it comes to me, the way things do in dreams, that I know the writing after all, the awkward loop on the bottom of the *y*, the prim, rigid *w* in *Waverly*. I've always known it.

Other people own black felt-tip markers, but no one else likes to keep a moral stranglehold on me the way she does.

"Thank you," I say, without turning away from the wall. "Thank you for finally just making something easy."

She breathes a small, businesslike sigh. "What are you even talking about?"

"Putting your honest-to-God *opinion* up there? You're usually harder to read, is all."

"Whatever," she says. "You're not making sense."

"But I deserved it, so it's okay. I mean, that's what this is, right? You had to. I needed to be corrected. Obviously."

"Fuck off," she says. There's something strangely naked about her voice, and I turn to face her.

The girl I'm looking at is not the girl I expected. Maribeth's cheeks are a bright, furious red. To my shock, there are tears in her eyes. I haven't seen her cry since seventh grade, when Peter Evanston took her two-subject folder with the Paul Frank monkey on the front and threw it on the roof.

She stares at me with absolute savagery. "I'm serious, don't even talk to me."

Something is molten inside me now. Something is hissing and smoking, eating through my bones.

"Sure," I say, and I sound so cool and flat. So *Waverly*.

"No problem. We'll just write all our meaningful communications on walls from now on."

The words are sleek and leaden in the ballistic chamber of my mouth. This is the poisonous part of my nature that Maribeth knows better than anyone. The part of me she has always valued most. I might look tidy and self-contained, but when the chips are down, I can be positively lethal.

I'm smiling, but it's not the smile she wants. In the row of mirrors, it looks predatory. How sharks with broken hearts would smile—powerful and hungry.

Maribeth stares back. Her mouth is angry, but her hands are scared, opening and closing like there's something there to grab if she could only find it. "Everything is always so *easy* for you!"

And I laugh. It comes spilling out in huge, inappropriate howls. I put my hands over my face and wail with the hilarity of her mistake.

"Don't laugh at me!" She shouts it—*screams* it. Her voice echoes in wounded yelps against the tiled walls.

Other girls have filtered into the bathroom between classes. They are gathering around us, ready to claw and pick like scavengers. There's a reason a flock of crows is called a murder.

I face the wall again and stab the offending sentiment with my index finger. "Tell me about that, Maribeth. I want to know all *about* that, because it is one thing to decide what I need to be, how I need to act, or tell me I'm weird or wrong or defective—and if I have the bad judgment to believe you, that is *my* problem—but to go around saying horrible, shitty things about someone you don't even *know*?"

The look she gives me is rigid. Defiant. "It's not like it even matters, right? Not to the cyborg. You'll hit *start*, you'll reset and adjust and *rearrange your priorities,* or whatever. When was the last time you cared enough about anything that someone could take it away from you?"

I stare back like I could melt the flesh off her face. "So that's it? You waited till now because that's how long it took to figure out how to hurt me?"

She doesn't answer, but most of the time, when someone doesn't respond to your accusation, they're not denying it. They're just not giving you the satisfaction of being right.

"I don't hurt you," I say. My tone suggests that I still might. "I don't take things from *you.*"

She looks at me with such pristine hatred that I feel it in the base of my skull. "You were supposed to be my friend, Waverly! We started the year with all these plans, all this stuff we were going to do and everything was going to be so good—we were going to take over the world, and now you don't even talk to me anymore!"

The implication that I have *ever* been able to talk to her is ludicrous. "What exotic foreign land are you *living* in? I'd have told you and it would have looked exactly like *that.* I'd have told you the truth and you'd have told me how stupid I was, how misguided. Because we need to be perfect, right? Perfect on the inside, perfect on the outside, or what's the goddamn point?"

Maribeth takes a deep, shuddering breath. "Maybe I could have listened more, okay? Maybe we should have backed off a little on Loring and the dance stuff. But why *Autumn*?"

Her voice is anguished, conveying so clearly that my association with someone like Autumn is the deepest betrayal I could have devised.

"I have no idea what I did to you," she says, "but I'd really like to know. I want to know what exactly I did to make you hate me."

The question barely makes sense. Hate her? I owe her so much. I learned everything I know from her. How to make people do what I want without having to say it. How to apologize for things I'm not sorry about, to hedge and falter and qualify, and finish even the most definitive statements of fact with a question mark. How to shove the realest things down deep, where no one can see them. How to smile on command, to fake my own incompetence. To signal that I'm insecure about my conclusions or abilities, when nothing could be farther from the truth. When there has never been a moment in my whole dogmatic existence when I didn't know exactly what I wanted.

And still, I have subscribed—willingly, totally—to Maribeth's animatronic version of me. Years and years of deferring to her, letting her correct my expression, my posture, my tone, until I'm nothing but memory chips and blinking lights.

I stare back at her, and in one long, slow exhalation, all the rage and the frustration just runs out of me.

"You didn't do anything, Maribeth. You were just being yourself."

Her jaw twitches. Her mouth is generous and beautiful. Venomous. She turns back to the wall, to the one perfect statement. "At least I was *honest*. You spent this whole semester acting like we're still friends. And really you don't even care that I don't know you anymore!"

I hold out my hand. "Give me the marker."

She makes a scornful noise and looks away.

"Give me that fucking marker."

She's bigger than me, the very picture of health, blond and glossy, pink-cheeked. I try to imagine myself as I appear to her, colorless now, except for the huge purple smears beneath my eyes, with my newly pierced ears, still painful, burning red at the lobes. In a perfect ecstasy of adrenaline, I understand that I scare her.

She reaches into her bag without taking her eyes off me. She puts the marker in my hand like she's handing over some kind of detonator.

"Go ahead," she says. "Cross it out. But no one's going to just forget."

I uncap the marker and step up to the wall. I cross out *slums,* cross out *poor white trash.* I scrawl my retort, writing so fast the felt tip starts to flatten and fray. The wall is so huge, so impossibly white, and the only thing left to say is blooming inside me like a mushroom cloud, slicing through the Kevlar and the composure, clamoring to get out:

is in love
Waverly Camdenmar ~~slums~~ with ~~poor white trash~~
Marshall Holt

I walk out of the building and across the back parking lot. The air smells like exhaust and burning leaves. The sky is so blue I can barely see.

In the shelter of the baseball dugout, I sit with my back against the wall and my head on my arms. The sound of the wind is sterile and faraway, a static roaring like a seashell. I focus on the feeling in my throat—that tight, gnawing pain that hasn't left since I shoved the needle through my earlobe. I'm raw to the touch.

I lean sideways against the cement and breathe very slowly, trying to get a grip on the desperate need to sob. I have peeled off my skin in front of everyone and I don't even care.

My hands are shaking like they will never stop, but so what? Once the audience and the breathless whispers and the last vestiges of Maribeth are gone, does the fact that I'm unraveling even matter?

I've lost something real, something I needed more than any canny, vindictive friend or stupid secret club. The rest of the world feels small and slow and faraway. My eyelids are hot against the pressure of my arms. I let my shoulders slump. The wind goes quiet.

I'm drifting away on something cottony, sinking into nothingness, when the strange, stuporous warmth is interrupted by a shadow.

I raise my head, blinking in the sudden glare. He's standing at the top of the dugout, silhouetted against the sun. I try to speak, to even just say his name, but all that comes out is a choking sound.

"Waverly," he says. "Are you okay?"

I take one huge, ugly breath, trying to find the words for what I am. Then I bury my face in my hands and cry harder than I've cried for anything in years. Maybe ever.

Marshall Holt just steps into the dugout, crouching next to me, tugging at my wrists.

He pulls his cuff down over his hand and begins to wipe my face, careful, careful. My makeup is running, leaving black smears on his sleeve. He just keeps doing it, touching my cheeks, looking at me like he's never seen me before, never hated me, never blushed or shouted or kissed me in his bed.

"Stand up," he says, taking my hands.

"I just want to stay here." I whisper it, so unspeakably scared that if I move the whole dugout will dissolve, I'll fade, he'll fade. We won't be anything.

"Come on." He pulls me toward him—gently, implacably. "Stand up so I can hug you."

As soon as I'm on my feet, he folds me against his chest. I close my eyes. I've never felt like a real thing anywhere but here.

"I'm sorry," I say against his shirt, grabbing handfuls of anything I can reach. "I'm so, so sorry."

"Waverly." He takes a step back and lowers his head to mine, our noses almost touching. "It's okay. You're not perfect. Whatever."

Perfect rings in my head, making tiny concentric circles, even though he doesn't sound accusatory. "Do you think I don't *know* that?"

"I mean, you don't have to be."

I stand with my hands clamped on his arms, looking up at him, this boy who knows me well enough to know that he can't solve me. Who knows me better than anyone. Knows me well enough to love me.

"Say it again."

He lowers his forehead to mine and whispers it. "You don't have to be."

"Is this real?" I say, mashing my mouth against the front of his hoodie. "Or am I just asleep again?"

"No, it's real. I mean, doesn't it *feel* real?"

But how can I trust a feeling, after all the times I've been with him, in his bed or in the nighttime squalor of his life? "My dreams are the truest thing about me—truer than real life. You're *always* real."

He smiles. "Then right now, I'm real in the real-life way."

"How, though? How can you be here?"

He smiles shyly and holds up his phone. Someone has texted him a sepia-filtered picture of the spill wall, complete with Maribeth's hateful graffiti and my terse, painful annotations.

The contact name at the top is "Awesome Pitbull." The message under the picture says *Merry Christmas, Holt*.

For a second, I can only look at it. The shape of my handwriting on the wall appears strangely out of proportion. It's disorienting, like seeing yourself on video, a sudden realization of how you look from some other angle, and I start to laugh.

With my eyes squeezed shut, I lean my forehead against his shoulder and laugh and laugh. *This* is why Autumn. Because she believes in truth, justice, honor among thieves—because she loves him. Because she was always the friend I needed, before I ever even knew I needed a friend.

Marshall takes the phone back, still smiling awkwardly. "When I said I wanted you to pick me, I didn't mean you had to, like . . . *announce* it. Seriously, this is not what I was asking for."

"I know." My words on the wall were necessary, though. The only way to say what I meant.

From the building, the bell sounds, blaring across the parking lot to signal the end of sixth period. I stand shivering in the shade of the dugout.

Marshall takes my hand and pulls me toward the steps. "It's cold. Let's go inside."

In my rigid former life, I would never walk into school with tears still visible on my face, never advertise the depth of my affections in the locker bay.

As we join the crowd, I lean into Marshall, acutely aware that I'm holding his hand. His fingers are laced with mine, intertwined in an intricate constellation that is as real as the people around us, real as the way my cells love his cells, or the way everyone in the bay keeps shooting us glances.

At my locker, I stand with my hand on the dial, savoring the feeling of Marshall beside me.

He leans down, his breath delicious against my ear. "Is this too weird? Do you need a minute?"

The question is astute and ridiculous. It's something no one else would even think to ask. I just smile and shake my head. Then I wrap my arms around his neck and kiss him like I mean it.

ACKNOWLEDGMENTS

My agent, Sarah Davies. In the simplest terms, she is truly a miracle.

My editor, Krista Marino, who patiently and painstakingly took this story apart and helped me put it back together so it looked like the one in my head.

My critique partners and incredible, indelible friends, Maggie Stiefvater and Tessa Gratton—Maggie, for always taking Waverly's side in everything. And Tess, for always taking Marshall's.

Emily Hainsworth, who read the first draft and said, "So, is Waverly actually a sociopath? I mean, it would be fine if she was. But is she?" Because that was a totally legitimate question.

Gia, for lending me all of Autumn's dance moves.

David, who knows what I like, reads what I write, thinks I'm funny, and watches all the horror movies with me.

Syl, we've been talking about this book forever and now I finally wrote it. Thank you for every time we ate chocolate chips and sat on the basement floor at the first house, and then on the porch at the other house, and all those coffee shops. And just for everything. In general. Thank you.

ABOUT THE AUTHOR

Brenna Yovanoff is the *New York Times* bestselling author of *The Replacement, The Space Between, Paper Valentine,* and *Fiendish*. She lives in Denver with her husband. To learn more about Brenna and her books, visit her online at brennayovanoff.com and follow @brennayovanoff on Twitter.